TINY PIECES OF SKULL

Or,

A Lesson in Manners

Roz Kaveney has been actively committed to gay, feminist and trans politics since the early 1970s. She helped found Feminists against Censorship and was deputy chair of Liberty in the 90s – she is still an active voice in print and online journalism and in social media. Wearing other hats, she has written extensively on popular culture in books like *Teen Dreams* and *Reading The Vampire Slayer*, developing an informal theory about what she calls the sense of 'thick texts' – the idea that it is useful to read most works of art with a sense of context, the other works they might have been, the effect of influence and the means of cultural production.

After abandoning poetry in her twenties, she returned to it in her late fifties, adopting an aggressive formalism as a way of queering the canon, writing poems on subjects excluded from the tradition by prejudice. Her first collection, *Dialectic of the Flesh*, has been shortlisted for awards including the Lambda. Well known for her sf reviewing, and for her involvement in a number of significant anthologies, she has returned to writing fiction – most recently, her epic fantasy sequence *Rhapsody of Blood* has received rave reviews in both the genre press and the mainstream.

Roz grew up working-class, queer and temporarily Catholic in London and Wakefield; she is embarrassed at how totally she fits a particular 'got the memo in childhood' trans narrative. Active in left politics from her teens, she was foolish enough to delay transition until her late twenties. She works in publishing and as a literary journalist.

TINY PIECES OF

SKULL

Or,
A Lesson in Manners

BY

ROZ KAVENEY

TEAM
ANGELICA

Published April 2015 by Team Angelica Publishing,
an imprint of Angelica Entertainments Ltd

Team Angelica Publishing
51 Coningham Road
London W12 8BS

www.teamangelica.com

A CIP catalogue record for this book is available from the
British Library

ISBN 978-0-9569719-7-5

Printed and bound by Lightning Source

This novel is dedicated to Neil Gaiman, one of its first three readers, who was an ally to trans people as early as the 1980s, who has promoted the careers of a number of trans people that I know about and who has sometimes been unfairly maligned by people in the community who have their facts wrong.

Annabelle Jones knew perfectly well what her American best friend Natasha thought about food.

It was one afternoon in the summer of 1979, and Natasha was staring across her slowly-sipped, calorie-free espresso at the overly generous sifting of chocolate on Annabelle's cappuccino. A spasm of distant pain passed across her carefully-crafted face as she watched the spoonful of sugar Annabelle had just added sink slowly through the foaming crust, raising small wafts of translucent powder as it went. She looked away, out through the lightly-curtained window, at the sheets of summer rain that were falling in the Gloucester Road, and paused for a moment in a way that was intended to arouse suspense or even dread.

'You'll never be a woman if you eat that cream cake,' she said finally, in as sepulchral a tone as she could manage.

'What does that even mean?' Annbelle found herself snapping. 'Lots of women eat cream cakes; look around us.'

The café was full of women of all ages doing just that.

Natasha glowered at her. Clearly this was not going to be something she backed down on.

'Yes,' she eventually conceded, 'of course you could eat them. But it would be better if you didn't. Mexica once told me we can never afford to relax. It's about being the best we can be. Like we're in training. Basic training. Very, very basic in your case. So, no cream cakes.'

'This cream cake in particular?' Annabelle indicated the admittedly rather large patisserie item in front of her that was currently overwhelming the side-plate on which it sat. 'Any cream cake ever? That's not a metonymy, is it? What is "a member of a class standing for the whole class"? And what does being a woman have to do with – '

'Listen, missy,' Natasha cut in, 'don't get smart with me. So I dropped out of high school before Rhetoric One. You just do not do that as part of a beauty operative equivalency.' And then with even greater vehemence, so that the people at the next table looked scared and guiltily shoved the rest of their cakes to the side of their plates: 'Any cream cake ever, except if you visit my mom. And then strictly out of politeness, and no meals for two days after.'

Natasha's own tendency was to the gaunt, almost the skeletal, but her well-supplemented cheekbones and full lips, and her liberal use of shaders, highlighters and a particular tawny blusher made her face less merely thin than dramatic and rich in aesthetically appealing contrasts. She looked meaningly at Annabelle, daring contradiction, and making Annabelle wonder with genuine admiration if she could ever learn to hold her face that still herself.

Annabelle knew – she had only to feel the slight tautness of the waistband of her jeans – that there was much to what Natasha said, if not, perhaps, in the terms in which she chose to say it. Annabelle had enough awareness, even in her present circumstances, not to challenge her friend by phrasing the problems concerned with limiting physical stereotypes politically. No-one had ever told Natasha that fat was a feminist issue, and she would not have cared even slightly if they had. Were Annabelle to do so, she would be told that she was making excuses again. With a sigh she pushed her plate to the side. There were far too many glacé cherries and bits of angelica on the cake for her to be able to defend it as a piece of wholesome nourishment.

'Oh, Annabelle, you mustn't let me make you do things you don't really want to. I'm just saying for your own good, you know that. So don't be fucking petulant, okay?'

The real problem was that Natasha had very little interest in food while Annabelle, equally genuinely, liked it a lot. In that respect they were simply entirely different types of human being, just as in one crucial other they were precisely the statistically-improbable same.

2.

Even from a distance the buffet table had looked promising.

The nibbles – on little silver plates – were those Japanese things with seaweed wrapped around them, and the sausages on sticks had a coarse graininess to them that implied they came from a really good butcher. Holding a cardboard plate with an unappealing and anachronistic Op Art design on it, and a plastic fork, and a glass of that red wine vintners seem to keep especially for publishers' parties and private views, was a reasonable answer to Annabelle's continuing new problem about what to do with her hands.

She knew she shouldn't have come; it was much too soon to have to cope in public with so many new people, as well as with old acquaintances who were meeting the new her for the first time. But Thomas had insisted, and when he was being nice to her he was so utterly, meltingly wonderful. She caught herself melting at the thought of his niceness, and administered to her conscience what would have been a rap across the knuckles had she not been holding a plate of rather overly greasy rice salad with bits of green pepper in it.

'Don't be wet,' she said, almost aloud.

'What was that again,' said a small, thin, dark American woman standing next to her, in a tone that indicated the suspicion something had been said she would be displeased to hear repeated.

Annabelle looked down at the other's acrylicly-reinforced fingernails and decided she had better explain.

'I was telling myself not to be wet about someone, that's all.'

She looked up into the other woman's eyes and noticed that she was wearing an awful lot of eyelash. Gosh, I didn't know the lower ones were back in.

The woman noticed her stare and responded in kind. 'Well, my dear, I must say that that is an amazingly graphic way of putting it. You English girls can be so coarse.'

'Oh, heavens, no,' Annabelle went on. 'Not likely, I mean, hardly.'

'Considering,' said the other, in so significant and conspiratorial a voice that Annabelle started to wonder what she knew, and whether....

'Wet is slang. I didn't catch your name. I'm Annabelle,' she said.

'Natasha.' Definitely conspiratorial, and probably sisterly.

'It's a way of saying, oh, sentimental and weak and stuff like that.'

'Well, you surely can't afford to be those, can you, my dear? Not right now, right? Too much taking care of business going on right now, right?'

The conspiratorial emphasis on 'business' pretty much confirmed what Annabelle already pretty much knew. 'And I suppose all of your business has been taken care of,' she said, backing an envious guess.

'Well, for sure, Miss Sharp,' said Natasha. 'But I must fly right now. There's a moustache over there that's going to be tonight's dinner.'

She insinuated her way back into the crush and disappeared. Annabelle had a sense of having missed, marginally, an important connection to possibility.

Thomas appeared, back from the self-promotion that they were here to do. He smiled, showing the perfect teeth that were one of his many attractions.

'I've talked to three literary editors in half an hour while you've been stuffing your face.'

'Gosh,' said Annabelle. 'That's quite good going, isn't it? Did you get any actual reviewing out of them, or was it just your beaux yeux they were after?'

'Well, possibly,' said Thomas. 'One of them asked if I was really here with you, or just your escort. She said she liked those pieces of yours, though I suspect she was more interested in scandal. Not a breath of which passed my lips, of course.'

He had on his shiny and gorgeous face that smirk which told people more of what they wanted to hear than his rather limited vocabulary could ever express, Annabelle thought in a sudden excess of ill-temper.

'Anyway, she was wondering... Oh, and she was going to ask you to review a couple of novels, so why don't you stagger over there and justify your existence by doing a bit of hustling for the pair of us.'

Thomas turned away and drifted over to a knot of people who were surrounding The Most Beautiful Young Literary Editor In Town.

Annabelle had watched him make a fool of himself over

that particular little miss before, twice: he really never did learn. He's not my boyfriend and occasionally his whoring himself around gets me work, so I shouldn't complain. Except this time he can't expect me to sit up all night feeding him Famous Grouse and telling him it's all alright. He can't do other than accept there are things I left unsaid before that are now, well, implicit.

She knew perfectly well, though, that it was going to be the same old routine: dear sweet old Jonesy, always a shoulder and a box of tissues and not much else.

The bloody arrogance of the man. He thinks he understands and can go on exploiting me. It's hardly over him that I made up my mind, is it, she tried, reasonably successfully and accurately, to convince herself.

'I have always found, my dear,' Natasha broke in on her depressed musings, 'that it is not a good idea to let people see that we are upset or annoyed. Your face is far too mobile. Luxe, Calme and Volupté is what La Mexica always used to recommend when I asked her for lessons, though when I got confident enough to ask her she said she had no idea what it meant either. Just what some john used to mutter when he came and she sat there smiling.'

'Oh, sorry,' said Annabelle. 'You caught me unawares.'

'Actually, though, looking serious and thoughtful and sad kind of suits the shape of your face, I guess.'

'Where's the moustache? Which one is he?'

'It didn't work out. Copy date coming up, he said, whatever that might mean. So I guess I'll have one more spritzer and then I'll leave.'

'It would be rather interesting to talk to you some time.' Annabelle thought she might as well try and learn what this woman could probably teach her. About eyelashes, at least.

'I don't take responsibility for people, not any more, even when they need help. Which' – and she looked at Annabelle with a cold and appraising eye – 'frankly, I have to say...'

'I get along,' said Annabelle, knowing pretty much what the other meant. 'I'm more a member of the bohemian intelligentsia than anything else, so it's important not to – '

'If bohemian intelligent means that you don't get your eyebrows right and wear black silk trousers with egg-stains on them, then I guess you surely are. I call it purely lazy, and that, my dear, we just cannot afford. You're almost worse than Carola.'

'Carola?'

'The last one who said it would be interesting to talk to me sometime.'

'What happened to her?'

'I guess I set her straight. But it was all such a lot of work just making her see what was wrong. She didn't even want her nose done, and the fuss she made about her lips...'

'I don't think I want to know.' Annabelle knew that acquaintance with what she thought of as The Knife was a feature of her future, but...

'Well, except for the nose, which isn't that bad considering, this is all stuff you need to be told, sweets. Frankly, this party is a bore; I guess it could hardly hurt if I let you buy me an espresso.'

Annabelle, to whom such a performance of reluctance was not unknown, wasn't sure whether she had succeeded in being granted an audience, or in being co-opted as one.

3.

The specific details of that first long monologue from Natasha eventually became hazy in Annabelle's mind: it was its general content that mattered. Decisions arrived at as holding actions against despair suddenly acquired a new dimension of sleazy but real glamour.

They sat drinking coffee in an unappealing, crowded but cheap pasta joint where people splashed the red and watery sauce off their tagliatelle in all directions, and where the pastries were stale enough not to tempt even Annabelle. But the backdrop to Natasha's stories was wonderfully other.

Of course it was entirely politically unsound to be even mildly fascinated by accounts of intimate dinners with presidential aides who came in the back way, with Vogue cover models and rock stars who once made the Top Fifty; all these things and people, that whole world of people being famous for rather more than fifteen minutes, was a transient foam trailed across the realities of class and gender war. And heaven knew Annabelle's position was from some points of view already too much one of complicity with things as they were.

There was something, she reflected, to the life lived without conscience and consciousness; and, besides, given the occasional horror and danger that lurked in the corners of Natasha's accounts, the miseries that went with the splendours, if Natasha had taken what she wanted, she had paid for it. She was sort of owed, really, and perhaps, after the miseries of the last few years, Annabelle was sort of owed a little as well.

After a bit, when Natasha had told of getting a chill after posing as a naked torchbearer at a cosmetics launch, but of how wonderful it had been to be actually in the same room as the team who had devised her favourite shade of pearly grey eyeshadow, Annabelle ventured a remark to this effect: 'It's sort of like,' she said, 'that thing of – gosh, is it Edith Wharton's – about "Take what you want, but pay for it"?'

'Who the hell is Edith Wharton? And sweets, I don't think you've got it quite right. They pay me. In theory, at least.'

Annabelle scraped foam and chocolate out of the bottom of her cup with her spoon and reflected that there were areas in this relationship where communication was always going to be difficult.

4.

The thing was, most of the time, her life was a lot better now. She was lucky in lots of ways, she knew that. Whatever literary editors and the occasional publisher said when she was not in the room, they still gave her work. Because however she was dressed, and however different she looked each time they saw her, they all knew she could make deadlines.

She'd always had good skin, and the pills she was taking were making it better, if anything. When she did her makeup she could bear to look in the mirror at her face now, because it looked like the version of her in her head.

But then there were the days running up to each time she went for electrolysis when she had to wear an extra thickness of foundation and powder on her upper lip and the two triangles each side of her chin, and she was convinced everyone could see; that her neighbours were laughing at her behind their hands. And then the hours afterwards when there was no makeup, and the triangles were red and tingling with shamefulness.

She was a bit tall and a bit loose in the gut, but her face was a nice shape, she thought. And then she looked at herself again in her enemy the mirror and felt like a terrible fraud who was just deceiving herself and no-one else. It was never going to come right and she had thrown away some parts of her life and was never going to get what she wanted and just looked stupid, like some sort of clown.

Then she would look again and it was like a shutter going up or a light going on and it was okay for hours at a time. Or even a couple of days, until she looked the wrong way at a mirror.

Mirrors were both the candid friend who would point out that one hair that needed to be tweezed, and the enemy who would tell her untruthfully that that top had been a colossal mistake like everything else; they were the flatterer who made her feel, as she did her makeup, that one day she would get to look at her face from every angle and not see a thing that she didn't like; the thug who shouted in her ear when she caught sight of herself naked that she was a monster who no-one would ever love.

And the thug had evidence. In Tom, who had never even noticed her in all those years, and would never see her, and now she was starting to see him and wonder how could she have been such a fool; and Magda, who had talked her into a pity fuck in the hope that somehow she could make Annabelle's limp bits into the key that would unlock her and change her mind.

Magda was her best friend in so many ways, even though they had met through Tom, and jealousy. Yet Magda did not understand, and Annabelle needed her to.

Perhaps one day.

*

5.

'Well, who is this Natasha, anyway?' said Magda in a half-interested drawl as she scanned the Guardian Women's Page for anything that might be at least vaguely sound enough to be worth reading. Magda was a good friend and amazingly supportive in the circumstances, but she would probably have been round less often if she ever got up in time to make it to the newsagent's before they ran out of the only paper she would be seen dead reading.

Annabelle turned on the coffee-grinder for slightly longer than was needed to give herself a moment to think out an acceptable answer.

'Well,' she said, holding her hands in front of her and looking down like a child giving a prepared recitation, 'she's a working-class kid from somewhere in the Mid-West that she said I wouldn't have heard of, and indeed I hadn't. Her father stopped chopping hot cars and got Born Again and wanted her to walk on coals to purify her. So she left. When she got to San Francisco, and she says you must never call it Frisco, she got in a lot of trouble.'

'I can imagine.' The face Magda pulled meant she was imagining something pretty lurid. 'And so she's, well, like you.'

'Yes.'

'But younger and prettier. Because it seems to me that you're moving into a world where that will always count against you. You're not just trying to become a woman, you're trying to become that sort of woman. It's dangerous as well as wrong.'

Annabelle decided that she wasn't going to go there. They had had this conversation before, and it never ended well.

'So anyway, she got into trouble. Because of being so young and naïve. Then she got off the drugs and managed to do a high-school equivalency while working in some sort of bar. And then she modelled for some hyper-realist or other and was the toast of SoHo or Tribeca. She says that angel climbing into the freezer of fruit at the Tate was cast from her, but I don't know for sure because she also says she's had a lot done to her face since then.'

'You started well,' said Magda, leaning over and picking lint from Annabelle's black woollen sweater to show they were still friends even if she disapproved. 'But my guess is that you're about to run out of apologia. For you as well as her.'

'Well, she's marginalised, isn't she? She doesn't really have many options apart from trying to be gorgeous. She's not at all as alienated or sociopathic as she might be; I'm finding her very supportive.'

Unlike some people, Annabelle forbore to say.

'Well,' Magda looked doubtful, 'I have to say that I am more than a little suspicious of her. Everything you've said, and as for those photographs as well.... As you know, I'm your friend, your dear friend.' She stood and planted a check on Annabelle's cheek, going slightly up on her toes to do so. 'And I will support you in what you feel you have to do in spite of my reservations. But this person seems to be everything in the world that I was worried you were fantasizing about. She may be very sweet to you, but her whole set of values sounds quite incredibly tawdry.'

'But she has been so sweet.'

Magda looked even more doubtful. 'Annabelle, you're so naïve. It sounds to me as if you are there at table with her to boost her sense of how wonderful she is.'

Annabelle considered cattily that Natasha was not the only person in her life who liked an attentive audience.

'But, Magda,' she ventured, 'doesn't everybody do that sometimes? Just a bit? People need approval. It's natural.'

Magda had very short cropped hair, but she managed to toss it anyway. 'Don't you ever talk to me about natural,' she said. 'There are hypocrisies to which I will not stoop.'

'The coffee should be ready by now,' said Annabelle, and went and got it.

'Thank you,' said Magda, who was usually polite to her hostess. 'But do think about this person and her effect on you. We don't want you turning into some brainless bimbo clothes-horse, do we?'

'Not much chance of that,' said Annabelle, in a tone which parodied, but included, regret.

*

6.

Annabelle found that the key to getting Natasha's memories out of her was to treat her to something first. Natasha was the sort of person to whom transactions were the natural mode in which personal relationships were conducted. Annabelle had made past years of gloom more or less bearable by acquiring odd little corners of London and Oxford, a few moments in any of which could be guaranteed to cheer her up. Some of these were just the sort of thing that a visiting American with rather glitzy taste would lap up, she thought, patronizingly and entirely correctly.

'So who was this Leighton, anyway,' said Natasha, trying, perhaps unconsciously, to strike a pose that would best show off her silhouette against the turquoise tiling. This particular room in Leighton House had always been a favourite of Annabelle's, though Thomas, in the days long before, when he did acid most weekends, had once had a very bad time in it when Annabelle took him there to calm him down, saying it was like being inside the eye of a housefly.

Not even a peacock; it had been a rather bad trip.

'Well,' said Annabelle, 'he was this mid-Victorian painter who did a lot of semi-classical scenes full of elegantly-draped semi-nude women, a lot of whom look suspiciously as if he would rather have been painting boys but, being a mid-Victorian, didn't know it. He was a pretty rotten painter really, but everyone seems to have thought he was a nice chap.'

'"Everyone" being other painters and other people who could afford large houses full of silly rooms?'

'Well, yes,' said Annabelle, heartened by this display of class resentment in someone whom she had assumed, being American, to be without such things.

Natasha looked at her in a slightly superior way.

'It's just that I've had johns like that, and believe me, my dear, they are the very worst kind. You've never turned tricks, have you?'

'No.' Annabelle wondered if she ought to apologise for it, and rebounded from that into what she realised sounded like arrogant moralism: 'I've always thought it would be a rather degrading thing to do, unless one had to, economically.

Besides, I'd be too frightened; I'd never get away with it without something awful happening.'

'Well, listen to Miss Prim,' said Natasha, and paused to examine her nail-varnish. 'But if you never have, never wanted to, and are never going to, why are you so interested in sitting for hours listening to me talk about it? Tell me that, my dear.'

'You're my friend, my shiny new friend,' said Annabelle. 'And I admire a lot of things about you, and it seems to be part of what gave you all that cool. If you think I'm exploiting you by getting you to talk about it then I suppose we could talk about the weather instead. And isn't this a wet June?'

'I wouldn't know,' said Natasha. 'I don't live here, remember? I just came over to deliver stuff to a dealer for my friend Hennie, and I couldn't see any reason to hurry back immediately.'

'What stuff?' Annabelle was suddenly nervous. 'What dealer?'

'Audubon drawings,' said Natasha, looking at her with great and plausible eyes and an air of mildly-abashing irritation. 'An art dealer. Well, kind of. I call him Mr. Carpets.'

Which sounded so anodyne that it probably wasn't.

Natasha perched on the side of the dry fountain in the middle of the room and tried to look reassuring. When an attendant attempted to catch her eye she stood up without being told and as if it had been her idea all along to stand as suddenly as she had sat down.

'Don't get so uptight. I'm not the kind of person to take foolish risks trashing around like Carola does. I have a position to keep up now; people in Chicago reckon I have real class, and give me respect. Real people, not just street trash and bar girls. Not that I don't still see them too. After all, they need a role model.'

She preened for a second, then pulled out a brush and redid her lips. As she put the cap back on her gloss brush and put it in her bag, she winced.

'You okay?' Annabelle was flustered because she didn't like the idea of her friend hurting.

Natasha looked a little embarrassed, as if she had been caught being less than perfect. She looked round the room. The attendant hovering nearby clearly didn't count, because she whispered, not especially quietly, 'It's my left boob; it's going a bit hard.'

She grabbed Annabelle's hand and shoved it against her chest. Annabelle was expecting something cyst-like, but she found herself with a handful of something that felt a bit like a cricket-ball.

'That's awful,' she worried.

'It happens sometimes.' Natasha tried to talk with bravado. 'If needs be, I'll have them out and new ones put in.'

Annabelle wasn't sure you ought to talk about these things as if you were changing the ribbon in a typewriter, but okay, Natasha was blasé.

Pretty much about everything.

7.

Annabelle had not expected ever to meet Mr. Carpets.

As it happened, though, Natasha rang her up a couple of days later. 'Annabelle, darling' – she obviously needed something - 'are you free tomorrow morning?'

Annabelle was almost always free. 'I've a deadline the day after. But I can work around it,' she said a little disingenuously.

'Only it would really be helpful if you could carry a portfolio for me.' Natasha sounded a little conspiratorial. 'Nothing is stolen – and it really is just the drawings. There's just some question of duty and licenses and authentication documents – nothing that could get you into trouble, but they might look at my visa and I only want to go home when I'm good and ready.'

Annabelle decided to trust her. What could possibly go wrong? And it was, ever so slightly, an adventure.

'Yes.' She was careful to sound tentative.

'Come to my hotel at eight and we'll grab a herb tea in the lobby, and I'll pass you the case under the table. Wear dark glasses.'

Annabelle felt as if she were being taught tradecraft.

'Gosh,' she said.

She must have sounded a little too excited because Natasha stepped on her quickly: 'That way my valued client doesn't have to look at your not-entirely-successful attempts at eye makeup.

It'll be okay in a while; I'll tell you what you're doing wrong until you get it right.'

This was not entirely reassuring, but the fact that Natasha was now being a cow again meant that she probably wasn't trying to lull Annabelle into a false sense of security.

It wasn't a very big portfolio. Annabelle had borrowed a large leather one from an ex of Thomas's who she hung out with sometimes, and it shifted around inside until she stuffed some copies of Vogue in with it, which she had brought in a carrier-bag in case of emergency.

'Nice touch,' Natasha said. 'They even look as if they've been read.'

Annabelle was quite hurt. 'Of course I've read them.'

Natasha snorted, obviously not convinced. 'Glad to see you did what you were told and wore dark glasses,' she said. 'Let's see what you've done. Because I know you're disobedient.'

Annabelle allowed Natasha to remove her dark glasses. She looked closely at Annabelle's eye-line and three kinds of shadow blurred in very carefully.

'Okay,' she said, 'actually that passes muster, but don't get cocky, missie. I'll arrive ten minutes after you. Try not to upset Mr. Carpets.'

8.

The office of Mr. Carpets was in one of those buildings in the lower part of Charing Cross Road of which the ground floors are bookshops or natty gents' outfitters. Annabelle went in through a rather grand entrance, the door of which had old and flaking paint, and into a long red-carpeted corridor that wasn't very well-lit. She didn't notice that the carpet was as shabby as the front door until her heel caught in a tuft that unravelled a little as she pulled it free.

This wasn't very reassuring. She pressed a button and a lift came down slowly into a metal cage with doors that took ages and then a certain amount of effort to open and close. She knew she wasn't all that fat, but she felt the floor and the cable give a little bit as she stepped in.

It creaked a little, and made her nervous, but the lift slowly rose and after a while, during which she tried not to think of the cable snapping and plummeting down, it got to the sixth floor and juddered to a stop.

The gate of the lift was stiff, but the outer gate had been oiled and opened smoothly. The corridor up here was brightly lit, and the carpet, which was black with gold ace-of-spades in it, looked new and was thick and springy under her feet – this all suddenly felt like far less of a chore.

There was a door a bit further down on the left and the brass plaque next to it said 'Scharpetti Imports', which made sense. Annabelle hadn't actually thought why he might be called Mr. Carpets. Before she could press the doorbell under the brass plaque the door was flung open and a very large man in a green velvet pinstripe suit strutted out magnificently. He had dark glasses on too, but his were small and flush against his eye-sockets as if they had grown there. Even blacker were the undone bow-tie which hung from the collar of his purple shirt and his shiny, slightly-platformed patent shoes. He really didn't need any extra height because his curly black hair brushed the top of the door-frame as he came through, but clearly this was a man whose heyday had been Swinging London and he was not about to let you forget it.

She'd expected him to boom, but what came out of his mouth was a honeyed, mild, tenor voice – not quite incongruous but almost. The accent was one degree off stage Italian; it probably had been Italian once and had then become cockney before deciding it was better off first time around, with occasional posh vowels in there somewhere.

'Aha.' Annabelle had never before heard anyone say 'Aha' as if they said it all the time and meant it. 'You must be this Annabelle my new good friend Natasha keeps talking about. You have something for me – bring it here.'

She passed him the portfolio, which suddenly looked as tiny in his hands as it had been inconveniently large in hers when she was carrying it: he was one of the few people she had ever met who made her feel petite. He turned on his heel and she followed him into an office which was all steel tubes and bright neon. There were rolls of carpet in the corner and Eastern carpets that looked expensive hanging on the walls. A desk that was a slab of marble looked as if it were floating until you saw the very thin, very strong-looking wires.

There was nothing on the desk until he put her portfolio down gently on it, opened the catches and took out the smaller one. With a cry of almost toddler-like glee he opened it and riffled through the folders within.

'Oh, splendid, the client will love these.' He nearly hit a high C in the middle of the word splendid, 'I'll make Mr. Datchet give Natasha some kind of special tip. Can you think of anything she'd especially like?'

Annabelle was at a loss. She had not a single idea about how these things worked.

'There must be something. Mr. Datchet is top of his field, and you girls always need something. Why don't I take her over to Harley Street and see what he can do for her – you come too, hold her hand.'

'Oh,' – light started to dawn – 'He's Mr. Datchet because he's a surgeon.'

At that moment Natasha arrived, and Scharpetti was all hand-kissy and embracy in a way that he had not been with Annabelle – who wasn't worried, precisely, though she thought that it really wasn't very polite of him.

She thought she'd better show some initiative and had best do it before his wandering hands found Natasha's cricket-ball breast and any chance of a tip went out the window.

'Sweetie, a word.' She pulled Natasha out into the corridor, yanking the door to behind them and continuing to drag Natasha along until she thought they were probably out of ear-shot.

'Client's a surgeon, and Scharpetti is talking about making him tip you in kind. Make him sort out the breast.'

Natasha kissed her on the cheek. 'Such a good idea, and you were saving me from his being turned off – you're such a little whore-in-training, darling. All the right instincts.'

She went back into the room, with Annabelle trailing nervously behind her.

'You know,' her voice was huskily confiding, 'I do have a little female problem that perhaps your client can help me with. It would be a wonderful favour if...'

'But of course,' he trilled. 'He's expecting me to come round this morning so let's go up to Harley Street straight away.'

Mr. Carpets filled the lift completely. Annabelle and Natasha decided they would walk down rather than wait.

'Is he always like this?' Annabelle was feeling a little overpowered.

'He gets things done, which is handy,' Natasha smiled sweetly. 'And the one time I let him have me he came really quickly. And is not the same size everywhere. He's generous, but I wouldn't want to upset him – he's got this thing about what's fair. He can get quite, as you English girls say, narky – we went for dinner and afterwards he counted out the tip very carefully to the last penny. One of the waiters laughed at him over that and he got very angry, very angry indeed.'

Out on the street Mr. Carpets stopped a taxi by just getting in front of it. Being in a taxi with him was less unpleasant than being in a lift with him would have been: there was room for them to breathe as long as they made sure not to do it at the same time.

And it wasn't that he was fat because he wasn't – there was just so much of him. He didn't sit still was part of the trouble, and he kept on being effusive and sucked the oxygen out of the cab even though all its windows were open. Annabelle started to feel quite faint; she lost track of where in Central London they were right up to the point where they pulled in outside a three-storey building somewhere at the unfashionable end of Harley Street.

However unfashionable the end of the street was, and however much less impressive the building was than the ones down the other end, Datchet's clinic was remarkable. The entry-hall and waiting-room had clearly had the benefit of Mr. Carpets' attention: there was a bird of prey motif which presumably Datchet had chosen, but it was carried out in the most minute of ways, from the hilt of the paper-knife on the desk to the plasterwork around the light-fittings in the ceilings which, if you didn't notice the unified theme, looked as if it had been there for centuries. The pattern in the carpet, the handles of the cupboard doors – Annabelle knew without having to check that all the leather-bound books on the shelves would have a bird image stamped into them

She hadn't sneaked a peek at the drawings when she had

them in her portfolio and now she wouldn't have to because she knew what they would show.

The sofa was reasonably comfortable. Mr. Carpets was pacing up and down while Mr. Datchet examined each of the drawings in turn with a jeweller's loupe. 'Those will do nicely.' He handed them back to Mr. Carpets. 'The usual framer, I take it.'

'Of course.' Mr. Carpets was almost offhandedly brusque about it, as if it were tiresome of Datchet even to raise the matter. 'Now, obviously I've paid the courier, but it's only fair that you tip her.'

Datchet looked a little annoyed.

You know how it is with girls like these two.' Mr. Carpets was very slightly dismissive. 'There's always something wrong with the plumbing or the upholstery – and she has a little problem I'd like you to fix for her.'

He waved a lordly hand and Datchet looked, slightly baffled, at Annabelle and Natasha. Natasha got up. Annabelle resolutely stayed where she was. If she were to be called upon to watch some grisly surgical procedure then friendship would dictate, but she was really not going to volunteer.

As a door opened into a room full of bright lights and tables and chairs with an odd plastic sheen to them – oh my God, easy to wipe down – Annabelle heard Datchet say, 'Now, what seems to be the problem?'

She became aware that Mr. Carpets was looking at her appraisingly.

'You're quite new.' His voice was cold but also somehow kind. 'I assumed you'd had a lot done, but you haven't. Mostly, don't – nice face, natural, best not to tinker. Your friend's gorgeous, of course, but there's a lot of things that could have gone wrong. I mean, obviously at some point you'll want the other thing done, I assume – not that everyone does, but she has. And very nicely too, I must say as a client...'

Datchet came back, snapping gloves off his hands. Natasha followed, looking slightly pained but otherwise cheerful. He turned back to her. 'They should have told you to do that; I always do. Massage the area with vitamin E and just use a little body English to break up that crust if it happens to the other one.'

He went over to his folder of drawings of birds copulating and started holding them up to the light. The blues and purples were, well, very blue and purple.

'Honestly,' Annabelle was shocked and a little worried, 'you were in there no time at all. What on earth did he do?'

Natasha took her hand and put it back onto the left breast, which now felt soft and yielding and slightly pillowy where previously it had been hard.

'I told him, and he listened and he put his gloves on to have a feel, and then he just sort of took my breast in his hand and cupped it and sort of twisted and suddenly I felt all the crustiness inside break up and go. It didn't even hurt much – it just felt, well, weird.'

Mr. Carpets, who had clearly been listening to all this, started to look impatiently at Datchet, and Annabelle found herself not envying anyone who got that glower pointed in their direction. Datchet was oblivious and went on looking at the drawings and the gorgeous tints they had been coloured with.

Eventually he put them away, and at that moment noticed that Mr. Carpets was tapping the fingers of one hand against the other arm hard enough to leave marks in the green velvet of his jacket sleeve.

Datchet looked at him as if he wanted to know what Mr. Carpets wanted to say.

Mr. Carpets' voice was no less honeyed and musical but somehow had a darkness to it. 'That wasn't much of a tip.' The darkness was like a cloud in the room.

Datchet looked flustered. 'I did what she needed. It just wasn't as bad as it looked and I knew what to do.'

Natasha tried to calm everything down. 'It's fine, honestly. He fixed me; I'm satisfied.'

Mr. Carpets ignored her altogether. 'I don't think that's a fair tip. I don't like unfairness.'

Suddenly he pointed at Annabelle.

'She needs tits and I'm sure she'd like to have them done. Right here, right now. That would be a fair tip.'

Datchet looked even more flustered. 'But I don't have a nurse booked in, or an anaesthetist. I can't just...'

Mr. Carpets' voice became colder and darker: 'Your nurse is upstairs, sleeping off the hangover she got drinking in one of my bars. Go and get her – sling her in a cold shower if you have to. And you can do it under a local – Annabelle here is getting her boobs for free, so she'll put up with that, won't you?'

'How did you know...'

'I make it my business to know. That's how I keep things fair.'

He clapped his hands and Datchet scurried from the room.

Annabelle was scared and yet at the same time thrilled. What was distressing about this was that it had nothing whatever to do with her, even though it would seriously change her life; it was about this bloody man and his ego.

She clutched Natasha's hand.

'What have you got me into?'

Natasha looked as scared as she assumed she did, but then pulled her features together into her 'I'm older and wiser and telling you things for your own good' face.

'Look at it this way, dear. This may be very slightly unpleasant for half an hour, but it will be done, and you know you want them. This way you won't do anything silly to get them. There was this kid in Chicago I heard about, went to a vet who hosted pumping parties – which is never a good idea because loose silicon can shift around inside you. But that never got to be a problem for her because he screwed up and put it straight into her lungs – she drowned on it, right there on his table. So he called his friends who owed him a favour over some race-horse, and they helped him get rid of the body. Feed at the dog-track, probably.'

Annabelle did not find this reassuring.

Mr. Carpets walked over and put a fatherly hand on her shoulder.

'Trust me, he'll give you a shot of valium and you'll be so off your face for half an hour you won't feel a thing. It will be just like going to the dentist – he took a bullet out of me once, years ago when I had some trouble with the Corsicans. And you're doing me a favour by being a good sport about it...'

Annabelle was momentarily aware that she had moved into a world in which it is always better to be owed than to owe. Did she want this, in spite of resenting how it was happening? Of course she'd be a fool to say no. Take what you want, but pay for it.

Datchet came back into the room. His nurse was with him and she didn't seem hungover. Annabelle looked at her and considered coldly that she clearly got a lot of surgery, either as a part of her pay or for sleeping with her employer. She was beautiful but sort of shiny – a shininess Annabelle recognised from Natasha.

I'll do this, she said to herself, because it's the right thing for me to do. I need to prove to myself that I mean it. After all, when I get the other thing done I'll need to be sure, and this helps me make up my mind. If Magda tells me that I'm thinking all wrong about being a woman, that I'm thinking in terms of surface, I'll tell her it's a commitment in my heart and I made a choice. Outward sign of inward grace, as the nuns taught us in catechism.

She got up from the sofa and went through to Datchet's office. You've got to come back a star, she said to herself as she shucked off her coat and her top and her padded bra, and put them on a chair by the door with her bag and her shoes. She made to take off her skirt and tights but Datchet gestured that she should leave them on.

'You're sure?' he asked.

'Oh yes,' Annabelle whispered, and she was.

She lay down on the table and smelled a mixture of flowers and chemicals as the nurse wiped her clean. The surgeon's hands were deft as he poked and prodded her.

'Nice development already – we'll go quite big. Not silly big so they look stretched, but you'll be surprised.'

Annabelle nodded and felt a needle slide into her arm and that was the only thing she felt. It wasn't like being asleep, it was like being somewhere else and watching from a mile away through a camera. She watched him cut – he cut on the left side first and she watched the nurse swab away blood and then she felt, though it was an interesting sensation rather than pain, as he cut through the fat under the breast tissue she already had and into the muscle beneath. It must be how a dead chicken would feel if it weren't dead, when you go in under the skin and put in the stuffing...

The implant looked a little like a jellyfish. Well, hi there, Annabelle said to it in her head as Datchet showed it to her, I'm sure we're going to be great friends.

Then she giggled, and by the time she'd stopped giggling, quietly so she didn't break anything or get in the way of anything, and she thought very hard about that, suddenly she was watching him do delicate little stitches on her right side and she'd thought he was doing the left first. Then the fog started to lift a little and she realised that she'd missed quite a lot.

'Just lie still for a bit.' Natasha held her hand. 'You'll feel like shit for days, but I think they're going to look amazing when the bruising goes.'

'Not so much of the bruising,' Datchet said, and his voice was full of professional vanity. 'I'll see you here in three weeks to take the stitches out and by then you'll have almost forgotten you didn't entirely grow your own. Vitamin E oil – here's a prescription.'

Annabelle tried to reach for it, but she still wasn't seeing quite straight, and Natasha took it for her.

After a while, she helped Annabelle stand. By this time Datchet had gone about his day, as had Mr. Carpets, and it was the nurse who helped them to the door and hailed them a cab.

'I don't have much money on me,' Annabelle said with concern.

'Mr. Carpets gave us cab-fare,' Natasha replied smugly. 'When he takes an interest he goes all the way.'

Three weeks later Annabelle went back, slightly worried that some other shoe would drop, that Datchett would suddenly be a lot less nice about it all. He was very professional about it, however, and couldn't have been gentler taking out her stitches.

'Best work I've done on one of you,' he said, preening. 'One of the best jobs I've ever done.'

But Annabelle wasn't listening to him.

He'd been right first time. Those three weeks had been strange, waking up and not even remembering at first, until the stitches caught or she found the area around them itching. And there they were, and someday soon they'd be just part of who she was and she wouldn't notice. Except when she wanted to.

*

9.

The restaurant was all white tiles and potted plants and tables with basket-weave and glass tops. Secretaries went there together for nights out, for daiquiris and steak sandwiches. Some were there tonight, and were clearly already getting right up the nose of the resident singer, a haughty blonde with cropped bleached hair, by squealing at each other through her best numbers. You could tell she was annoyed by the way she made 'Told me love was too plebeian/Told me you were through with me and' sound more like a declaration of class revanchism than a harshly flirtatious rebuke to an imaginary lover.

'She's good, isn't she?' said Thomas, whom a primrose yellow shirt and red blazer did not suit either together or separately.

Annabelle had been avoiding him. It seemed for the best.

'Yes,' she said. 'The voice is sort of muscular under the velvet.'

'Annabelle, you don't have to say you think people are good just because I fancy them.'

'I didn't specifically know that you did.'

'Well, I do. That's why I got you to meet me here. So that when you leave, in about ten minutes, I'm already here to see her.'

'I take it,' said Annabelle, sensing enough grief in the immediate offing that there was little to be lost by being at least slightly aggressive, 'that I am supposed to leave not only in the not drastically distant future, but after some homily or other?'

'Well, yes,' said Thomas. 'I've been thinking for some time that we should see a lot less of each other.'

For once, finally, he was showing sensitivity to what she wanted.

'Perhaps acknowledging each other in a distant sort of way,' she said, 'in the anterooms of literary personages to whom we introduced each other. Or did you, now I think about it, ever actually get around to introducing me to anyone?'

That was, she reflected, an almost perfect example of a rhetorical question, and he, of course, ignored it altogether, except to sniff loudly.

'Well, look, Annabelle, you're doing what you think you have to do. But I don't see why I should be expected to afford the consequences of being seen in people's eyes as regularly associated with you.'

She had been a fool ever to care about this cowardly bourgeois little shit.

'You mean that the whiff of sulphur which hangs around me might stain your cricket-flannel reputation?'

'I never asked you to hang around. I've been understanding but I've got my own life to get on with, and there is really not much of a place in it for you. Especially not now. I mean before I could sort of pretend not to notice what you felt, but now It's all too tongue-hanging-out trusty dog.'

'Bitch,' said Annabelle.

'If you insist,' said Thomas.

'But I've never pressured you or anything. And I have been sort of convenient to you, from time to time.'

'A worrisome thing/'ll leave you to sing/blues in the night,' contributed the singer.

'You've been like some bloody secretary, hanging around mooning and trying to be convenient and indispensable. Annabelle, being useful and being fancied are just things from two different worlds. You're so difficult to talk to sometimes. You spend the whole time scoring suffering points.'

'Maybe that's because people insist on making me suffer.'

'It seems to me that most of the suffering you set up for yourself. After all, you don't seem much happier now than – '

'I could hardly,' said Annabelle, 'expect things to be peachy-keen overnight, could I? I never talked about it as a quick fix. That may be what other people seem to think I thought, but not what I – '

Annabelle shut up suddenly. The gaggle of secretaries at the next table were squealing at each other a lot less, and were now leaning on their elbows to dedicate their attention to her argument with Thomas. She tried to cultivate repose and chewed meditatively on one of the glacé cherries in her pina colada. The singer didn't seem to be looking in Thomas' direction all that often, so perhaps he was not the person in the world most qualified to moan about the intrusiveness of unrequited love. She reached into her capacious bag, extracted a tissue and blew her nose.

Thomas sat forward again and stopped running his finger down his sideburn. She had always found that gesture appealing, just because of the way it seemed to reveal vulnerability peeping out from behind the complacency.

'I mean,' he said, 'look at you now. I'll admit you've got the whimpering down pretty well pat, but I don't have to be Magda to find it pretty significant that half the time these days you seem to be mainly interested in the freedom to go around snivelling. '

'I prefer to call it being in touch with my feelings,' said Annabelle, straightening her neck combatively.

'Why not try being in touch with other people's feelings a little more? You live in a world of fantasies half the time. I bet when I asked you to meet me here tonight you half-thought that it was going to be some sort of bloody tryst at which I finally admitted...'

Quite suddenly, she was laughing at him. 'Oh, give me some credit,' she said. 'I can't put my hand on my heart and say that I don't ever have daydreams, but I do have some sense of what they are, and of what the bottom line is. And what the bloody bottom line is, it seems to me, is that one way or another you are saying that you can't afford me. Like you said at the start.'

She got up to go and then thought better of it because, damn it, there were other things she wanted to say.

'Well, goodbye, my love. It was nice deluding myself about you, but I shan't again. But yes, Magda is right. She always has been. About a lot of things. I should take her advice and follow her example more often.'

'That is so typically cheap; she wouldn't talk to you about me.'

'Dream on,' said Annabelle. 'But I know about the stuffed hippo.'

'Oh.'

Tom was looking especially unappealing now – fear never suited him.

'You see,' said Annabelle, 'Her solidarity with me may be a little ambivalent. But that is politics. And we always, my love, talked. I may dream, but I have always had enough information available to me to be a realist, even in my dreams.'

As she leaned forward to say more, the straining buttons of her jacket gave in and came undone. Tom's eyes suddenly focussed on her chest and his mouth dropped slightly open.

'I love you/ just the way you are,' added the singer, whose repertoire seemed to extend from the sublime to the banal.

'What?' Tom was suddenly very flustered.

'My life is moving on in all sorts of ways.' Annabelle twitched a shoulder gently just to make sure he saw that they were really there. 'And just think, you won't have to know about any of the changes.'

'What have you done?'

Annabelle glanced down. 'Moved on,' she said with satisfaction. 'But,' she went on, as she finally and definitively rose, 'you are quite right. I need not to be around you anymore. Too much of a reminder of old times. We both have careers to think of. And new things in our lives.'

Annabelle tried hard not to overact silent dignity as she left, scoring with her heel the instep of one of the more obnoxious of the secretaries at the adjacent table. There are, at times, advantages to being slightly overwrought and slightly drunk.

'One for my baby/ and one more for the road,' added the unfortunate target of Thomas' affections.

10.

Coffee in the Gloucester Road espresso bar was becoming such a regular fixture between them that the woman who ran it kept dusting the table and calling Natasha 'Signora' so that she could eavesdrop a little more efficiently.

'You need a break,' Natasha said, unwrapping the free amaretti that had been left on a saucer. She wasn't going to eat them, but she liked to set fire to the paper. Later Annabelle would somehow or other sneak them without Natasha seeing; she usually managed. 'I mean,' she continued, 'whateverhisnameis sounds like bad news, candidly. I'm glad you told me about him, though: I was beginning to worry, what with your hanging around with that feminist and all. But the crap he's handing out you don't need.'

'So what do you think I should do?'

'Look, Annabelle. Not for very long, perhaps, but I think I know you. You'll just sit around this Goddamn city being lazy and fat and Goddamn charming, and you won't ever get a thing done worth doing, or that you want to do. And then you'll turn forty, and it'll be raining, and you'll turn on the gas.'

'You can't poison yourself with North Sea Gas. You can only blow yourself up. And the neighbours, and I am much too socially responsible to do that,' Annabelle added, awarding herself a gold merit star.

'Whatever. Look,' Natasha said earnestly, 'I'm going back in a couple of days. I mean, it's been real nice, but...'

'So?'

'Okay, see, we're friends, right? And I know I said I wouldn't get involved in helping out again, but, shit, why should you pay for Carola, right? And you surely need help, my dear. Come along with, or when you can. You must be able to get the money somehow. Review a book or something.'

'I don't think that would pay for my flight, somehow. But I'll think about it.'

''Cause I should be a connection once I'm back.'

Years later, when articles about power dressing started to appear in Cosmo, Annabelle realised why Natasha wore a suit with such narrow lapels and such singularly unappealing shoulder-pads and epaulettes. 'I need someone to do the office work; the deal's all set up and I need someone for files and letters. I don't care to handle all that. My talent has always been for selling.'

'But,' Annabelle said, taking a quick look at the brochures Natasha had shoved under her nose, ' is selling fluffy sweaters, vitamin removal creams and Mickey and Minnie personalised matching calculators for loving couples on the rhythm method quite the same as selling – you'll pardon the expression – your body?'

'Sure,' said Natasha, and, damn her eyes, ate one of the amaretti. 'It's all the market, isn't it? If you go out and sell, and what you've got's the best, people'll buy. This john in Chicago, he was a professor, and he explained economics to me, and he said it was all real simple. He said I was a perfect example of what makes America great; hustling my butt off at all hours no matter what the weather – nor rain nor hail nor savage service. When I told him I was visiting here he said maybe I should stay. People like me are needed to stop the rot, he said. That's what they need, you and a billion dollars – and I do not need to tell you, my dear, that that is what I looked like that evening. But I don't deal wholesale. So come and work for me. I'll get you in shape – I got you your tits already, didn't I? And no cream cakes.'

She crushed the other amaretti to crumbs in her fingers and put the result in the ash tray with the burnt fragments of its paper. Natasha often made actions sort of final.

11.

'Well, franchement,' said Magda, waving a trowel under Annabelle's nose, 'I think you're fucking crazy.'

'But I'm at such an impasse. And it does sound like quite a good idea, really. Where do you want these put?' Annabelle pulled up a handful of white tendrils from the old sink Magda was using as a planter.

'Honestly, Annabelle, you are so useless sometimes. Look,' Magda said, suiting action to words, 'you shake off as much soil as you can and then you stick them in the bucket over there. No, the orange one. And then when that's full you empty them onto the bonfire. Do I have to spell everything out?' She was anxious to be finished before the rain started.

'Actually,' said Annabelle,' I think you do have to spell things out, maybe. Not about the gardening. Can't you see how I'm starting to feel it would be a good idea to get away, and be where no-one will know me? I mean, you and bloody Thomas seem to think I'm so predictable. And somewhere else I could at least escape that for a while.'

'Our regarding you as predictable, Annabelle, is largely a reflection of the fact that, quite candidly, you are, but is more importantly a recognition that you are, like all of us, a product of your own personal history. One of my objections to – well, to all of this – has always been that you're trying to ignore history, to step outside it and start again, and running off to Chicago is not going to change your past.'

'Do you really think that you know the whole of what my past is, really, inside? And as for my future...'

'Unless,' said Magda, doing non-specific but vigorous things with a trowel, 'you regard yourself as some kind of totally free agent, untrammelled by history, sex and class, you have to admit that one can have a pretty good idea.'

'So perhaps I get to go to Chicago in order that a historical role can be fulfilled.'

'More likely to get yourself slashed in some sordid barroom where you shouldn't be in the first place,' said Magda, patting a tomato plant firmly into the soil in its growbag. 'Things end in tears.'

'But tears that are at last authentically mine, perhaps,' said Annabelle.

'Oh,' said Magda, staring at Annabelle's breasts in a tight-lipped way that seemed to indicate that she was not going to mention them, ever. 'And of your friends, you know.'

12.

People were odd at the airport. She'd meant to sneak away but had relented at the last moment and dropped them postcards.

Thomas was obviously relieved that she was going, but somehow it wasn't upsetting that he was. Part of what had always attracted her to him was that he played by the rules, and the rules dictated that on this occasion he be as nice as he possibly could because he was not going to have to be so for very much longer. He opened a bottle of not very good champagne and produced some lumpfish caviar on slightly battered saltines from a tin box, and she sat and drank and looked wistful, knowing perfectly well that it wouldn't make the slightest difference, or would even make things worse, if she swore and threw things.

Magda stood around shaking her head a lot and looking knowing and sad. She said there would always be place to stay at her flat when Annabelle came back. She did not actually say, 'With your tail between your legs,' but as Annabelle knew that there was some possibility that she was right, she couldn't afford to take offense at being moralised over when she wasn't looking.

Magda had a new friend, or at least one Annabelle had never met before, called Ariadne, but she rather got the sense they
were an item from the way Ariadne glowered at Tom when he
kissed Magda hallo.

Ariadne did not approve of Annabelle at all; even less of
her various decisions. She persisted in telling her and Magda so
rather loudly, and was rude to Thomas when he tried to shut
her up by forcing more champagne on her. She had that
certainty not only that her ideological position was correct, but
that none of those present could possibly have come across
such ideas before and have failed to be converted by them.

Annabelle stayed cool; she valued Magda, and this person
was important to her. Besides, she had no especial gift for being
at her most ladylike when losing her temper, and it was
important that she leave a good impression.

But the things Ariadne said rankled, and on the plane Annabelle wrote her a long postcard, which she posted at the New
York Port Authority as almost her first American act. It said:

'Well, yes, of course my dear, we are all liars and unnatural.
It is in the nature of things that we are. Falsehood has become,
if you like, my first name and my last. You will cavil at such a
use of the word 'nature'; tough. I am hysterical, though you
would double-deprecate my use of the word; I am untrustwor-
thy and unreliable. I am a thoroughly bad lot, at last, and I am
really enjoying it. Given that once I was, presumably, at least
superficially none of those things, imagine the freedom of
making a choice which involves becoming them, even if
thereafter the corruption of my – I believe the word you used,
perhaps with some special meaning, was integrity – proceeds
without further volition and without a break.'

She posted this, and then, almost immediately, posted an
afterthought. It said, 'And my tits are real. The opposite of real
is imaginary, and I know what imaginary tits are like, and these
are not they, not ever again.'

13.

To survive in a new country, Annabelle had decided that she

believed, you had to make yourself love it. One way of doing this, for her, was to eat a lot of its food.

She had pleaded to Natasha the necessity of cheap flights and of seeing New York, without which, Natasha was the first to admit, one could not fully understand the American experience, could one? And since it was in so American an image that Natasha seemed to intend to make her make herself over...

She did the museums, of course, and managed, in the Guggenheim, to get acro- and claustrophobia simultaneously amid some not very good French stage designs. Trying to find a bit of Times Square that actually looked menacing she stopped off in a rather opulently dubious bar where naked youths, she had heard, danced on trampolines most evenings, and she got herself bought drinks by telling fey young executives with gold monograms on their briefcases what happened in the second series of *Rock Follies*.

But all of that was just the surface; the real point was that moving around as a tourist gave her the appetite to tackle mountains. Special Breakfast – Links, Crispy Rashers of Hickory Smoked, Eggs Anyway You Like Them, Pancakes, Toast, Jelly, And All The Coffee You Can Drink. Oh, and our own meat loaf, golden hash browns, and chef's salad; Reubens and Italian Meatball Subs and Tuna and Beansprout on Caraway to go; Knishes and Calzones and Egg Rolls and the American idea of a samosa; icecream mounds that took as much willpower to get through as they would have done not to try.

Years later the opulent taste of American food was what stayed with her as hers, fully paid for, apprehended and digested. Everything else – the Hudson Valley, photogenic in autumn red, seen from an observation car while playing Botticelli with a witty dyke in a leather jacket with too many silly zips and a doper who would rather have been doing charades; the George Washington Bridge in a chequer cab and lightning over its towers; the Loop at dawn as she strutted home on a loose heel; even all the most personal encounters and escapades – all of that was something which, more or less, she had read in books or had seen in the movies, or might have done had she bothered to go to the Scala for that particular allnighter. The tastes of food were the bit of America she knew she had perceived entirely by and for herself. The tastes of food, and, of course, occasional pain and terror.

14.

The table she was sharing was utterly spotless by English standards, which meant that for America this place was slightly low rent and unbuttoned. If Annabelle had needed any confirmation of her certainty that she was not really as greedy as all that, it lay in the stack of hotcakes, apple, cheese and walnut Danishes, seven pieces of bacon, four sausage patties and the heaven knows how many eggs that went into the omelette in front of the man sitting opposite her. But he seemed to be in need of it; he was on that scale in all directions. As early as eight on a mild September morning he was oozing sweat into the surfers and palm trees on his shirt.

'I'm sorry to bother you, sir, but could you pass the ketchup please,' Annabelle ventured, aware that this was the first person she had spoken to in the US apart from waiters, clerks, taxi-drivers and others who are paid to be polite.

'Sure-er, lady. You're English?'

'Yes, indeed. Everyone seems to notice that. I don't know why.'

'Yeah,' he said in one of those aggressive ways that seem to come naturally to a particular sort of large man. He flipped open a leather wallet. 'You know what this is?'

'A police badge, isn't it? Detective Bunckley of – why – Chicago.'

'Ten years ago and on my own turf it would have been a lewd vagrancy bust, lady.'

'Really, how interesting. And how things have changed for the worse, officer.'

He was clearly struggling under all the fat and muscle to think of something really devastating to say. But when the police are in a position merely to be rude to you they are never nearly as good at it as the average five-year-old, who is in that position all the time, and so gets the practice. Annabelle smiled to the waitress for some coffee, and made a little tent of her hands.

'Do go on,' she said.

'I was in New Orleans last year. They're everywhere there, and they're so pretty you can't tell even if you look hard. You're not though.'

'I'm sure that an experienced and dedicated police officer like yourself has been looking hard at us all for many years. But they tell me that I have a certain raffish charm.' She sipped her coffee in a manner intended to convey that she, at least, was too polite to continue this conversational sparring.

'Well, now', she finished her coffee and left money to cover it and the tip. Breakfast could be skipped this morning. 'I've so enjoyed our little chat, officer. Do you have breakfast here every day at this time?'

'Sure.'

'Then I won't. Bon appetit, and adieu.'

'Listen, punk, even in this city, you put a step out of line I can make that au revoir.'

'Well,' she said, 'I am indeed sorry, officer. That just means, I suppose, that I will have to conduct myself with unusually absolute decorum. Not too difficult, I find. Like you said, I'm not one of the pretty ones.'

She walked out of the coffee-shop trying hard neither to stride aggressively nor swing her hips in a manner he might consider an arrestably satirical sashay. A noise of heavy breathing, and a mild ox-like odour behind her told her she shouldn't have pushed her luck. Or do you never let them see you're scared?

'I guess I was kinda out of turn,' he said. 'No hard feelings, though? I was wondering...'

Not the proposition, surely? Not even a pig could be that gauche. And much too much of a pudge, cherie, even with the muscles as well.

'Yes?' Easy on the Fenella Fielding breathiness there, girl.

'When you go back to London, if I gave you my precinct house back in Chicago, could you get me something I've always wanted?'

Help.

'I always wanted one of those hats your – er – bobbies wear?'

'Well, gosh – I mean, gee, I'm sorry, but the last time I was

having a little social chat with the super at West End Central,
he was explaining they're having to be really careful about
letting them go. Sad, really, but what with the demand, and the
cuts – you know about how we have cuts; do you have cuts too?
– they're trying to make ends meet by bottling up the market
until the going price shoots through the roof. Apparently – ' by
this stage they had drifted back to his table, he had sat down,
and she was punctuating what followed with bites of his walnut
Danish – 'apparently the Swiss Guard, you know, the Pope's
ones, started the idea a while back with all those various metal
things, cuirasses and so on, that they have to wear. A keen law
enforcement officer like yourself ought to know about the
market; I mean, it's legal and everything.'

'IAD wouldn't go for it,' he said with a beagle look of sorrow
and regret.

'Gosh, then, you've got a problem. Cos the only way usually
now is to organise swaps.'

How does one get out of this silly conversation without of-
fending this frightful thug?

'Why are you doing this anyway?' he said. 'You're not cheap
street trash like most of them. You're polite, and you don't do
all that bitchy stuff, and you've got class, I mean the accent, and
you show respect. Why do it? Wash your face and cut your hair.
And get rid of those. You know it makes sense. They won't be
able to put it back if you change your mind.'

'One of the things,' said Annabelle with hauteur, 'that I really, really like about Americans' – she was backing towards the
door while retaining the last couple of shards of the walnut
Danish – ' is that amazing warmth they keep telling you about,
that deep capacity to care and share and worry and not mind
your own Goddamn business.'

Thank God there was a cab, and she was in and off to Lex-
ington and Second before he could shamble out after her.
Presumably they can't shoot you for social chitchat. But thank
heavens, if he was typical of the Chicago Police Department,
that she wasn't planning on breaking any laws.

In a way she hoped she would see him again, though not be
seen by him, and only if something humiliating was happening
to him. A pigeon would do, she thought coarsely. Maybe it's
because he likes boys, she thought, though she knew it was not

remotely likely. And if he did, it wouldn't be that way; it would be running a baseball team for Holy Name and being a role model and leading them in the rosary, not touching them in the shower. Perhaps he's on the take – how else could he pay for a breakfast like that every day? Perhaps he'll just fall over and die, but that's not going to happen just for my convenience. It was the humiliation that she hated. He hadn't even felt he had to explain that he'd read her; had just called her 'lady' with such perfunctory fake politeness.

15.

But that was the only moment of New York that she felt as one of threat. It was September; the sweats and the sudden twenty-first floor window flare were softening, and had not yet been replaced by bitter slipperiness. In the early morning the city was quiet, warm light on glass, stone and good brick. Annabelle often regretted the tourist's prudence that kept her out of Central Park; from the perimeter, it looked like a place to be. That was its point perhaps; not only an artificial paradise, but a lost domain as well. The Village was outside expectation; small-balconied and dormered houses whose proportions were foreign rather than just International Unpleasant.

The rattle and clang of the subway was a way of travelling more different from the Tube or the Metro than either was from the other. Its map seemed to make sense, but didn't. And one actually could take the A-Train. Look, kid, she was being told, this is always going to be a damned noisy, unpleasant, boxed-in way to ride – so we will make that its point, make it frightening and confusing too, and you'll bounce out of your station with adrenalin flushing the dirt through your skin.

And they were all foreigners. After a bit, Annabelle noticed this. The fixed and painted smiles were there all the time – on pickets outside the New York Times, on the waitresses who brought her her seventh cup of coffee, on the rather seedy assistant with the worrying cough in the second-hand bookstore as he said, no, they didn't have it, but she could try the store down the street, second left, and across the intersection two blocks down. Smiles for everyone. Smiles for her

because of the accent. She felt such a fraud; they liked it so
much and she knew how less than perfect it was. Her vowels
had that Yorkshire flattening, the ends of words that West
London nasality, and none of it had been improved by the
alteration in pitch. But, what, being foreign, they did not know
could not hurt them, and reaped her dividends; always best be
sure and keep them smiling.

This was the city of Natasha's legends as well, this place of
sunlight, architecture and gluttony. It was here that Maria
found ten thousand behind her pillow one morning and had
her ring finger cut off for a cheap diamond the same night;
hither that Mexica returned with the shape of her skull altered;
here that she tried to make pointed teeth fashionable and only
failed when she bit the wrong columnist; here that silicon and
bourbon ripened Alhambra into a peach so close to bursting
that sheiks queued in the lobby, anxious to have her before the
debacle.

Annabelle knew she would have to move on; the Arabian
Nights is no place to get your head together. And Natasha had
hinted at nightmares too. 'You need seasoning a bit first,
sweets. One look at you now and those bitches would cut your
heart out and sell it for chili sauce.'

16.

'I've been spending too much money,' she announced over
breakfast to someone called Brett, whom she remembered,
vaguely and through the mists of a slivovitz hangover, having
picked up in a bar in Brooklyn the night before. What had she
been doing in Brooklyn, and what was she doing in this
apartment, and where, come to that, was it?

'Why do you think that?' he said in a voice as smooth as the
rather good hot chocolate he served for breakfast. 'What else
are you going to spend it on, apart from having a good time?'

'Well,' she said, 'I'm supposed to be in Chicago.'

'Who says?' he said. 'You'd be welcome to stay here. I need
a room-mate and, if you wanted, well, we were both drunk last
night, and I do assure you it could be a whole lot better.'

Her memory of what had passed between them was that he

had been sort of amiable and floppy. This was probably more welcome than anything more exciting or demanding, but there was no point in telling him that because he'd have probably thought she was being nice rather than truthful, and in any case she had Destiny to confront, and Destiny was more liable to be in Chicago than to be a black craftsman printer in Brooklyn. She made her adieux and left with only moments of regret, moments that soon became useless when she dropped the piece of paper with his address and telephone number on it in the process of getting notes out of her purse to pay the cab-driver.

She stopped off at a particularly nice cake shop in the Village and had a serious overdose of éclairs because she was going to be under serious observation thereafter; went back to her hotel, paid her bill, packed her bags and got a cab to Pennsylvania Station.

'This your first time in the States, lady?' the cabbie said, doing one of those smiles that show off a moustache to best advantage, and giving her a clear picture of the superiority of American dental work.

'Yes,' she said. 'That's why I thought it was time to see a little bit more of the country than just New York.'

'We like the Big Apple round here,' he said, 'but I see what you mean.'

'Do people really call it the Big Apple,' she said incredulously. 'I thought that was just for tourists.'

'You're a tourist, aren't you?'

'Not that much of one,' Annabelle said.

After that he seemed to be quite a likeable person. He smiled at her all the way to Pennsylvania Station so hard that she worried he was concentrating on doing that rather than on driving.

'Do you need any help?' he said when she tipped him rather generously. 'I don't have to go look for another fare right away, if you need help with your bags.'

So she left him with her bags by a pillar and went and got her ticket, and then gave him another tip when she came back, and he helped her load her cases onto a trolley and pointed out which way to go. It wasn't Track 29.

She thought about watching the continent go by but decided it would be more sensible to take some sleepers and doze

her way west. Friends had told her that if she insisted on
travelling by train she really wouldn't want to have to look out
at Pittsburgh and Cleveland and Gary, Indiana. In the moments
of the twenty-eight hours that she was fully awake she glanced
from the windows and saw furnaces and smoke and dirt, and
was grateful that she had friends who could show her the ropes.

Eventually it was time for a late breakfast and a lot of orange juice and coffee to flush out the sleepers, and Chicago just
an hour or so down the line. She felt like playing her Weill
tapes and went to the case up on the luggage rack. The tape
player had gone, and so had the tin box with most of her cash.
The nuns in the neighbouring seats, who had been there ever
since New York, had seen nothing; they explained that they had
made vows of poverty and so could not possibly have taken it.
It must have been the cabdriver, Annabelle eventually realised,
retrospectively distrusting gold teeth so ostentatiously dis-
played. No music, not much money and, when the train pulled
in at Chicago, on the platform, no Natasha.

17.

For a while Annabelle paced the platform, coming down hard
on the heels of her boots as if she could tread on necks. Then
she went and looked in the coffee-shop. Then she rushed back
to the platform in case Natasha had turned up late and was
getting impatient waiting for her. By this time she had that
vague feeling of itchiness that panic produces by making you
remember that you have been on a train for twenty-eight hours
and did not wash quite as thoroughly as you might have done
the couple of times you went along to the washroom and tried
to get clean.

Eventually she found a phone-booth. Natasha didn't let it
ring too many times.

'Well, I would have sent a telegram,' she started in what
might almost have qualified as apologetic terms, 'but Carlos
thought it would be a waste of time because you'd probably
already bought your ticket and would want to come anyway, so
he stopped me going down to the post office. You know how
good men are at persuading you not to run an errand at just

that moment. And anyway he thinks transatlantic phone calls put the mercury in tuna and stuff like that. He said if it was your karma to be here then you'd be here and there was nothing I ought to do about it.'

'So I can't stay with you? Is that it? You did ask me. It wasn't my idea.'

'Carlos,' Natasha said in the aggressive tone one adopts when explaining a discovery one has just made to someone whose scepticism annoys one, 'Carlos says that that was just your karma working through me.'

Annabelle hardly liked to mention the robbery; any more lectures on the workings of the Great Wheel and she would very probably be sick.

'Of course,' said Natasha – you could see the shit-eating smile down the phone – 'now Carlos is with me. And his ideas for the business are so sharp. He told me I needed a professional, not to play around with amateurs.'

'So he's, ah, professional.'

'Since you raise the issue, sweets, he is, though I probably shouldn't tell you after what Carola did, what with you two being the same and all. But he said he was sorry and that it was because of what her coke was cut with that the deal went the way it did. And I put the fear of God into her for that.'

'You've told me before that you have this tough side.'

'Of course when I say the fear of God what I really mean is the fear of me. She got the first plane out to the Coast the moment I showed her my toenail clippers. And look, I know I asked you to stay, but things have changed, so don't guilt-trip me about it. And there are lots of good cheap hotels in this city where they don't mind, you know. And the privacy will be good for your self-discipline – you won't have your feminist friends telling you it doesn't matter about being fat. I'm sorry about the job, but there'll probably be a bookstore or something that will take you on. Or is there something you could sell? Come to that... I'm sorry if I've dropped you into this, but I've told you enough times that you could learn the ropes if you had to. If push comes to shove, sweets, there are worse things in the world, you know, and you probably always wanted to be put in a position where you had to, really, anyway.'

And Annabelle did know precisely what she meant, though

she had thought she could breathe the slightly sexy scent of wickedness that had been part of Natasha's charm from the start and not end up one way or another having to pay. When you are a tourist, you don't expect it to get real.

There was a tinge of wistful regret in Natasha's voice; the worst of it was that she went on meaning well, but just not very. 'You could try the Chesterfield, I suppose. It's conveniently located for all the right sorts of bars and clubs, and Carola used to live there. I'd offer to give you a ride, but Carlos says it would be encouraging exactly the sort of dependency you Brits have to grow out of.'

Annabelle managed to organise herself sufficiently to find out how to get to the Chesterfield on the bus. There had better be no cabs for a while; money was strictly limited and there would be more important things to spend it on than them or cream cakes.

Chicago was as confusing as any city is when you first get there, and she was at this point too anxious to concoct for herself, from her passing impressions, phrases that would serve as first steps towards constructing for her the city's ambience. The bus pulled through a grubby bit full of shops and office-buildings, then through a very smart bit full of shops on the other side of a not-very-special-looking river, and then the gaps between buildings started to stretch out and the buildings to be a little grubby again. She asked someone, smiled through the usual comment on her accent, and got off at the next stop.

The Chesterfield was almost by the bus-stop. It had carpets and a coffee-shop, both more or less clean. They were quite polite on the desk as they took most of the money Annabelle had left as an advance payment.

As the lift door closed she heard the desk clerk say to someone on the intercom, 'Yes, I think so. Fucking place is getting full of them.' But she chose to pretend it had not happened; she had had enough unpleasantness for one day and wanted to lie down, not remonstrate with someone she might need to placate some day.

The room was long and narrow but overall a decent size, and it did have a bath, even though it was not a very big one. Annabelle had no great fondness for showers because she had never worked out how you were supposed to get your feet clean without scalding the back of your neck. There was a good large mirror with a reasonable light within reach of the bedside lamp for side-lighting, if you remembered where it was and didn't trip over the cord. The bed was lumpy; many had passed through it. Without bothering to do more than throw her clothes in the direction of the armchair and splash her face, armpits and crotch with tepid water, she threw herself onto it, sobbed gently, and rapidly and consolingly fell asleep.

18.

Then she had a failure of nerve. She had these occasionally, though had managed to miss out on the one she had expected after the scene with Thomas. So she was overdue. She sat alone in her room with her head in her hands for a couple of days, periodically getting up and pacing, then lying down and sleeping fitfully, dreaming of lost luggage, delayed letters and other straightforward examples of anxiety nightmares. What on earth had she been thinking of and what had she got herself into? She wasn't going to ring Natasha – she had that much pride, she was pleasantly surprised to find – but she knew that if she didn't ring, Natasha was going to assume blithely that she was making out okay and not ring her.

Even if she did ring Natasha she would likely as not end up talking to Carlos, and she didn't think she could manage that without the risk of being unforgivably rude. She had a good idea of what he would be like, she thought; his hair would be short but sort of Redford floppy at the front, and there would be some sort of slight ridgedness to it at the sides and back to demonstrate that he and his barber cared enough to want to show that they took trouble and the men's fashion magazines. He probably had a moustache as well. Surely he didn't wax it? She wouldn't, she thought with an enjoyable malice that she knew meant she was coming out of her gloom on the other side, be at all surprised. Oh God, and Gucci trainers, and designer jeans, and tee-shirts with the names of famous stores and – no, not a medallion, not even one with his birthstone, but probably a copper bracelet against rheumatism with his allergies and blood-group tastefully engraved on the inside.

(All of this proved in the event to be more or less right, except for the brand of trainers. He worked for Gucci, and if he didn't wear the product except at work his boss Salvatore might bitch about his loyalty status, but couldn't use ripping the company off as an excuse for canning him.)

In dark glasses and a trench-coat she sidled out to a supermarket a block or so away and bought a cheap packet of cold ham and an economy-size bag of apples and a very cheap transistor radio. For the first day all she could get it to tune into were the soul and country stations, which was better than no music at all, but soon made her remember how much she loathed the music of the underprivileged: she had enough cheap bravado and self-pity of her own to cope with. Eventually she lost her temper and threw the damned thing across the room. The back was a bit cracked, but it started working properly.

It was definitely time to stop being depressed, because the first things she got as she spun the dial were David Bowie singing 'Rebel, Rebel' – strange how potent cheap coincidence is, she thought – and the icier camp of Poulenc's flute sonata. As omens go, not bad. As the Poulenc tinkled to its close and she finished putting on a restrained face suitable for asking bookstores for jobs when you haven't got a green card, there came a knock on the door.

19.

Outside, trying hard to lean into the doorframe like Lauren Bacall, was a tall redhead in a dark green suede romper-suit whom Annabelle had never seen before in her life. Her legs went on forever, without pausing even momentarily to be a bum.

'Are you alright?' the redhead asked, slurring, and there was a growl in the syrup there somewhere.

'Oh, hi,' said Annabelle, hoping against hope that her face passed muster. 'I've been having a bit of a gloom. But I'm alright now.'

'So you are English, then,' said the other, in a tone that mingled breathiness with awe. 'I heard that bastard of a desk clerk say something about there being an English sister hiding out on this floor. And since I live just along the corridor – and I just love your accent – can I visit?'

'Surely,' said Annabelle, being as gracious as she could to the first human being who had addressed her in days. 'It's very kind of you to call. I'm Annabelle. You're...?'

'Alexandra, these days. It used to be Alexandria, but I decided that was a bit obvious and tacky, really. These days, I'm trying for a more genteel personal style. And this, hon, is Randolph.'

She was not, after all, wearing a snake-skin belt. The rather gaudy python unravelled itself from the suede fringes that sprouted from the midriff of the romper suit and nosed after the Planter's Peanuts Annabelle had put out for herself on a saucer. After flicking its forked tongue experimentally over a couple it decided it was not really all that interested in them and slunk back up Alexandra's leg to her waist. She was now languorously ensconced on the bed; after a few nervous twitches the python dropped back into what was presumably sleep.

'Oh, hon, I'm always doing that and forgetting to ask. You don't mind snakes, do you?'

Actually Annabelle had used to mind snakes terribly, but then she had dated a herpetologist who was also a junkie, and had the economic habit of using a favourite constrictor as a tourniquet. Once she had been in the same room with that going on a couple of times the edge had gone from her phobia.

'He seems quite a nice snake,' she said politely. 'Do you wear him all the time?'

'Oh, for sure,' said Alexandra. 'He's my partner. Whither thou goest, and all that. And you can't leave the best thing in your life lying around in this hotel. Too much hungry Puerto Rican envy tippy-toeing down the corridors, if you take my meaning.'

'One does seem to get robbed in this country,' said Annabelle. 'I can't understand it. I've hardly ever been robbed in London, and I've only been here a week and a half and a New York cabdriver rifled my bag and got my tape-player and most of my money, and he even had the nerve to grouch about the size of the tip.'

'Hey, don't go all Un-American on me, hon. You just gotta be smart, is all. Don't trust anybody except your friends. And don't put temptation in their way, come to that.'

'And there's another thing, actually, since you mention it. Do you by any chance know an expensive piece of smug treachery called Natasha?'

'Hey, you said "actually", I mean, like that. But yeah, Miss Elegance, herself? I couldn't say we were dear and close friends. But years ago, when, hon, she was not what she is today, not by any means, I picked her up a couple times when they bounced her on the sidewalk. And a couple times since she's favoured me with a distant grin from those siliconed lips as she whizzed past in that Porsche she has. What's she to you?'

Annabelle explained. She hardly played it for sympathy at all.

'Well,' said Alexandra, dabbing her mascara with a tissue. 'You are a klutz, aren't you? They did tell you about not taking sweets from strangers, and coming in outta the rain, and Santa Claus, and all that? I've decided' – she stood and drew herself up to her considerable height with a fluid twist of her hips and calves, and Randolph hissed quietly and lethargically – 'I have decided, hon, that you and I are going to be great friends. I'll get your ass out of the sling in which it finds itself, and you can teach me to speak like an English lady.'

'That's most awfully kind and sweet of you,' said Annabelle, 'but Americans never seem to understand about my accent. It's nowhere near as correct as all that.'

'God, so it's true about England, isn't it? You really do have this thing about class. Listen, hon, it's a good voice and it will serve you well, and it's the best one I'm ever going to have to learn from.'

Annabelle reflected that life was bound in the circumstances to be constantly a matter of approximations and of compromises.

Alexandra fussed around the room for a few minutes, and cooed in a suitably impressed way over the labels in a couple of the dresses which Annabelle now filled out perhaps a little over-generously. She suggested they went for coffee, stressing in advance that it would be her treat. Annabelle graciously agreed that this would be pleasant, but did make the slightly theatrical point of using the padlock she had bought for the wardrobe. Once the issue of one's lack of street sense had been raised, one could never make too much of a point of trying to acquire its superficies.

'That's better,' said Alexandra as she locked the room door.

They talked a lot over coffee, and Alexandra insisted on buying them both a sandwich as well.

Annabelle realised quite quickly that Alexandra was not necessarily all that good an exotic dancer, because if she had been she would not have been living in a fleabag like the Chesterfield. And she would probably have had a spare snake. She waved her hands around an awful lot. If one had wanted to flatter her – and eventually, once she'd spent several days refining the precise phrasing, Annabelle brought a spark of pure delight into her Kohled and spangled eyes by raising the matter – one would have compared her movements to those of a Javanese temple dancer. But in a small coffee-shop what they mainly did was make you keep a close watch for the tasselled lampshade, the ketchup bottle, and the taller bits of crockery.

20.

'Well, of course,' Alexandra confided over her second iced coffee, 'it was Mexica who taught me every little thing I know.'

'So she really exists? She was one of the bits I assumed was just Natasha fantasizing.'

'Oh, for sure,' said Alexandra. 'She came by back when I was just an unhappy little girl in the Coastguards, and she gave us a show. Not that the others knew, of course, but I did. Sort of natural affinity. And she invited me backstage and none of them could understand why, and they made foul, coarse remarks about it, so fuck them, 'cause I surely wasn't about to tell them. She was terribly sympathetic and nice that time, and she said that from one look at me I shouldn't, just shouldn't, be there. But I had to finish out my time, because you don't want to spend time in those stockades, hon. Terrible things can happen to you in there, even if you're careful. Not that terrible things don't happen to you in the Chesterfield Hotel. So I sat on my bunk and kept quiet for a couple years and read *My Life...*'

'By Isadora Duncan, you mean?'

'Clever kiddy.'

'Just a guess.'

'And then, when they let me go, I went straight to New York. Mexica wasn't there then; she was off in Switzerland, having that thing done to the shape of her head. But it was her who got me there.'

'And she hadn't made you any promises.'

'Well, no, but you shouldn't be hard on Natasha, is sort of what I'm saying. You'd still be in London, doing whatever you'd be doing there. And don't feed sauerkraut to Randolph; it's not you has to spend the evening with a farting snake.'

'So how did her head look afterwards? No-one ever seems to say.'

'I couldn't see any difference really, but I always thought she looked a bit like a lizard anyway. A real beautiful lizard, of course. If it made her feel more at ease with herself then I guess it was money well-spent. I never understood how they could do it without affecting her brain a bit; I guess they put a tuck in it or something. Not that La Divina was ever a full load of bricks anyway. When she came back we had lunch and she told me about not doing cream cakes and I showed her the act I'd worked out and she told me "Darleeng, get yourself a snake for Chrissake. It'll give you something to do with your hands, and maybe with your evenings." Which was maybe a bit smartbitch when you think about it, but happens to have been the second-best bit of advice anyone ever gave me. Randolph is awfully jealous – did I say "awfully" right, hon? – and I have to be real relaxed and at ease with a guy before he calms down and stops trying to bite their toes.'

'Doesn't that restrict you emotional life a bit?'

'Yeah, but it makes it feel real secure. Anyway, you'll meet Mexica sometime. She doesn't live here, of course. She doesn't live anywhere, she doesn't believe in it. But she passes through on the way. Of course you'll have to put up with a little bit of viciousness, probably. I mean, you don't do nearly enough to the ends of your eyebrows. Or is there some reason for that? I don't see British *Vogue* very often these days. Mind you, she usen't to want to bother much herself, which is why she did what she did to hers in the end. But you surely must've been told all about that, hon?'

'Well, gosh, I'm sorry, Alexandra, darling, but I have to admit that in amongst telling me about the finer points of the neglect of my own eyebrows – and yes, it is bone-idleness, not some fashion pointer or feminist principle – in ticking me off, sweet Tasha did omit to tell me about whatever it is you mean.'

'Well, sorry I'm sure. You needn't get snippy with me. I'm not bitching you up or anything. Just trying to help, is all. We've all been there, more or less, and it's quite a nice face, considering....'

'But you see, darling, that's just what Natasha used to say, but when you got past the considering, what she was considering was that I needed to have nose and cheekbones and chin razed to the ground, and salt sown in the ruins, and to start over again from scratch.'

'I don't mean anything that major, hon. She's just fussy. No, one day Mexica was sitting in this hotel bar in Miami where they do très ornamental Margaritas. She doesn't drink: she feels she owes that to the memory of the Alhambra. But she does think the right full glass can be an attractive accessory. Some PR fag across the room made a Remark. La Divina is awfully sensitive when people bitch at her in Spanish. Maybe she doesn't understand the rest of the time; I always meant to get a phrasebook. Anyway, what he said was something about her eyebrows. So she stuffed her ice down his ascot and squeezed her lime over his moustache and she said, "Okay, maricon," and she walked right out of that bar. And when she went back in there the next time she had had them electrolysed out and the most perfect bow arches you ever saw tattooed in. It was the principle of the thing.'

21.

Alexandra discussed Annabelle's financial predicament in a helpful and constructive manner.

'You are just going to have to get yourself some money, hon. What a good thing I knocked on your door.'

She was, herself, between proper engagements, she said, and had been ever since her agent had been careless where he put his cigar ash and Randolph had responded by sinking his teeth into the agent's wrist.

'It's not that pythons don't bite; it's just that you don't have to worry about poison or anything when they do. But this little fat guy, he goes on and on about tourniquets and serums even though it was only a scratch. And since then he hasn't been coming through with the goods.' Instead, Alexandra was hostessing down at the Ace, and Diane let her do go-go work as a way of keeping herself in trim.

The Ace was a run-down mansion just down the block and at the end of a side-street. You could tell it had been rather grand once because the club area was essentially a converted reception area and ballroom, with second-floor ceilings that had cherubs on them. It also had some rather fine Deco stained glass, and periodically people from the Design Faculty or the Art Institute would turn up at the bar with the excuse of wanting to look at it.

'Diane,' Alexandra explained, 'doesn't really like it because they don't spend much on drink, so she encourages them to come mid-afternoon, when business would be slack anyway. That way she can increase her average hourly turn-over for the books, and they can talk about rich colour-values and go ooh and aah without disturbing Randolph and screwing up my act. She did suggest to the bosses that they auction it, or even give it to the Institute, but they said they keep the building up as an investment, not for what she makes them from the club, and their architectural advisers said the house would be more valuable with the glass in place when the time came to sell. You'd never believe how thorough they are in artistic matters.'

Diane was small and neat and had probably been born wearing black silk sweaters and designer jeans; there was a tight body structure to her that made you as nervous as she was. Just not as productively so. She was essentially anonymous – you remembered the loose shaggy perm, the big glasses and the row of bangles, and not much else. She did a good job at the Ace but always seemed too efficient to be limited to it, as if it were a warehouse in which she was being stored against need.

(Years later Annabelle worked for a literary editor in London who seemed to be the same person, but it was probably just the same energy, tough, strained competence and vigorous pointing of the hands. Annabelle decided against checking out the resemblance, or the magazine's backers, though they too were awfully thorough in artistic matters.)

'Waifs and strays, I see,' said Diane. 'Still, we could do worse than the voice, and it might mean I shift some of that Gordon's I got a case of on consignment. You can work bar, can't you? Everyone can work bar,' she continued, before Annabelle could answer. 'Teeth and smiles and cleavage, and chatter to them so long as no-one's waiting parched and it doesn't distract from the girl on stage or the ones who are sitting with them, because it's them that are making us the money. You keep your tips and I pay you flat rate too. I do that with everyone these days now Mayor Byrne's got so tough on B-Drinking. Can't say I'm sorry; did it myself before they put me in as manager. Rotten way to make a living, I always thought so, and either the standard of your booze or the standard of your girls is bound to suffer in the end. And it's hell on the potted plants. Right, well, you can see where everything is; get Alexandra to do your cheekbones for you, dear; they need to look more dramatic in this lighting.'

Annabelle went back to the Chesterfield to prepare. She had severe doubts about all of this. It was just the sort of thing that everyone said would happen to her if she went to the States: craven complicity with sexism and probably with organised crime as well. Ariadne would have sniffed loudly as if everything she had ever thought had been instantly confirmed, and Magda would have fussed around, given her good stern advice and increased the volume of her reading list.

But what do you do in a foreign city with no money when the one friend you have in the world thrusts a job on you, and insists on restructuring your use of blusher? It takes real principles to be ungracious, and Annabelle knew she just didn't have them in her. And it was this or hang around outside McDonald's waiting for people to drop their fries. If you will the ends, you will the means, and she supposed that it proved Ariadne and Magda were quite right about her.

*

22.

On her third night a dreaded presence squatted at one end of the bar. It probably wasn't the visible presence of a uniform instead of a silly Hawaiian shirt that made him look more menacing, though it did make his fat look harder.

'Why,' Annabelle said in a nervous trill, 'Officer Bunckley. What can I get you?'

'They said there was a new girl here on the bar and it was one of you lot and it was a limey, so I thought it might be you. This is a small city so be very careful what you get up to, because if I catch you outta line, your ass is green. And I'll have a Bud. On the invisible tab, if you take my meaning.'

Annabelle did. She supposed he drank canned and bottled beer so that no-one would be tempted to spit in it.

He went off to be unpleasant to a couple of the girls at a table too far away for Annabelle to be sure that he was being unpleasant except from the commiserating shrugs and grimaces that the one he was mostly not looking at kept making in her direction. Annabelle relaxed and continued to try and explain the house policy to a visiting Rumanian trade delegation whose French was better than hers, but not much. Eventually they understood that it was just like clubs in Rumania, i.e. a rip-off as far as all that was concerned, and they moaned at each other in some soulful dialect and ordered a round of triple bourbons and sat at the table next to Bunckley, adding a note of impatience to his girls' grimaces. Annabelle noticed him move his chair firmly away from this new source of contamination; clearly he didn't like Communists either.

There was no-one else to be served for the moment so she relaxed. Randolph was snoozing in an empty ice-bucket and Alexandra was telling stories again, sitting on the bar, swinging her legs in a clock-time but restrained alternation.

'I thought you used to be on the circuit, Diane, and you never heard about Earthquake?'

'No, Alexandra,' said Diane, in that note of tired tolerance she standardly adopted in such conversations, and which she was allowed to get away with without being bitched out because she was, after all, the boss. 'I have to allow that I really never did. It's a big circuit out there, and you girls have your own grape-vine, anyway. You're like these Armenians I know, everyone's each other's fifth cousins.'

'Well, like you say, Earthquake was a sister, and she got real ambitious after Mexica looked in on her act and told her it wasn't bad but needed something, a little extra to give it a real zip. With me it was Randolph; sometimes I think Mexica just says it to be polite, and others I think it's to make us insecure. But, anyway, around about then there was this disaster movie, and a lot of cinemas got talked into hiring these sound-projectors, subsonics I think they call it, that make the place shake like the San Andreas fault let go. And when the movie bombed these gadgets were on the market all over, right. So Earthquake had this real neat idea.'

'I saw that act once,' said a guy at the bar wearing a Shriner fez. He had apparently originally come in the Ace during a convention and only went away ever again to sleep and get money, but even after years no-one knew his name. He was too dull to bother to find out, and only ever had enough money to pay for his drinks and a tip, so it wasn't worth trying to gold-dig him. 'I forgot that was what they called her. When she got heavily into the grinding, this thing happened, and the crown on my front tooth shook loose.'

'Yes, well, that turned out to be the problem,' said Alexandra. 'She was out on tour and her agent was reading *Variety*, and he noticed how many show-lounges had fallen down a couple weeks after she played them. Not built as strong as cinemas, I guess. So he called her up and they went off to Barcelona together, because he always wanted to go there to look at this cathedral, and he reckoned the management'd find them anywhere. And they did, but they weren't very annoyed with her, except for going off without asking first, for which they disciplined her a bit, but not so it showed, cos they wanted her to do a whole lot more touring. What the agent forgot is, places are insured, right? And they own builders, too, so it was handy all round. I don't know what happened to the agent; they didn't need to be nice to him.'

*

23.

'Oh God, so you're working for that old harpy Diane,' said Natasha, when Annabelle called in on her for tea. 'And you're mixed up with Alexandra, too. Well, I guess it just means you've found some sort of appropriate level. At least it's not the Hawaiian girls.'

'I can't stop people being nice to me,' said Annabelle, trying not to sound ironic to an extent that might jeopardize her right to a pot of Earl Grey.

'No one has to let those people be nice to them.'

'I have to keep eating.'

'You'd be much better if you didn't. Carlos says that the real proof of the superiority of Indian thought is that they all manage to do without food so well. We just couldn't do it – much too materialistic. But he says he'll work on that with me after yoga has got my sexual responses sorted out. We're working on that right now; he thought it was the priority.'

'How considerate of him,' said Annabelle, forgetting for a moment about the irony.

Natasha didn't notice; she often didn't. She had had a deep purple streak put into her raven hair, and had cut a tear in the knee of her jeans, which she had carefully stitched the ends of and covered in safety pins – she had explained on the phone that she was going through a punk phase.

'And how is Carlos?' Annabelle brought herself to ask.

Natasha looked soulfully round her room, at its tubular steel furniture, Perspex coffee-table and well-stuffed cushions.

'Still awfully good. And he's making a real job of the accounts. I had a look at the books with him last week and I couldn't follow them at all, no matter how much he explained his system. Oh, and I had a call from Carola yesterday; she doesn't like it in San Diego at all. I could tell from her tone of voice as she talked about the sun and all. But I said 'toenails' very distinctly and dauntingly, and she knows me well enough to have got the message. I can't understand her; I took the mousy little wimp that she was out of that scuzzy antique store of her aunt's, I reorganized her life in detail, and I gave her, practically gave her, a whole new outlook and face. And then she turns on me and betrays me viciously. Of course she takes too many drugs. Deformation professionelle, sweets.'

The latter concept was one which had occurred to Annabelle in other contexts. In this particular one, though, after mixing gin and tonics for Japanese businessmen a few hundred times and watching them slurp them down in seconds, she had come to think that perhaps the sweet-factory principle was universal. She herself was less interested in drinking than she had ever been. Perhaps it just meant that she was secretly happy. And perhaps it was different with coke.

She had much for which to forgive Natasha, and one ought to have some pride and not come calling. But, well, her apartment was one of the few places in Chicago where Annabelle knew she could get Earl Grey on an afternoon off, and the lithographs on the walls were bad enough to be mildly amusing.

The only trouble was the view. Natasha hadn't mentioned which floor the apartment was on when she asked Annabelle to stay. She probably thought you could cure acrophobia that way, and she was never one to leave her dear friends with a problem, a blemish, or anything that was unreconstructedly them.

The door clicked open, and a dream of men's white suiting strutted into the room.

'Hello, my ownest. I just popped in to pick up some dispatch forms. Oh, I thought you'd be alone. I guess this must be Annabelle. I can tell from your descriptions.'

'And, for just the same reasons, you must be Carlos.' The moustache actually was waxed at the ends.

'Oh, my most darling,' he said to Natasha, 'you are so right: in spite of it all, she does have this gorgeous accent. If she's going to have to be around I'd use the chance to learn to copy it, if I were you. Not right for my image, of course, but for you it could be chic. You have to think image when we're thinking expansion. I looked at the order books again, my loveliest. Going places.'

He pecked Natasha dexterously where his moustache and her lip-gloss would not contaminate each other and, snatching up some papers from a side-table, span from the apartment like a dancer. Natasha turned from watching him go, and sighed; her eyes were fogged.

It is always alarming, as well as gratifying, to discover your friends do, after all, have their weak points. Natasha's fierce quest for perfection was such an absolute that to find her flaws out was a real crisis for Annabelle, who was obliged in some important matters to rely on her friend's judgment. But – and she knew she was prejudiced against him, and he just wasn't her type to start off with, and Thomas wore even more dreadfully precious clothes, and she bore him a grudge because of the way he had messed up her plans – but, honestly, he was such a cheap gigolo.

'Goddamn it,' said Natasha. 'I hadn't wanted you to meet him. Maybe we should have gone to a coffee shop or something. I mean, sweets, you're no threat or anything, of course – you don't mind my saying that, do you, because you know it's true, and your realism is one of the most attractive things about you, I've always thought. But you are Carola's astrological twin, and you can't be too careful about the stars. Well, what did you think? Isn't he great?'

'Well, I don't know about that, and I'm not going to, am I? But he seems to make you happy, and that's all a friend ought to care about, isn't it?' The euphemism kid rides again, she thought. 'Tell me, did he buy the lithographs as a present, or were they a joint purchase?'

'Oh, he got me to buy them from this friend of his to improve my taste. He thinks that when I was in London I lost touch with modern American values. That's part of the down he has on you, sweets. It's important that things be Now, he says. And water-lilies just are not that, are they, sweets? He says that the Post-Impressionists just are not tenable any more. He was impressed that I'd bothered to develop any taste at all, of course, but he said that I'd just have to...'

'Tear it down and start again from scratch?'

'Why, sure, his very words.'

'Just reminded me of something.'

Annabelle was not sure, seconds later, whether she had had the nerve to say that aloud. Natasha gave no sign of having noticed, even if the remark had been vocalized at a level she could have heard.

'He says,' said Natasha, looking large-eyed and confiding, 'that it is important in a relationship such as ours that I not exercise my will too much. He says my will is much too yang, or maybe the other one. In the circumstances. I've got to learn to go with the flow of my environment, he says, and not try and change it by unbecoming aggression. He sets up all these exercises for me, like cheating at solitaire so as to lose.'

'In the circumstances? So he does know, then?'

'Well, if he didn't I'd never have let you in the apartment with those eyebrows and everything. I mean, friendship is friendship, but a girl has to look after her own interests, hasn't she? No, someone told him when we first met, someone trying to turn him against me for purposes of their own, but it didn't work at all. He says I'm much too beautiful for it to matter much. And he thought it would be a healthy opportunity to explore neglected areas in his own psyche, and he thought he could do me a lot of good in the process. What you do not understand, Annabelle, is that in this country we can combine self-interest with consideration of others' best interests. There just is not a conflict. He says that is what's wrong with you Brits, and why I shouldn't get too involved. So, anyway, we continued to get to know each other, and he found out enough about the things that were left over as wrong with me from before that he could tell me all about them.'

'And the business with Carola? How does that fit in?'

'Sometimes, Annabelle Jones, you are just not very gracious, are you? But, since you have to be so tacky as to ask, he has assured me, cross his heart, that she got round him by appealing to his better nature, saying that she really needed him, and he felt sorry for her. She's so pathetic really. When her nose isn't stuffed full of money to give her confidence, she's just a wet little mouse. She told him awful lies about me bullying people. He had to listen, he says, because even from her warped perspective he might find out something important about me. He does take making me over very seriously, you know. And she got him ripped.'

Annabelle thought quite hard about letting it go, though managed to keep her forehead clear of furrows while she did so. It would be safer and much more non-aggressive to do so, and she knew what Carlos would say her saying anything aggressive proved about her. Magda and Ariadne too, probably. She decided to enjoy it, rather than just perform it as a sisterly duty.

'Natasha darling, it has been a lovely cup of tea. Gosh, it

really has. And the lithographs are nice, and thanks for show-ing me the one with the pink trees and the green spiders. Somehow I am so very much fonder of you than I was when I got here, and I really think of you as a friend again. Really, don't worry about me, because things are going to be all right for me in Chicago; honestly they are. I'm being made to stand on my own two feet, you see. And you did get me here. But, oh honestly, my dearest darling Natasha, I really have got to say it.'

'Say what?'

'Aren't you getting carried away more than a little on the most awful tide of bullshit? I mean, we are friends after all, and you'd tell me in seconds in like case, and you tell me about my eyebrows and things, and I don't mind, really, because I know you mean it for the best, and it often is, and nor should you mind. But he is quite frightful, you know.'

The most attractive – the only attractive – piece of art in the apartment was the vista of Chicago stretched out across the window. Long straight roads that disappeared to infinity across each other, and just enough diagonals and curves round the lake and along the river to keep it from being a board-game. And Twenties houses, and the John Hancock Dark Tower looming, and the river, and the dying lake. For a second Annabelle looked out at them all intently. Doing so made a useful and emphatic point, and she needed to practice doing that by being still. Also, anyway, she might soon be outside the window with them.

Natasha hadn't gone pale, but it would have been hard to tell. She always wore such major slap, even for a sisterly cup of tea.

'Oh, you are a bit hard on him,' she eventually said, dis-missively. 'I know he's not your type, but then look at what your type is, frankly. And you just don't understand where he's coming from. It's because you're a foreigner, I guess. And since you really don't fancy him, maybe that means there's some-thing wrong with Carola's chart.'

'But I'm not talking about my feelings. Don't you see that, considered objectively...'

'There you go again, being all yang and analytical,' Natasha said in the lofty tone of someone on an inside track, and pointing her nose at the ceiling in the manner of one whose inside track is also Higher Things. 'You're just not in touch with yourself yet, you see. But I've got to move on, and I need some love and affection. You wouldn't have time for that right now, but I've got where you want to be going and I can tell you it's logical. You just don't know what I want, or what you'll want.'

'Okay, Natasha,' said Annabelle, putting on an Older but Wiser face in response to her friend's posing. 'But I did say it. Remember that. And you know I mean well.'

'Oh, sweets, it's just your pain speaking. When you say stuff like that I know it isn't just bitching, because you are not, my dear, subtle enough to say things in an emotionally convincing unbitchy way if you were. Of course I forgive you, and I only thought a bit about breaking your nose with the table-lighter. Which would be a really unfriendly act, considering.'

24.

For a few weeks, then, this was the rhythm of Annabelle's life. She spent a lot of her time with Alexandra in the hotel and at work, and came to realise that she and the tall, leggy camp redhead were friends, even though they came from different planets; this last being a fact of which Alexandra seemed most of the time charmingly unaware. But then Annabelle never actually raised the issue in so many words, just turned the radio station over when Alexandra winced at Schoenberg or Carla Bley. Alexandra's relentless tide of anecdote washed over her; it was a relief to be around someone who didn't even notice that they were doing all the talking.

'You know, hon,' Alexandra eventually said, 'you have it in you to be a great whore, in spite of not having the looks. You've got really good at looking really interested when I tell the same story for the third time; it's a useful talent, and it does you credit.'

'Well, gosh,' said Annabelle,' it's not that. Actually, they're very good stories, and someday, if I listen carefully, I might be able to pass them off as my own.'

'Flatterer,' said Alexandra, and slapped her friendlily across the cheek. 'Like I said, you're such a little whore.'

Annabelle spent most of her afternoons off with Natasha, and tried very hard not to venture further subversive thoughts about her friend's paramour, not even the merest whisk of a tail around a distant corner. Whether Natasha had said anything to Carlos or not he never turned up in the flat again when Annabelle was there; he must have had some sensitivity to be so competent at conning people, she supposed, and she wouldn't be worth dignifying even with a row. It was comparatively easy to avoid thinking about him as long as she stared melancholically out of the window and averted her gaze from the lithographs, the tubular steel chairs and the mobile of revolving puce and silver prisms that soon joined them.

It was a little colder now in the evenings but she still had her beaver coat; luckily she had been wearing it at Penn Central or it would have gone the way of all fur. She had a pair of hunting boots that even Natasha admitted had a degree of chic, though not with non-designer jeans.

On days when she was going to be with Alexandra Annabelle shaded her cheeks and the sides of her nose and did her lip-lines one way; and when she was going to see Natasha she would do them another, the way Natasha liked it. She would make as sure as was consistent without actually using the fire-escape that she got in and out of the hotel without Alexandra's seeing this; she felt innocent of disloyalty, but she knew both sets of cosmetology lectures were well-meant, and that her friends would be hurt and feel competitive if she got careless. There is such a thing as tact.

All the lectures on self-improvement stuck in a way. She saw a doctor for her shots in a part of town that you reached by riding the El through acres of burned-out apartment blocks with charred rafters sticking out and casting shadows like a Piranesi prison. She went to see a Hawaiian sister in an office over a gun shop to have hot needles stuck into her upper lip and round the corners of her chin. Natasha was magnanimous and gave her a case of some cream made from dead baby chicks, and she rubbed it into her face and her breasts every time she had a bath, and she brushed her hair a hundred and fifty times, morning and night. She even started touching her toes and doing sit-ups, but decided it was necessary to preserve some autonomy and stopped. She went and read in libraries in the mornings, and spent her sandwich money in second-hand bookstores and never even thought about cream cakes. Slowly her figure changed from what she would have called pudgy to what she had learned in New York to refer to as zoftig, and Natasha eventually noticed enough to sniff and say she supposed it was some sort of improvement.

By now Chicago was America for her, far more convincingly than New York had ever been. New York was still The City, as was London. Both were Babylon, rich in ivory, silver, gold and the souls of men; both were prosperous and fallen. Chicago lacked that sense of scale and of the metaphysical. It was provincial, and knew its limits. For that reason it had a sense of home, of the Leeds of her adolescence. The likeness was no more than an analogy, and could never pass for an identity. There was the brashness of the Age of Gold in common, and a capacity for being vulgar, because when you've got the brass no-one can afford to call you on it. Both Leeds and Chicago had art galleries better than you might have expected. But Leeds never had that much money, and Atkinson Grimshaw is not up to Monet.

A lot of the people were fat; the cities had that much in common. In Leeds, though, it was chip-butty bloat rather than mere over-eating. Chicago was bumptious enough to have forgotten Depression. Leeds had never recovered its nerve; rightly, because Depression was back there again, and you found what you never found in Chicago, grass between the cracks of the mosaic tiles in the underpasses of the motorways of the Sixties. Where Leeds, at best, had had architects for whom Pevsner was prepared to make a case, the whole point about the buildings of Chicago was that it had had architects for whom no-one ever felt a case needed to be made; splendidly arrogant dark towers and bright lights and green glass waterfalls, and flowerbeds and trees on unlikely heights.

The arrogance was nervous. There were those acres of charred brick and wood as a reminder of something else, and places where you knew you never went. If it was laid out like a board-game, there were dangerous squares. The dark towers showed you that you could win, but you had also to know that it was possible, terminally, to lose. Annabelle avoided thinking of this at night, and she spent her afternoons thinking of the smaller beauties of arty little streets.

25.

'What do you do all the time, hon, inside your head, when
you're not here?' asked Alexandra as they strutted around Old
Town together one afternoon, killing time before the Ace
opened. 'I know you go away a lot; not that you glaze or
anything – '

Annabelle had been looking up from a tourist boutique full
of uninteresting sweat-shirts and strip-club frontage at the
higher storeys of the Lloyd Wright School of buildings they had
been tacked onto. She returned to herself with mild confusion
and an instant ingratiating nervous smile, and tried to cover up
by repairing her lip-gloss.

'You're a quiet one,' Alexandra continued, 'and you're always looking at things when you ought to be looking out. This
is the street you're on, and you've got to watch out on the street,
not look at the buildings. It's not a picture gallery out here; it's
a shooting-range. There are hawks out, and I don't just mean
it's getting a bit cold. I really don't mind it, being your friend; it
has sort of fringe benefits, I guess. Just, you need watching all
the time, and some of it you might watch out for yourself.'

'Oh, I'm sorry, Alexandra. I don't mean to be a burden, or
to take advantage, or anything. But bits of this city are just so
good to look at.'

'Yeah,' said Alexandra, joining her in repairing her makeup
in a handy mirror in the boutique window, 'some of its wallets,
and a very few of its cocks. Hey, Miss Priss, don't you ever go
out to get tackily laid? Or is it just one endless round of refined,
genteel, intellectual pleasure?'

'Well, yes, but I used to be in love, and that makes it hurt
to think of, somehow. I haven't here, because I'm told this is a
dangerous foreign city and yes, I do know about the ravening
beasts and birds of prey out here, and what I know is that if you
don't know the rules it's safer to live like a nun. I went to this
joint called the Regency one time in London and I didn't know
the rules there, and this boy asked me to dance, and I snogged
with him a bit, and this very large man hit me in the face the

moment he saw us together. I had a black eye for days. I ruined his suede boots for him, though.'

'Oh wow,' said Alexandra, 'what did you do? Slash them?'

'I was on the floor and I threw up on them. When you hit a new world there are manners to learn, and you either learn manners by getting slapped hard on the wrist, or by simply sitting still and watching what the grownups do. I don't like getting slapped, and that leaves me with being quiet. What the grownups do, though, is often so very boring that I suppose I do let my attention wander a bit.'

'Well, pardon me, hon,' said Alexandra. 'I'm sure that's what's best for you if you think it is. You can trust me, anyway; and I don't mind us going round as a pair for a while, anytime you want. I mean, you're fit to be seen with. I'm glad you listened, finally, about the eyebrows; it's an improvement. If you ever feel like hunting as a pair that's okay too. Two bitches can be safe, right; it's not just you that doesn't feel safe getting laid without someone riding shotgun. And if we ever go down to the Chatterbox.... The Chatterbox is full of malice and loveliness, but if you are careful, or have a friend to watch out for you, it can be a good place to get your meat. I am just so wholly glad that right now it's no longer the place where I have to go to get my bread as well.'

26.

Business was slack in the Ace that night, and Annabelle was discussing Grimm's Law and the Great Vowel Shift with the only customer at the bar. His approach was quite distressingly mechanistic, but as long as he kept buying gin Annabelle wasn't going to correct him too volubly. Alexandra was so bored she was listening to the conversation, not that that helped her much.

'You mean,' she said, in a tone more of incredulity than of genuine intellectual enquiry, 'that one day in the Middle Ages everyone suddenly swapped their vowels around? Sounds a really dumb idea is what I think.' Randolph poked his head out of the empty ice-bucket at the sound of her raised voice, and she peered into his dark eyes for confirmation.

Suddenly there were whistles being blown all over the place and the Ace was full of uniformed police who did not look like customers for Tequila Sunrises. Annabelle's philologist was too drunk or too embroiled in intellectual passion to notice their arrival until one of them tapped him on the shoulder. He looked round, gulped down his drink and cringed.

'Yes, officer?'

'Time to go, sonny. Place just closed for business. What's your name?'

'Ah... Ah... Grimm, Officer.'

'Oh, sure,' said the cop, 'just like your brother. Any stories you want to tell before you leave? Or any complaints about the service?'

'Only,' the philologist lurched towards the door, 'that this bargirl has views about linguistics that are fundamentally unsound.'

'Everywhere I go,' said Detective Bunckley as he sauntered up to the bar, reached over and opened himself a beer, 'I hear complaints about your attitude. You get nowhere in this town with attitude. Done anything about my helmet yet? No? Let's see if there's any of your business here I can be minding for you. I knew I'd be seeing you again, lady; you're not so smart.'

Irrespective of what they were or were not wearing the girls got rousted out onto the night-time street. Annabelle was glad of her plumpness; it had kept her in the comparatively conservative clothing appropriate to bar-work when you're not competing, and now it kept her warm in the cold. Alexandra was wearing one of her dance outfits, and the others stood around her to keep her warm and protect her from passing drunks.

'Form the wagons in a circle,' she said.

Diane had been paying off a captain who had been moved over to Serious Crimes and had forgotten to tell her. They found twenty-seven violations. The lemon slices Annabelle was putting into the gin were fresh, and they should have come out of a bottle; the lights were not put up full when people looked at the stained glass and someone had sprained an ankle on the low stage; there was no separate toilet for Randolph; the hat check was done by whoever was not working at the time, rather than by someone trustworthy and specially designated. Some of these were harder to believe than they were going to be to pay off, but you don't argue with the Vice when they still might cart everyone off in a paddy-wagon.

They searched everyone's bags for drugs but didn't get lucky; they took most of the girls' money away 'to check it for forgeries.' And you didn't go down to the station to ask for it back.

After she had made the necessary phone-calls Diane went to the wall-safe and found enough money in petty cash to take them all out for chow mein. Alexandra had been out for Chinese with Diane before, and something was clearly on her mind, because she wasn't concentrating on her chopsticks. Noodles were splashing soy and corn-starch on her usually immaculate silk blouse. The others went off to get their coats, but she gestured with the spare rib off which she was picking shreds of pork that she wanted Annabelle and Alexandra to stay behind a second or so. She looked sufficiently embarrassed and apologetic that Annabelle knew she was going to be fired. She had seen that expression on bosses' faces before.

'Look, I'm sorry,' Diane started. 'I'm really sorry, kid, but Bunckley's such a weird bastard; you never know whether he stays bought, and he never does anything so important that anyone really bothers to sort out his affairs for him. But even before tonight I'd had to tell management about you because it's my job to let them know anything that affects business.'

'So?' said Annabelle, for the sake of appearances.

'Well, they don't want to take any risks, so I've got to let you go. I told them you give good gin and tonic, but they don't drink it and none of them are that interested in good service. They don't cream off tips, you see, so why should they be?'

Annabelle was tight-lipped and trying to be gracious. She knew that it wasn't Diane's fault and she was determined that she was not going to give her a hard time for it.

'Well, Diane,' she said, 'it's been super. Thanks for everything. And do you mind if I steal just one more of those ribs?'

'Hang on,' said Alexandra, drawing herself up to her full height even though it made the sequins hanging from her leotard jingle. 'This is just not good enough, hon; it's really shitty that they should do this to you. Look, Diane, you know how Bunckley gets on sisters' cases; it's not fair. She's been a good worker, and if she goes...'

Yes, well,' said Diane, in a tone of embarrassed boredom. 'I was going to have to come to that even before the raid. I've got instructions, and you know how it is. There's some girl being brought in from out of town. Now, I'm sure she's not as good as you, but someone up in the office was making her on his vacation. And at that level, as far as they're concerned, you don't cut it; you can't. Also, that agent of yours has been putting in the bad word about dangerous snakes, not that he can talk. What can I say? Be careful, both of you. And maybe I can see you again when all this calms down. You're good girls, hard workers. Goodnight; God bless.'

They snatched a last spare rib each from her plate and left disconsolately, chewing.

27.

Alexandra had never prevailed upon Annabelle to go down to the Chatterbox with her, but economic necessity worked where her vague need to get laid had not. It was just about how she had imagined it. A block down from the hospital and, perhaps more importantly, from the morgue, it practically backed onto a precinct house.

'Sometimes they raid it on their way back from getting in coffee,' Alexandra said as she pointed out the convenience of its location, 'but that means they haven't had to go far, and unless they've got heartburn from those meatball subs they tend to be in a good mood. Which, believe me, girl, when you come to get arrested, is important.'

Alexandra was not at all pleased to be going back to this place as a serious proposition, Annabelle realised. This was not going to be any fun at all: it was going to take all the attention she could muster up. Thank God there were no good buildings to distract one.

'Now, you don't have to do anything, hon,' Alexandra continued. 'It would be better if you just watch me the first few times, and watch out for me too, of course. I can go on buying your sandwiches for a while, hon, but not forever, right? And you've done it all before, haven't you? Likely you kind of enjoyed it; that's part of why we're both here doing all this depraved stuff. Just look carefully before you touch; you're the merchandise, but act as if they are. Remember, let them do all the talking. If they've spelt it out or shown you anything, it's entrapment; if you spell it out, they can bust you. Not that they tell the truth all the time, but they play by the rules, mostly.'

'Why should they, ever?' asked Annabelle, slightly incredulous at the idea of ethical policemen after losing her ten dollars to them in the Ace.

'Internal Affairs, hon. They have to watch their asses at that end too, as well as arrest records. We're an easy bust but, bless 'em, we can end in tears for them, too, unless they're real slick. And we can be slick too.'

They were pacing outside the building. Alexandra was in no hurry to go in, nowhere near as much as she had been to get home, change her clothes from the Ace and come out again. It meant giving up some part of her to go back, maybe. The neon sign was working fitfully, and not flickering so much as shining in a half-hearted way, as if it had it in mind to give up soon and go to Florida.

'Mexica showed them that time, you see, hon. She had those teeth with the points, and they could do real delicate work, they really could. One guy had her blow him, and then busted her. And she offered him seconds to beat the bust, and he took them, and the bust stood afterwards. Smart bastard. In the night court, though, she had them drop his pants, and she had put these hickeys all over his balls, so she got him for entrapment. His friends got her a few nights after and slapped her around, but IAD found her real cooperative. She knew a lot. And she got them too. After that they let her alone round here. And that's how she got the diamond put in; they broke the original cap, you see.' Noticing the look on Annabelle's face she went on, 'Oh God, hon, I know. I'm whistling in the dark. I'm worried, too: I shouldn't have to be here, and you shouldn't be here at all, we both know that. But there's the rent to pay, and soon they'll be charging me extra for the heat I gotta have for Randolph.'

There were two men in white suits in the lobby, standing on a piece of red plush carpet that might have curled up at the edges had they not been there to hold it down. The larger of the two was very large indeed. He just stood around being that – it seemed enough of a function for him to have. The smaller had a lounge-lizard smile, and an indeterminate and oily demeanour that he had obviously been taught at Villain School.

'Why, Alexandra,' he said, showing his fillings. 'Welcome back. It's been a while, hasn't it? Still, I always expect to see you girls again eventually. There's always room, and I run such a nice place you can't keep away. Shame about the Ace, wasn't it? Careless girl, Diane. You have to keep briefed. Leeches change jobs and they're not going to tell you, are they? This will be the English girl. The one Bunckley likes so much. Usually the only English around here is muffins but hey, nice tits. They said you were friends. She knows the score? That's kosher then. Two dollars membership. You lost your card? Careless girl. Have to buy a new one. And one for you. Go on through. Nothing's changed. Take care.'

All this was very slow. You stood there shuffling your feet on the carpet but had to keep listening without interrupting. It was an affectation, and was intended to be menacing as well as irritating. It worked.

Inside, a bar stretched most of the length of a long room. It was covered in dim coloured lights, mostly red but others, randomly, blue, green or amber. There was no clear scheme or anything: people had brought in spares and plugged them in when the red ones burned out. They were low-wattage but no-one dusted them a whole lot either. There was a lot of smoke in the air; Annabelle's eyes started stinging almost at once. It felt like she was blinking away tears of shame, but she knew it was her contacts.

At the back were two pool-tables, which were being used by a number of black men as big as the larger man at the door, and by three or four smaller blacks with missing limbs. These latter seemed to be the ones who were good at pool. They only ever passed through the front of the bar, and people didn't try to hustle them as they passed. A waiter brought them their drinks. You had to go past them to get to the ladies; you did so very quietly and carefully. No-one ever screamed near them; it would have been bad policy to make one miss his shot, and even the craziest, most fucked-up girls never forgot that.

The toilets were, of course, quite disgusting; flooded, without paper and stained occasionally with blood, not always from carelessness with syringes. One of the reasons why it was a good idea to go to the Chatterbox with a friend was that you really did not want to go into the powder-room alone.

As they walked in, the air was suddenly full of purrs, trills and venom.

'Hey, Alexandra, keeping Randolph nice and warm?'

'Boy, what an unlucky snake!'

'Hey, English, got any unhygienic lemons for us?'

'What did just walk in, sister?'

'Ah don' know, but it is surely slung low to the floor, sister.'

'Hey, doggies! Biscuits from mama? Or want to go walkies?'

There were a lot of faces at the tables and round the bar, and all of them were extravagant and trashy in paint and glitter and none of them were even slightly friendly. Alexandra tightened her neck muscles and her smile, and managed to slither towards the bar in as unobtrusive a way as was consistent with not looking scared. Annabelle did not so much hang back as stand in a way she hoped looked confident, competent and ready, though for what she was glad she could not imagine. Against her standard practice and advice when working Alexandra got them stiff Martinis. They were needed. They found themselves a table towards the back of the girls' area, and sipped nervously. Soon other new arrivals were getting a milder dose of the same treatment, and Alexandra and Annabelle were being merely ignored.

'Christ, Alexandra,' Annabelle said, 'is it always like this?'

'If I was still well in, it wouldn't be. But they hate it when you get some class, or have it. It wasn't that bad: no-one tried to stop us getting to the bar. Then they do this whole "You bumped into me and you owe me a drink" scenario, and that's when the nail-files and toe-clippers come out and faces end up on the washroom floor. But we'll be all right. Just be careful. Stick with me, kid, and we'll survive the night.'

28.

A tall, sullen bottle-blonde was standing by their table, suddenly. She wore black thigh-boots and a leather chemise and had long black lacquered fingernails, with one of which she speared the olive from Annabelle's drink.

They stared into each other's contact lenses in sudden challenge. Annabelle knew the other wore contact lenses because one was slightly out of alignment and she could see brown ringing the frightening fluorescent blue.

'Hey, English!'

'Indeed,' replied Annabelle.

'I called to you before. Maybe you don't hear so good.'

'My hearing is excellent. But, I fear, we have not been introduced.'

'Now I got your attention, right? I don't like the fucking English; what do you say to that?'

'But why on earth not? Most people tell us we are utterly charming.'

'You killed the Führer, for one. That's why.'

'Oh, in that case,' Annabelle said, rising to her feet, 'how about Rule Britannia, you Nazi bitch?' They intruded on each other's personal space for several seconds before Annabelle continued, 'Now, fuck off before I lose my temper, bomb Dresden and ruin those silly fingernails.'

And she went away.

'Holy mother, hon,' said Alexandra, gulping mouthfuls of Martini in panic. 'I said be careful. That was Inge, and she's the baddest. She only thinks she's German, and she's very well-connected, to relatives, I mean; they didn't disown her like they usually do. She always carries, and sometimes it's a Luger. Hon, you just do not answer back when one of those girls starts in on you. You sit there, and you take it, and eventually they might go away.'

Annabelle didn't pursue the political dimension of the situation. She suspected Alexandra of not having any principles; it was part of her charm. 'You didn't notice,' she explained, 'what I was doing with my foot when I stood up. In those heels I'd have had her instep smashed before she could pull anything. I know I weigh too much, but it has its uses. I did it to a groper once in the foreign language section of Hackney Library. Besides, don't people round here respect spirit?'

'Only when it's theirs,' said Alexandra.

Nothing further happened that or any other night. Inge

took the line that bluff had been called, and that Annabelle was maybe alright in that she hadn't pursued the issue; had showed restraint. Annabelle smiled sweetly at everyone, and didn't push her luck. Since Annabelle wasn't being pushy, for Inge to have started anything further would have been tacky; for anyone else to would have been presumptuous. Annabelle and Alexandra couldn't have fitted into the upper levels of the Chatterbox's hierarchy and seemed to have managed to opt out. They didn't want a place in it: for them the bar was a place to work and make some money, not a way of life, not a pecking order.

29.

It took several hours before they had a bite. You got to the Chatterbox early to be sure of getting yourselves a table, and so did all the other sisters, except for the few heavy enough to demand a regular place at the bar. The men came along later, after dinner and enough drinks and shaking off those companions who wouldn't have understood. They didn't have to bother about finding a place at the table. Some of them didn't want one; some were high-rolling show-offs who wanted to stand at the bar being competed over in screams and bitching, desiring the spice of the sudden flash of a sharpened comb. Sometimes they didn't find their way home easily, or at all.

Annabelle and Alexandra were being sensible and were looking for johns who would be sensible as well. After that first Martini they stuck to Cokes, and not so many they had to make that dangerous stalk to the washroom either.

The first two men who tried to join them were real country boys, drinking Bud from the bottle. Annabelle wasn't sure what their lack of shaves and their check shirts meant, but when Alexandra told them sweetly that she was fearfully sorry but these seats were reserved Annabelle imitated her sweet but frosty and unwelcoming smile. Soon after they left, slapping each other on the backs and guffawing, and Alexandra relaxed.

'Just tourists, being smart. You never quite know with that kind. They could have just sold the farm and be looking for some new action, but mostly good ol' boys are bad news. They think it's real smart to take us back then say we have to pay them, haw haw. And then they start slapping us around a bit. Me, I don't take the risk. I got out of one of those towns, and I figure anyone who stayed in the hills doesn't deserve me. But at the same time, I hate to pass up a trick.'

After a while two other men came and joined them. These were much more the right sort of thing. There was a convention of accountants in town, and they were over for the weekend from Minneapolis, they said, though the chances were it was probably really Pittsburgh. They almost always told those silly lies, as if one were interested, which of course one was pretending to be.

'The barman said you two were more refined,' said the more nervous one, who wore a red blazer and matching ascot.

'This is so,' said Annabelle, placing a large tip on the tray that had just arrived with everyone's drinks.

'Sounds like you're English,' said the one with the bow-tie and the blue tint in his glasses. He was the more outgoing of the two, the one whose palms were not sweating.

'This is also true,' said Annabelle.

So they talked for a while about Annabelle's being interesting because English, and it became clear that the one with the blue glasses was more interested in Alexandra, but that his friend wasn't especially disappointed, and was a bit shy. Annabelle was hugely relieved; he wasn't going to have any set ideas about whatever happened if he hadn't done things before, so all she had to do was be arrogant and take things for granted, and he wouldn't know if she didn't get things quite right. Because, while she'd done things before, she wasn't sure how you did it while cosseting people's egos if they were paying.

She and Alexandra managed to look interested in accounting for twenty minutes or so as the two johns discussed some coup they had pulled at the conference over a hated rival with some computer programme or other. You were not supposed to look too interested, luckily. People like this sometimes got paranoid and accused you of industrial espionage if you asked them questions. You just kept yourself blanded out.

Annabelle's thought he ought to make some sort of effort. 'Your eyes,' he said, 'they're attractively distant and mysterious and lofty.'

'Why, thank you, kind sir,' she said, 'but actually it's my contact lenses. They're starting to hurt a little.'

'Well, we can't have that,' said Alexandra's. 'It must be the smoke in this bar.'

'Yes,' said Alexandra, 'poor darling.'

'Well,' said Annabelle's, 'we could move on, I guess.'

'Yes,' said Alexandra's. 'If they felt like partying I got some Jim Beam in my room, and none of us smoke. If they felt like partying.'

'We feel like partying,' said Alexandra. 'Probably.'

'Well,' said Annabelle's, 'I'm sure we'd give them cab-fare and stuff.'

Alexandra's looked at his friend impatiently.

'We don't discuss that here,' he said. 'I told you.'

'But we discuss it eventually,' said Alexandra. 'I have to buy my girl her eye-drops.'

'Of course,' he said. 'But there'll be some action.'

'Surely,' said Annabelle.

'And with you two, it's slightly special action, right?'

'Depends on what you're used to, maybe,' said Alexandra.

'Because I told Bart here what happened to me last year when I found this place and didn't know. And he thought it sounded wild. We tell each other most things. Because we're brothers. You two are sisters, right?'

'Well, I suppose so,' said Annabelle. 'Oh sorry, you mean really. Oh no, we just do our cheekbones the same way.'

'Oh, because you look alike,' said Bart.

'Must be the rotten light in here,' said Alexandra, suddenly tight-lipped.

Annabelle was glad to get out into the open; her brain was frosting with ennui. It was nice to pass those hostile little faces with even a furtive accountant on your arm. It was appalling that she should slip into the habit of thinking competitively, but it is nice to go in and win, occasionally. He was holding onto her arm partly because he was nervous and partly because he was drunk and unsteady, but maybe he liked her a little, and this was not going to be too embarrassing and humiliating. The whole thing could be a lot worse. Really it could.

Mostly he wanted to touch her breasts, gently and tentatively, and every so often glance down to her crotch. After a bit he asked if he could see and it only seemed polite to let him. He looked long and hard, and suddenly she really did not care that he could see her.

Or even touch it, even more nervously than he had her breasts.

The encounter was, unexpectedly, sensitive and tender and rather sweet, and not involving or upsetting at all. He was going to go away, and sometime in the future other things would turn out to have been temporary as well... And then she realised with pleasant surprise that she hadn't felt mirrors be horrid to her for ages.

30.

And that was how their evenings went. They went to the Chatterbox and looked as strong as they needed to, but made no trouble and no issues out of anything, and the girls at the bar left them alone. They sat patiently over soft drinks and waited for supper to introduce himself. They always hunted as a pair, the first to pull keeping the john waiting until they could go back to the hotel as a foursome. They stuck to middle-aged businessmen with hungry eyes. People who were drunk and pushy were a risk, and the businessmen sort of understood that sometimes you have to wait a little before you can clinch a deal. Annabelle's contacts went on hurting; there was something in the air of the place to which she must just have been allergic.

Afterwards, uptown a few blocks in the Oak Tree, they would restrict themselves to buttered eggs, toast and coffee for their late breakfast. Most of the Chatterboxers would be in there being ostentatious about what they'd scored; a hundred-dollar trick meant steak. Inge always had filet mignon with her Eggs Benedict, but there was some suspicion her connections meant she didn't have to pay anyway. If you stuck to something solid but modest it meant no-one could rank you. If you played that game, deciding that you just felt like a croissant and a cup of hot chocolate could be socially very humiliating.

'Prostitution is just like school-teaching really,' Annabelle remarked. 'Both involve spending an inordinate amount of time in conditions of considerable discomfort, making an effort to keep a smile on your face and a yawn away from your lips for the benefit of people whom, were it not for the money, you would not care to meet socially.'

'Well, listen to Miss Thing,' said Alexandra, throwing a sugar lump into Annabelle's cleavage. 'Stop showing off how poised you are. I hate it when you rehearse all your lines. Way you talk you'd never think you blew that black guy in his limo last night on the way to work. Have you no pride? A decent self-respecting working girl just doesn't go with men who drive Chevys. He hadn't hoovered in there for years.'

'There isn't much in the way of dirt you can't brush off boots,' said Annabelle, 'and it was only fluff anyway.'

31.

'I didn't bring you to Chicago to do that sort of thing,' said Natasha, who was wearing a black business-suit with no safety-pins, and a pair of glasses which she didn't need, and which were presumably intended to make her look more censorious. 'If you no longer care about yourself, you ought to show me more respect. People are saying – and by people, I loosely mean that suntanned Polish ingrate Carola – that I brought some innocent little – ha! – thing here from London on one of my whims, and then left her to starve in the lowest of dives. Your friend who hangs out so appropriately with a reptile has been free with her mouth as well. It is not so. You came here of your own free will. I hardly promised anything, I just said I'd see. You could always use your return ticket, you know. You do have that still, don't you?'

'But darling,' purred Annabelle, 'I'm not starving at all. I'm eating, and not too much either, before you ask. I'm not taking drugs and I never have more than one real drink a night unless that's what someone is paying me to do. I'm paying for my shots, and the Aloha Beauty Parlor. Like you said the other week, there is certainly some sort of improvement. I'm not leeching off you and I'm not leeching off Alexandra.'

'Yes, but you're certainly sucking something, even if it's not blood. That isn't the point anyway. Not at all. I'm glad to see you coping after your fashion. I suppose you're not doing all that disastrously given where you were when we started. I just wish it wasn't at the expense of my reputation.'

Annabelle had just about got stillness and repose down pat now; she needed them.

'As Carlos has pointed out,' Natasha continued, 'a promising young businesswoman already compromised by her background cannot, just cannot, afford to be seen around with low-rent trash. Even if it has a nice accent. You cast a shadow on me, sweets. Carlos says it might cause difficulties with the loan officer.'

'Darling Tasha, unless your bank maintains a constant watch on your living-room windows with sniper scopes... There are fifty-eight apartments in this block. I could be visiting any one of them, and the only way your loan officer could possibly know that I go and hustle in the Chatterbox is if he's one of the people I go there to hustle.'

'Carlos says they have ways of knowing. Anyway, it's his apartment now. I let it from him as a tax shelter. And he doesn't want you here.'

Annabelle ventured a sob. People had been known to accuse her of guilt-tripping. 'So this is good-bye,' she said; how fortunate that she was wearing black too – it made melodrama possible. 'We can forget all those intimate little teas in the Gloucester Road; they never happened. We never knew each other. Mr. Smooth can scrub me from your life. Well, Tasha, my dear, since we have got to this point, there are one or two things I may as well – '

'Oh, sweets, don't over-react. That's not what I said. What I said is that you can't come here because it's his apartment and he says you can't. I'll come by the Chesterfield and we can go for tea. But do go away for now, because you're making me feel bad and Carlos says that guilt is bad for my complexion. Christ, though, sweets, did you have to get so sordid just to make me feel bad?'

32.

Actually Annabelle rather agreed with Natasha, though she was never going to say so, because Natasha was hardly morally entitled to comment. The aphorisms were more or less bravado, and even most of the insouciant way she had with tricks was for Alexandra's benefit as much as her own. Alexandra saw herself as being on the skids, slithering back into a way of life she thought she had managed to get entirely out of. The way things were with her agent it was clear that she wasn't going to get back to dancing for a while, and if Alexandra was going to swan around being Annabelle's Virgil Annabelle had to keep a song in Alexandra's heart, because falling back into remembering happier days was only going to bring her down.

Annabelle was having to dare herself to go on, because if she let herself weaken at all she would lose her nerve altogether, and that would leave her sobbing in a hotel room out of which she would sooner or later be thrown without her luggage. A tacky bar full of psychos and fairy-lights had not been part of her agenda; she had envisaged a new life in America almost as quiet and gentle as the one she had had in London, just a little more depraved and fun. Natasha had largely created her current situation, and Annabelle wasn't going to let her off the hook by going soft, admitting she hated it all and going home. Natasha might be annoyed at her now, but if Annabelle ran away she was going to get, and deserve, Natasha's contempt.

Some days, in spite of everything positive about how she knew she now looked, the mirrors were being very mean indeed.

It was all rather more miserable than could be made tolerable by the odd glass of sherry or pleasing cornice decoration or Brahms scherzo coming slightly tinnily over the rather better radio that was one of the wages of sin. She wasn't here for refined pleasures; they were available more cheaply in London, because in London she knew where they were cheap. Annabelle had come to Chicago with a vague idea of sleeping with pleasant men with quiet manners, unostentatiously trim bodies and the sort of informed mind that her wit could entertain even if she was overweight. What she was getting – at best – were nervous company lawyers with greying chest-hair who went on about their expense accounts and the cheapest flight back to Denver, and who looked anxious in hotel lobbies and got her noticed by the detective. She thought about going home, often.

Ultimately the deciding factor was Mr. Gucci: what had happened to her was a consequence rather than the purpose of Carlos' game-plan, but that didn't mean she was prepared to let him win if she could possibly do anything to come in sneakily from behind and land a killer blow. He obviously thought he was well into his endgame. Getting the flat and excluding her from it were both so crude. What amazed her was Natasha's capacity for continuing to pretend to herself that she was deceived: she really couldn't be that daft, could she? Still, there must be something Annabelle could do. Perhaps the best thing for now would be to get more information. Even when knowledge is not power, it is always liable to be interesting.

33.

When she got down to actually thinking of her next move it was obvious, really.

Annabelle's memory was not all that good, but by working at it very hard, and leaving it and coming back to it sideways, she eventually got the sound of Carola's surname. It either began with a J or a Y, and you could eliminate at least two of the possible vowels from what followed on. Carola was Polish, so Annabelle supposed the connection between spelling and sound might be even more loose than usual; but presumably the odds were against its being the Polish equivalent of Cholmondely.

She had plenty of time to sit in her room and work through the phone-book for the most likely candidates. She knew the broad area where Carola lived, and that it was an apartment block. That made it possible to go through the list of possibles with a street map and eliminate almost all of them. She got it right second time; the first time turned out to be a pet-shop, and the guy who answered made her an indecent proposition and offered her some Siamese fighting-fish at a cut rate if she came by.

'Hello,' she said tentatively, on this second call. 'Is that Carola?'

'Oh, hi,' said a silky smokiness at the other end. 'Who is this, please?'

'Well, you don't know me, even if you are Carola, but...'

'Oh, wow, hi, I guess you must be Annabelle. I was wondering if we'd ever run into each other. My dear, everyone has been telling me about you. I could tell it was you by the accent. But I guess you must get tired of people saying that.'

'I was wondering if I might meet you for a coffee sometime.'

'Sure, that would be neat. I'm sure we have a lot of dirt to dish to each other, right?'

'Well, yes. It was something of the kind I had in mind, actually.'

'You sound adorable, my dear. I can't wait: why not come over right now? You know where to come?'

'I'm sure I can find it on the street-map,' said Annabelle, preferring not to reveal how she had got the number in the first place.

'It's so nice to have you call. I'm sort of an expert on the gaunt goddess, after all. Come by as soon as you can, my dear; for some of us, at least, this remains Hospitality City.'

34.

The white-haired doorman in the rather silly purple uniform looked world-weary and tolerant when Annabelle asked to be put through to Carola's apartment. She got the feeling though that it was nothing particularly to do with her; rather more to do with the other visitors that came to see Carola in the line of her profession, and with the tone of the building going up – or down.

My, the girl had a lot of locks and deadbolts on her door. And isn't it strange how you can always tell that people are looking at you through one of those peepholes: you never know whether to wave or not. Carola took no chances, but Annabelle supposed she could not really afford to.

Natasha had mentioned an aunt; the flat had a couple of nice chests, and several of those chairs which are valuable because people were uncomfortable on them in New England in the late seventeenth century. There was a rather unpleasant batik of cockerels fighting on one wall, and a couple of posters from Janis Joplin concerts on another. These were okay, actually, because it was clear from the tattiness of their corners that they had been up on the walls of a number of apartments over the years before they were framed. Otherwise the flat had little in it worthy of negative, or any other, remark; and you didn't have the feeling that antique-dealing had been a vocation for Carola she had angsted over giving up for coke-dealing.

Carola wasn't the sort of person who bothered being virtuously uncomfortable on Colonial furniture; she was the sort of person who spends a lot of time lying around on irregularly-mounded cushions of various sizes and of colours not chosen for their quiet blending with each other. She was a smallish person with intense and over-made-up eyes, a delicate nose that was at least one size too small for her face, and white and very regular teeth. This last was less the product of endless virtue in the matter of candy bars than the result of the fact that, with the sole exceptions of the antique-dealing aunt and her own trade in recreational pharmaceuticals, her entire family were dentists, and she was thus by way of being the orthodontic equivalent of a captive audience.

'It's really most awfully nice - '

'Goddamn it,' interrupted Carola. 'Don't be so Goddamn English at me all the time; I don't think I can bear it. You look a tad frazzled; is it just the stairs, or could you do with a V? Or two Vs, maybe.'

She pointed to a large glass ashtray that was sitting in the middle of the mirrored top of the coffee-table, and which was full of small white tablets. Annabelle, who had few bad habits, looked askance. She had never known before that she was capable of looking askance, but there you are.

'Jesus, sweetheart, it's only valium. Just a calm-down, right?'

'No thank you.' Annabelle didn't want to be impolite but she liked her mind just the way it was. Valium during surgery was one thing, but...

'Suit yourself, kid. Don't mind me, I'm just an addict.'

'Oh, sorry.' There are more guilt-trippers than one in this city.

'Didn't she tell you about that? It was my loving father, the tooth-pulling bastard. I was such a neurotic kid – well, of course, all sisters are – that whenever he was left alone with me when Ma was doing her late surgeries he'd slip me a batch of tablets to shut me up so he could get on with his scale model of the Alamo. When they realised he'd overdone it a bit he got off the child-abuse charge by writing it up for the journals. It's a real tear-jerker the way he wrote it, a classic case history in paediatric circles. I tell people that's why I do so much coke; I need to put some spikes back in my lines before they go completely flat.'

'Does it work?'

Carola shrugged. It was hard to tell how much of this was her telling jokes.' I'm still pretty laid back a lot of the time, but that could just be my personality. You know, you don't seem a bit like me, not really. Which just goes to show how little the astrology bit is worth.'

'Look, Carola,' Annabelle said, 'what is all this stuff, anyway, about you and me and astrology? Darling Tasha keeps making dark and significant comments about it all, but whenever I push her she says it's probably better I know no more because the knowledge might ruin the spontaneity which, she says, is one of my few charms.'

'You and I were born same time, same day,' Carola said. 'Same time in different time-zones, but the earth rotates so same stars near as dammit for the pair of us. She reckons that makes us sort of twin sisters. To begin with we're both sisters, right, and then there's the nuns – you're sort of Irish and I'm Polish, but that's all the same for her – untermenschen, the pair of us. We both pass out a lot, and we both majored in English. We both let her push us around a lot, too. I mean, that may not strike you as the rules of evidence or logic, but for her it's close enough. It gets her off the hook, too; if we're how we are because of the stars, nothing she said or did means that much.'

'I see. Well, can we come back to that later? This next bit is going to be difficult. I feel like I've got an awful nerve.'

'Try me,' said Carola, avidly.

'I've been thinking things through,' said Annabelle. 'Things I've been told that don't quite add up. I'd like to check my guesses. First, you didn't seduce Carlos at all, did you?'

'Other way round, sort of.'

'He came round here – to score some coke, maybe?'

'Right.'

'And you sat around giving him a taste. He got chatty and said how worried he gets about Natasha's insecurity in her identity?'

'It was put more crudely than that.' Carola's voice was full of mild self-contempt. 'But yes, more or less. You worked this out without any hints, did you?'

Annabelle felt her cheeks go round with utter smugness. 'I have the advantages of paranoia and hatred, and being smart, in my way. He said it would be really useful for him to go to bed with you just the once – for her sake, so that he could get a perspective on how she felt, and on her insecurities, because you seemed basically more together than her. Right?'

'That's uncanny,' Carola said. 'You should do it in public. He's a smooth-talking bastard, Carlos. Of course, I was sort of ripped at the time. I shouldn't be when I'm doing business, but in theory it's different when it's friends. You know how it is, no-one ever said I was Little Miss Self-Control.'

'No,' said Annabelle, 'I'm afraid they never did.'

'I did find him quite attractive, though: I don't like Natasha so much that I'd fuck someone just for the sake of her thera-peutic needs. The good sister's never got that far into my head.'

'And then he told her?'

'Now you're being naïve, by dear little Sherlock,' said Carola. 'It was much grosser than that. He told her he was here, and when to pick him up with the deal. She used to have her own keys, which she threw at me that evening when she walked in and found us in flagrante. She broke my favourite Lalique vase. That slick bastard had even worked out in advance precisely how long it would take him to talk me into it.'

Annabelle was shocked; she felt revealed as a country mouse. 'So it's not just the money, is it? He really does actually hate her as well.'

'Guess so,' said Carola. 'I don't reckon he thinks much of the rest of us either. I mean, it adds up, doesn't it?'

'A sister did him down some time?'

'I don't think so. I think it all has to do with Mr. Salvatore.'

'Who he?' asked Annabelle.

'Carlos has this boss at the store called Mr. Salvatore, who is very cool and very well-tailored and charming and sort of like Rossano Brazzo and has been trying to get into Carlos' pants lo! these many years, as who can blame him? Mr. Salvatore, like many others, finds it hard to believe that anyone as neat and pretty and devious as Carlos can really be as straight as he always says he is. Carlos hates it when guys put the make on him, or says he does, but he is kind of flirtatious, even when he's telling them no way. Anyway – '

Carola's tone gave subtext to what she was saying, but her eyes remained innocent of malice for a sentence or two more.

'One reason why he has a charmed life is that Mr. Salvatore is so very well-connected. They wouldn't let Carlos in on it because he's an artichoke, or whatever it is they say, but he has nice manners, so... If Carlos ever is really in trouble all he'll have to do is put out a bit. He likes and doesn't like having that option. It doesn't take his balls off, but it sort of nibbles at them. And so he doesn't like sisters.'

Annabelle shrugged resignedly. 'Nothing to be done about it all, is there?'

'Not really,' said Carola. 'And who would want to? She's let you down. She won't listen to a single word that I say. Just hisses "toenails" through clenched teeth down the phone as if it was supposed to mean something. I don't know what she told you about my going to San Diego, but it was business not her demented phonecalls driving me out of town.'

Annabelle reserved judgement on this; she was not necessarily going to believe every single word that her new friend uttered.

'But it just isn't fair,' Annabelle said. 'He's getting away with it. She can be such a silly bitch, and that bastard is making himself a handsome profit out of making her even sillier than she was already.'

Carola lay back further on the cushions, trying to be a Persian cat and not having quite the degree of indolent malice that she was aspiring to. 'Darling Annabelle,' she said, 'why on earth should we bother ourselves about it anymore? You don't owe her that much, you know. We both knew the score about ourselves, and we'd have sorted things out for ourselves in our own sweet time, but she came into our lives bursting with silicone and confidence and told us all about the Charlene Atlas ninety-day plan and stuff. It's not her sweet and loving nature, you know: it's not the kindness of being a sister. It's all just ego. It makes her look so good, you see. Mexica used to do it before they cut her brain out, but you'll know all about that from Alexandra. Natasha does it because she thinks Mexica is the best, and the way she might end up taking over as the best is to do at least some of the same stuff. She needs to prove she's got the winning formula by making others do it.'

'Well,' said Annabelle, 'she's not getting it right right now, is she? I mean it's okay for you; you've graduated to a point where you don't need to trust her opinion on anything anymore. I do, though I suppose that's because she's left me not trusting my own judgement for trusting her in the first place.'

'You seem to be doing okay, Annabelle,' said Carola. 'You seem to be on your own flow. You worry too much, but you're coping and you don't even seem to need any valium to get you through. Your worrying about her does you credit, my dear, and it also proves that you're coping better than most of us would, because you've got yourself the free time from somewhere and the space in your head to actually worry about what happens to her.'

'That's just because I'm so incredibly virtuous,' said Annabelle. 'No, actually it's sort of because I want to go on having the right to be annoyed at her for letting me down, and I wouldn't have that right if I didn't feel an equivalent obligation to at least worry about her.'

Slowly and ironically Carola crossed herself. 'Holy mother,' she said. 'It sounds to me, my dear, as if the good sisters got well and truly inside your head in the end.'

There was a sound then as, not especially unobtrusively, all the deadlocks opened from the outside, and a good-looking young man with short, neat dark hair in a white suit entered the room.

'Hello, Mark,' said Carola. 'This is Annabelle, of whom you have heard.'

'Oh, right, sure,' he said. 'Hi there.'

'Just reminding him he knows the beads, dear,' Carola remarked to Annabelle as Mark went over to the drinks cabinet and poured himself a generous Scotch. Annabelle looked a second time at the suit and the slightly walrussy moustache. He had a degree of style, a certain unostentatiousness about having style. It might be better to reserve judgement on this one; he might be something quite interesting.

'Beads, Carola darling?' she asked.

'Oh, sorry, that's one of the things I'd thought she'd have told you about. She picked it up from Mexica too, I think. Beads means, well, you know, all this and everything when you don't necessarily want to name concepts, and we don't, a lot of the time, do we? It's a necessary part of having manners.'

'Oh, you mean like being sisters, or being friends of Dorothy and all that.'

'Honeychile, that's about it, but I don't think we're in Kansas anymore,' said Carola.

Mark slumped on another set of cushions and glugged back his drink as if he really needed it. He was clearly not interested in social chitchat. Annabelle could tell from the impatient way he was moving his feet on the parquet.

'Look, Carola, sorry to break up the kaffeeklatsch. I really have to talk to you about some stuff; bad news from the airport.'

Annabelle was already on her feet and pulling on her beaver coat. Part of making a good first impression on interesting new men is showing that you have the discretion to know when to shut up and leave.

'Dears,' she said, 'it's been lovely. But you have business to attend to, and I am far too much of an innocent bystander to want to be here while you do. After all, what I don't know, I can't talk about, right?'

'Well, yes,' said Carola. 'Sort of like Wittgenstein. Nice of you to be so considerate. A pity, though: I was going to cook up a mess of pork chops in a while. But Mark and I probably have to go see these men. Come by again soon, and we can bitch up Natasha some more; it's really so nice not to have to do it all by oneself. Say goodbye to nice Annabelle, Mark.'

Mark looked at her properly for a moment, seeing her as a person rather than as an obstruction, she hoped.

'Ciao, nice Annabelle,' said Mark.

*

35.

When she got home to the Chesterfield, Annabelle knocked on Alexandra's door and found her wrapped in a slightly bedraggled dressing-gown, paying especial attention to her paint.

'Do you mind if I don't come down to the Chatterbox this evening?' she asked.

Alexandra looked positively relieved. 'Honey, I was surely hoping you would say that, though I hope it doesn't mean you're planning to stay home and grouch. We've got to have ourselves some desperate fun sometime, and it seems to me that time is now. We've been slogging away in that damn pit for weeks and we need a night off. It's alright being a whore, but you must never let yourself get compulsive about it. There are cocks in this town that don't have dollar bills wrapped round them. That's where Mexica went wrong, you see.'

'Gosh,' said Annabelle, 'criticism of La Divina.'

'I'm not blind to her faults, you know, hon; just grateful enough for past help that I don't go on about them the whole time. I've noticed, though, that she is not a fully happy person.'

Alexandra paused between sentences, either significantly or to concentrate on the mirror. She was going through an elaborate procedure with little tongs that was intended to put a curl into her false eyelashes.

'It's all money with her now. I suppose it's partly upkeep on the bod, or maybe she pays them in installments. I was working with some other chicana one time who said she ended up without much feeling, and that that's why she's so interested in money instead. But then some bitch will always say something like that about anyone who's made it all the way through. Silly, jealous children – though when I last saw her in New York she was turning five hundred-some tricks easy. I saw her in a bar one night and she got me to pick up the tab because she didn't want to make change and she figures I owe her everything anyway. After, when we went back to her hotel for a talkette, she allowed that it was her turn now, and had me wait in the lobby while she took the driver up for his five dollar fare. Oh, she was fair, she allowed for his waiting-time as well. Afterwards she walked him back down and he said she was the best in his life, ever. So she made him give her all his cigarettes too.'

36.

Then they had to work out where to go and what to do. Annabelle didn't push her luck too far on the movie, but there was
no way she was going to see anything with Burt Reynolds in it –
except possibly *At Long Last Love*; and Alexandra said she
thought he was cute but she would respect the feelings of
someone who was, after all, a visitor and could not be expected
to be at all times in touch with the finer points of American
culture. Annabelle suggested that they went to see *Days of
Heaven*, which was on at one of the uptown quasi-art-houses,
and Alexandra said she supposed that would be all right, and
then ended up crying all the way through and saying she didn't
mind going to art movies if they were that sad, and who was
that hunky guy? Sam who?

She had been to Texas before. With a guy she met in the
coastguards, when they were both on furlough.

'He was just a farmboy, hon. There wasn't anything going
on. It didn't occur to him, and I was such an innocent then
anyway. Daren't go there now of course; nor try and find out
what happened to him. There are things we just have to let
alone, and places we just don't go back to, and places we have
to leave if we're there. Shame though, really: it is that pretty,
just like in the movie. And I'd be a good farmer's wife, keeping
all the hands happy with pie. And barn-dancing, and everyone
being surprised how spry I was for my age.'

After the film they went down to the Ragazzo.

'Safer there, hon,' Alexandra said. 'I mean, even I'm not
perfect or safe, not really, but you – well, the eyebrows have
improved, but... There'll be alright; it's kinda mixed. A lot of
guys dressed as lumberjacks, but plenty of them swing the axe
with both hands, and even the ones that don't can be fun to
chat with.'

Annabelle had other ideas about the rest of the evening.
She popped out to the lobby to call Carola, and Carola answered and said why not, it had only been business earlier, and
yes, she thought Mark at least wanted to be friends, and no, she
couldn't give Annabelle his number straight off. But as it
happened she thought he was going to be down at the Ragazzo
later on anyway; not that it was especially, except for business,

his sort of place.

It wasn't Annabelle's, either. She had never seen especial merit in going to places where she looked comparatively klutzy on the dance-floor and there was lots of different-coloured smoke and epilepsy lights and Donna and Gloria cooing over endless chunker-chunker-kerchunker and men who, when they weren't flexing their Charles Atlas muscles, cracked essence of armpit under their noses and acted like naughty hot sticky schoolboys.

Alexandra was bound to get wild and insufferable. She had left Randolph sleeping off some mice in the pocket of her rabbit and was in the mood to dare you to dare her to do something outrageous. She was spoiling for a chance to make an exhibition of herself, and Annabelle knew that she was going to be considered a spoilsport for not especially encouraging her.

Annabelle spotted Mark looking strong and silent at the bar, and squirmed her way through the masses to his side.

'Hi, Mark,' she yelled over the music. 'Carola said I might find you here. You drink Famous Grouse, right?' She thrust some notes at the boy in shorts behind the bar and got herself a Gordon's and Schweppes.

'Say, that's real nice of you,' Mark yelled back as she passed him his glass. 'You remembered what I drink from one meeting.'

'We aim to please,' Annabelle replied. 'And we have a trained memory.'

'Sorry about this morning. We were having troubles. Those guys can be so temperamental.'

'I can imagine,' said Annabelle. This guy didn't especially sparkle as far as dialogue went, but maybe he would be better in places where he could actually make himself heard. This was not in any case the place for the deep and meaningful. Eye-contact got them onto the dance-floor without further attempts at conversation. If I look hard enough into his soulful browns he won't notice I can't do much with my feet. Oh, okay, he relies on perfect teeth and stamping from the hip, so that's cool. Not flamenco, but tasty enough. Oh dear, though: cerise suede. Even if he's not a hiding to nothing one way or the other, such taste, my dear. Then she noticed that his eyes were firmly fixed on her breasts, and it occurred to her that maybe she'd have a chance. He knows, and he is still staring.

Alexandra got tired of holding their drinks and arranged with one of the oiled boys in niches round the wall to take over his spot when he needed to go to the bathroom. Annabelle thought this was going to be embarrassing, but decided to put a good face on it when Alexandra came over to tell her.

'Break a leg, honey,' she said.

'That's not a nice thing to be saying, missy,' said Alexandra in hurt tones.

'Oh God, I'm sorry,' said Annabelle. 'Don't they say that here? All my actor friends do it. It's like saying good luck, only not, because the Furies – the Kindly Ones – might be listening. It's like not whistling, or peacock feathers in the Scottish Play and stuff.'

'What are you talking about?' said Alexandra. 'Sometimes your mouth moves and nothing comes out that makes any sense at all. You're foreign, did I ever tell you that?' But she was clearly mollified, and pecked Annabelle on a cheek in a way that implied that no irrevocable offense had been given.

In a way it was Alexandra's finest hour. She was actually very good at this sort of thing; she'd obviously never really been trying down at the Ace. She could bend in all sorts of places that Annabelle couldn't. That top helped; Annabelle hadn't really appreciated the cunning of it when it had come out of the wardrobe. Obviously Alexandra had been intending to do something like this all along. There were more slits in it than one would have imagined; some of them might be seams going, but surely not all.

The hair and the falls she had put in swirled around her like comets. What a pedant you are, Annabelle Jones: etymology everywhere. The crowd loved her, and the applause, and even the sexual responses, were only partly in quotation marks. They clapped the rhythms and she dipped, kicked, strutted, writhed and soared.

Alas the boy she had evicted had been wearing rather too much oil on his pectorals, and some of it had dripped and puddled on the plinth beneath her stilettos. Alexandra threw herself into a pirouette that turned into a fatal spin and a squeal of pain. Gallant hands caught her and bore her shoulder-high to a couch in the lounge. Annabelle pecked Mark an apologetic goodbye on the moustache, and went to help organise a cab to the emergency room of the nearest hospital.

There were mild problems about the name on Alexandra's insurance records with one of those incredibly hatchet-faced, whining angry harpies they always have on the cash desk in American hospitals. Alexandra was far too euphoric to be any good at all at dealing with the situation. Annabelle got called 'Lady' one time too many, and her accent went up several degrees on the peerage scale, and eventually they got Alexandra down to X-ray. She giggled helplessly when they asked her if she was possibly pregnant, and Annabelle said that meant no, and not to pay any attention to her. The young intern looked confused, and the technician winked, and Annabelle winked back, and nothing further was said. This was a relief because Annabelle really could not handle the education of young American doctors at this time of night.

The injuries to her wrists and ankles were sprains, it turned out, and the nurses bandaged them tightly and sent Alexandra straight home.

She was still flying past the pain. 'I told you I was good, didn't I? See, I was, hon, I really was, in spite of all this. Yours was nice; you should have got him to come with, or maybe not such a hot idea. It was nice of you to leave him and come with me.' Short phrases burbled her to sleep.

Great, thought Annabelle, she gets glory and ends up in bed for a week or so, and I end up having to pay the rent for both of us. Her eyes were stinging from cigarette smoke; she knew they would continue to do so for days.

37.

Things were premonitory in the Chatterbox next evening: it was like going into a dark cloud, and only partly because they hadn't bothered to replace the large number of bulbs that had burned out over the weekend.

Water had puddled from the toilets almost as far as the farthest pool-table, and the players, especially the ones with all their limbs, were grouchy in consequence. People were waiting to go past them to the Ladies until the last possible moment, and even then put the trip off until they were absolutely sure no-one else was already in there waiting with a grudge over a Coke not bought last week.

Inge and the other bottle-blondes were sticking to one side of the bar, and Martha and the Pantherines were looking sullen and righteously angry on the other. Things had been particularly tense since Thursday, when Inge had brought in an egg-plant and had sat at the bar, dismembering it with her nail-file.

'That's some sort of Sicilian thing she's doing,' Alexandra had explained, ever the good tourist guide. 'And I don't mean the preparation of food.'

'Waste, really,' Annabelle had said. 'I quite like aubergine.'

'Do be quiet,' said Alexandra. 'These things get taken really seriously.'

This evening Annabelle was a bit doubtful about where to sit, and so she went over to a group of Hispanics who were looking nervous at one of the tables in a far corner. She didn't know any of them well, but the Hawaiians, who were the only people Alexandra had thought it safe actually to introduce her to because a couple of them went to the same electrolysist, had clearly decided not to risk their perfect complexions by being there that night.

The Hispanics were no more friendly than usual, but out of sisterly feeling they thought they ought to tell her that there was this other girl – Ninette, they said – whom Annabelle didn't know, and she was in the hospital, badly cut, in a coma.

'She stayed friends with all she could, but some bicha decided to fuck her up anyway. They're all crazy on drugs round here, except us. We do downers; no-one goes crazy on downers. But look out, English. Right now round here unaffiliated means unsafe, and there ain't no way you can buy yourself protection round that bar. Word in your ear while you still have one, eh chica. You're not bad for a stuck-up ugly bitch, but this place is turf now.'

'Gosh, thanks,' said Annabelle, and sipped harder at her Coke.

'Don't feel you have to go right away, chica.'

She got up and left. Behind her, the ironic one was rebuked in whispers: 'Bruja, that one. Even her friend. Didn't you hear? Put the make on some guy she was with and she put on the eye.

Told her to break her legs. So okay, she only managed a sprain, but that's better mal d'ocho than anyone round here ever managed. Don't offend her, not ever. She's not as nice as she looks.'

38.

It was still only twilight outside: she had gone down to the Chatterbox early, and a wasted evening now lay in front of her. Clearly the place was just not going to be safe for her by herself; it seemed it wouldn't be safe even when Alexandra was back on her feet again. When she was, maybe it would be time to pack up and use the ticket home, because it must be the case that if Alexandra weren't lumbered with looking after her she would have more options. It was important not to be selfish, probably.

An arm slammed her to the wall.

'Spread 'em,' a brusque voice said.

She did so. A hand pinched her ferociously at breast and hip.

'Okay, cocksucker – Oh, I'm sorry, it's the nice English visitor lady.'

She could just about see his face in the dark of the alley he'd shoved her into, a face with dark glasses of the sort that might as well be a mask, and the worst teeth she'd seen in the US. A badge was flashed at her from a pocket of the dark suit he was wearing, and she was vaguely aware that she hadn't seen it properly; but then her eyes had been hurting so badly she hadn't put her lenses in.

'You're busted.'

'On what charge? Don't I get my rights read?' She had seen TV and knew about this stuff.

'I don't need a charge to bust your kind, scumbag, and when your rights come is when I feel like it, not when you ask. Okay, let me see your bag. No drugs, nothing at all? We'll go in the lining later. Don't move; don't lie to me. People get shot real easy in this city, and me, I don't have to answer questions about it afterwards. Your hotel room. Now. Don't ask about warrants, or it will be your face that gets less pretty.'

Obviously the man was mad; he was manic or speeding or

both. It never occurred to Annabelle at the time that he might not be a cop. Everything she had seen of the Chicago force since she got there – the graft, the change-stealers, bad character-actor players like Bunckley – fitted the bad news as she had picked it up from films. You could tell the police from the criminal psychopaths only because some of the former had the grace to wear uniforms.

Mainly as he dragged her along the sidewalk to her hotel she was thinking how this probably had something to do with her being seen talking to Mark or going into Carola's apartment-building, rather than with her failure to get Bunckley his police helmet. How this was because she had been vulnerable enough to let loneliness and friendship and lust persuade her to hang around with them without knowing absolutely precisely what they were doing.

She wasn't thinking straight, she knew that much. She was terrified of what might happen to her in a US prison. The couple of times she had been picked up in London she had known she could talk her way out of it, but here innocence was unlikely to be much help without money. She was foreign; did she even get a public defender? And in a place like Chicago did they even have public defenders? She felt like throwing up – sick with terror; you really could be, then. Somehow she kept going; as long as they weren't in a police station maybe it wouldn't be real.

The desk clerk paid no attention as they entered, luckily. People brought guests in and out of the Chesterfield all the time and you didn't get tipped for asking why they were holding hands so tightly. She managed to get and keep her back straight, and keep tears out of her eyes.

'Smart kid,' the cop said in the lift, 'not trying to run. I got backup all over. We wouldn't want you hurt before you can help us out.'

They went past Alexandra's room. I hope she's sound asleep, Annabelle thought. I don't want her deciding to come in and getting involved. Hopefully she'll assume if I'm back this early I'm with a john, and won't butt in. No reason why she should get hurt too.

In her room he looked round at the tacked-up poster for an Erté show, the stacks of books. 'Fuck it,' he said. 'Where's

Garland? Where have you hidden Garland? You people always have Garland on your walls. Have you used your Garland poster to smuggle drugs in?'

Annabelle finally realised that, unless the sweet-factory principle fails to operate with narcotics cops, this man was a bit odd.

'In a while there'll be some questions, but in the meantime I want you to look at this.' He was out of his trousers and reddishly semi-erect, but what he meant by 'this' was probably the thin blade he was waving around.

'Oh,' said Annabelle, 'you're not a policeman. I see.'

'Easy meat, kid. You're such easy meat. But I've been of use to the police in my time – course I have – man like me, knows how to handle himself, knows a cocksucker when I see one, no matter how pretty, knows what to do with a knife. I'm always of use – company, cops, syndicate, you gotta stay tied in, and me and my friend here' – that pass could have taken her eye out; his hand seemed to wobble a bit for an international dagger-man – 'we've been of help, you know.'

He used his free hand to shove her to her knees; he wasn't very strong, but she wasn't standing up very convincingly. She wasn't going to fight, she thought. Ninette fought, probably; maybe he won't hurt me if I don't fight. His pubic hair smelt of sweat and semen and dirty laundry and old shit and blood. He ground against her; he wasn't any harder.

With his free hand he tweaked her left nipple hard. She'd been worried that her new breasts wouldn't be sensitive but there was a downside to the fact that they were. 'Do something, cocksucker. Hey, that's funny. I told you what to do without meaning to. It's in your name, freak. If I feel a tooth, you lose three, right; and my friend is just waiting to chew your face. That's better; oh, that's good.'

This man was unwashed and foul. She was going to be riddled with germs. Least of her troubles. He started to pull on her silk scarf, like a halter. He pulled out of her mouth, crouched behind her, and tugged down her jeans and knickers.

'Don't be smart. Stay where you are. Smart bitch moved on me last night. She ain't feeling so good. You won't be smart. Hurts, don't it?'

It hurt more than she had expected; lubricant and affection

had made it more than tolerable in the past. Ninette's stale blood was in her mouth, and for a moment she had to check the knife was still by her face because it felt like she was being cut down there.

'Nice and tight; nice and tight. Just what a man needs. Next I'll cut that pretty face, or those tits.'

He was really a lot smaller than her, and this was going on long enough that she was getting cramp in her left leg. Without any rational decision, and as if her conscious mind had simply let itself forget the knife, she jack-knifed straight and in the process kicked him very hard in the right kneecap.

'Fuck, oh fuck,' he moaned.

She scrabbled forward out of his reach, trying to wriggle her jeans up as she went for one of the bureau-drawers. He lunged forwards too, and beat her to it.

'Going for the gun?' he snarled, holding the drawer closed. 'You want a real good pistol-fuck, that it?' He couldn't stand properly, but he was still bouncing around with the power to hurt that his knife gave him. He opened the drawer and glanced in: no gun, and her Swiss army knife was in the drawer below.

Her eyes on his, Annabelle reached into the drawer. 'Actually, no,' she said, suddenly calm. 'I thought I'd do you a favour, you see. These are tarot cards. You've been so charming. Sit down and I'll lay you a pattern. Your fortune.'

Was she getting away with this? For the moment at least he wasn't hurting her. The pack got properly, if quickly, shuffled; she made him use his left hand but he just took the knife in his right. She laid a crescent because that would give her more time to think. He started to turn the cards, which wasn't his job the way she did it, but that was his problem. And actually it was his problem because, though she hadn't faked it even a bit, there really were a lot of swords in the layout, and a couple of Major Arcana that in that company weren't so hot.

'Ah, well, the meaning of all this is quite complex.' She was stalling, but he caught the concern in her eyes and he looked freaked out by it: he wasn't used to pity from his victims. Without ceasing to look at him with amused compassion like wise women are supposed to, she banged her left fist down hard on his right hand, grabbed the knife by its blade up near the hilt with her right, and tossed it up on top of the wardrobe.

She'd never been able to bowl, but underarm she was really good.

The cards, of course, never lie. She slapped him very hard with the full reach of her long left arm, clawed his face forwards into the top of her skull, and kneed him in the balls. This isn't really happening any more than that was. I don't act like this; I wasn't really that stupid, was I? Thank heavens I learned to do all this at school.

She left him on the floor, then went back and kicked him a couple of times in the side of the head. She picked up the room-phone from where it had been knocked to the floor and dialled Alexandra's room.

'Hi, desk,' she said mendaciously. 'Could you call the police to room 201? There's a sex pervert here; he's been subdued already. They'll be how many minutes? Why, thank you.'

'You haven't really called the police,' he said, struggling to his feet and pulling up his trousers. Some of the bluster was back, in spite of the nosebleed. 'And if you did, I'll say you tried to roll me.'

'Your choice,' she smirked, because the next few moves were clear, and she started to buff her nails on a file from her manicure set. 'But the knife's where a shorty like you can't reach it, and there's blood on it, and the blood isn't mine or yours, and my fingerprints are only on the blade, not the handle. And then there's your little police badge that you got out of a cereal packet. I really don't think you'd be wise to stick around; use the fire-escape while you still can. The police might not like people like me, but people like you they hurt.'

He zipped his trousers gingerly, gave her a long, cool look, and was out of the door. She followed; if he went for the lifts it might still mean trouble. But no. Alexandra stuck her head round her door as he passed and Annabelle lip-fingered her back in. He banged out through the emergency exit. She ran up and slammed it: once it closed, it couldn't be opened from the other side.

Annabelle ran back to her room and dialled out on the phone.

They answered at the lobby of the Chatterbox right away.

'Hello, Jimmy,' she said, 'how's the race war? Yes, this is English. Listen: it was a guy who cut Ninette; nothing to do with Inge or Martha. The same guy who followed me out tonight, early on. White suit, shades. Anyway, he's stuck on the fire-escape at the Chesterfield; you know the bit that swings down to the street is jammed, don't you? I thought you might decide to take an interest because it's been cutting into your profits, right? Besides, he goes around saying he's syndicate and getting into rooms with that and a fake police badge, and they can do without the bad name, can't they? Thought you'd see it the same as me. Why yes, how kind. I'm okay, really.'

She hung up. What am I in, she giggled to herself, a Clint Eastwood movie? I forgot to tell the guy the Mafia don't read you your rights either. I wonder if Jimmy will bother, or if he's got down by now. I suppose if he's desperate he could jump. I hope they kill him. Would Ariadne say that was the right political line?

Alexandra came in then, and held her as she drank a large glass of neat gin and burst into sobs. She had hoped to avoid the worst possibilities of her new life, and here they were all coming up like lemons, and some of it was her own fault, but things hurt, and it wasn't fair.

But after a bit she sneaked a look at a mirror, and it didn't dare say a word out of turn.

39.

After more gin, and a long hot bath, and some chicken teriyaki they called out for, and a lot of stroking of the back of her neck by Alexandra, she got some sleep, and when she woke she couldn't remember the bad dreams.

In the morning Alexandra took charge; this was a routine she knew, sort of. She hobbled into the lift and they got a cab down to the free clinic on Clark so they wouldn't be confronted with another dumb intern who needed to be told everything, and who would want them to involve the police. An ageing hippie with a medical degree and a beard to his waist gave Annabelle a Wassermann and the other obvious tests, and some shots in case she had picked up an E. coli infection. Then Annabelle insisted on going uptown; she said she had something to do, and wouldn't be more specific until they got to the

John Hancock and into the express lift to the observation platform.

'But hon,' said Alexandra, 'I thought you suffered from vertigo. I mean, you always said how badly even Natasha's window affects your stomach, and in a mood like this... They won't let you jump, and really you shouldn't take it that much to heart, you know.'

Annabelle looked down from the tower at the dark, bright, rich and dirty city, and shook a histrionic fist. 'From now on,' she intoned, 'it is war between us.'

'Oh, thank God,' said Alexandra. 'You're making a literary reference.' She paused a moment, then reflected, 'You know, all in black pretty much suits you – it's a look... And almost no makeup – now you're a bit thinner, you bring that off too.'

She passed Annabelle a lipstick. It was black.

'Go with the theme, sweetie, go with the theme.'

Even though money was short, they took a cab back to the Chesterfield; Alexandra was still limping and the seats on Chicago buses were harder than Annabelle felt like bearing that morning.

They found Inge sitting in the lobby. In daylight she went for Joan Crawford suits in indiscreet shades of red, cut so the shoulders looked as if they were padded, and wedgies that looked as if you could actually walk in them. She also wore an eye-patch and carried a black cane with a silver top which looked as if it came apart; no-one was going to be allowed to think she had gone soft.

'Hi, Inge,' said Annabelle, in a world-weary sort of voice. 'How's tricks?'

'Tied to the furniture and bleeding, of course. What do you think, English?'

Annabelle had never seen Inge smile before, but of course she would have an amethyst in one of her canines. Mexica's influence on the sisters' dentistry had gone on being deleterious for a long time.

'Since I was looking in anyway,' Inge continued, 'Jimmy asked me to say that your acquaintance has been given a long lecture on the error of his ways. When we heard, we took up a collection. Hey, you did pretty good: it was hardly worth your calling in, except to clear up the misunderstanding about Ninette; even before he jumped off the fire-escape when he saw the guys coming, the state you left him in – guy said it looked like my style, and that, liebchen, is a compliment. Anytime you want to take up – but no, not really your thing, is it? And you'd look terrible blonde. Now, you weren't thinking of going back to the Box for a while, were you? Ones who don't think you're a bruja think you're a jonah. I mean, the collection for you ended up bigger than the one for Ninette because a lot of those bitches just don't want you around. Silly, really, but I'll see you sometime. Because you wouldn't want to be going back too soon, would you? And this'll mean you can take it easy. Sorry I ever thought you were a wimp. Sieg Heil and stuff.'

She handed over an envelope, stamped and turned on her heel. Annabelle nodded graciously; you have to accept a salute.

One of the largest of the black security guards from the Chesterfield peeled away from the wall, where he had hitherto been leaning unnoticed, and followed Inge out. His presence made Annabelle realise what the crinkliness of the envelope had at first not; that the girls down at the Chatterbox had really been quite generous. Oh well, she thought, treat it as sickness benefit. After all, as long as no-one gets too explicit it might not actually be blood money, not as such. Because they are men, Jimmy and his cohorts, and possibly it was just a serious talking-to they gave him. They might think him almost entitled, really. They don't have to like us to take profits from us, after all.

Alexandra told her to stop brooding, and Annabelle put most of the money in the hotel safe. They went for late lunch to what turned out to be a rather nice little pseudo-French bistro Alexandra had spotted in a neighbouring side-street. She ordered a bottle of Chateaubriand because she thought it would be a good idea to build up Annabelle's strength, but had to drink Perrier herself because of the painkillers and antibiotics.

They ate intently. Alexandra got sufficiently involved with the Bearnaise that her lipstick was allowed to stay smudged for minutes at a time. Suddenly she tapped Annabelle's shin with her foot, perhaps too enthusiastically, but she meant well because, 'That's him, isn't it?' she said in a hiss.

Annabelle took out a mirror and looked over her shoulder. It was Carlos all right, and he was either making great play with affecting not to notice her, or paying even more attention than he seemed to the small, skinny woman with him. She was dressed in couture fetish, all white leatherette and silver chains.

Alexandra wanted the pair of them to go over and bitch him up. She thought it would do Annabelle good to inflict a little pain and embarrassment. Annabelle thought, though, that with the pair of them semi-crippled they would make too grotesque a scene for it to be really worthwhile. Besides, she said to her friend, placing a hand firmly on her arm, was it not time that the pair of them stopped acting as if they had no class? Ladies of leisure now, dear, for a few weeks at least.

40.

In the late afternoon Annabelle felt well enough to pop out and take a turn around the block on her own. She was browsing in a bookstore when she was tapped on the shoulder. She spun, trembling but aggressive, and almost took out Mark's throat with the new Calvino.

'Hi,' he grinned. 'What's shaking, kid?'

He was utterly oblivious of her mental state, it seemed, and she couldn't help resenting that. He was still nice to look at, albeit more abstractly so than had been the case before last night. But she needed a friend, and she ought not to stop talking to men because it had, after all, only been one loony, had it not? She paid for a stack of thrillers and made him carry them round to a neighbouring coffee-shop. She was still very jumpy, but coffee might be okay if she had a lot of sugar in it.

'Don't you want anything to eat?' he asked. 'They give great cream cake here.'

'No,' she said. 'I'm not hungry.'

'Surely a girl like you doesn't have any bad habits she needs to get rid of.'

'There are,' she said firmly, 'a lot of bad habits which I need to give up before they get me into any further trouble.'

'I'm sure,' he said, and placed a hand on her wrist, 'that someone as smart as you need never get into trouble.'

Steady, girl, she told herself; he almost certainly hasn't heard about it yet. How could he; you haven't even rung Carola, and he'd be part of different grapevines to Jimmy and Inge. He's being flirtatious, not crass. And you couldn't inflict that much damage with a sugar-sifter, anyway.

'Actually, Mark...'

'Eckshually. You really do talk like that all the time, don't you? It's really you, all that voice and everything. I thought it was like eyelashes, or Alexandra's falls.'

'Mark, sorry, sweetie,' Annabelle said, 'but stop it a second, okay? Yes, I like you. We're friends. But no smooth-talking right now. Things happen, things I'm not going to talk about to you. I'm all grise and grim today, so if you want me pleased to have you around me, then your best bet is not to try too hard to be amusing. You're probably saying to yourself, who does she think she is? That's a good question, and I'm not sure the answer comes all that readily to me today. But I could really do with you as a friend right now; but I mean a friend, not someone to sit around being groovy at me.'

He was sensitive, a bit, because he stayed anyway, and was tactful even without knowing what it was he was having to be tactful about, and he did and said nothing that even her most touchy and irrational side could object to. They had several coffees and he carried her books to the door of the elevator, and then he smiled goodbye.

Look, she was still hurting, and it was all much too soon even if it meant she didn't get a second chance. Alexandra said it was just like getting back on a horse or a diving-board, but, well, it wasn't, was it?

Over the next few days she handled the situation progressively less well. Mainly she sat around in her room and brooded, and Alexandra came to know better than to pop in with cheery comments. Annabelle had put herself on autopilot, and people on autopilot tend to programme themselves to bite off the heads of people who try to serve up cheery, interfering chatter.

Annabelle popped out to the doctor, or to the electrolysist, when she had to. At the odd hours when she felt like eating she would go down to the coffee-shop in the hotel and glower people out of talking to her. Every couple of days she would stroll over to the bookstore and collect another stack of detective stories; she felt more at home living in her mind now than living in her body, but even her mind couldn't stand too much effort. She threw on her jeans and a blouse to go out and took them off the moment she got back to her room.

Alexandra got bored after a while, tired of restraining herself from coming in. She felt Annabelle was overreacting to something that was highly unpleasant but which, after all, hon, was a risk we all take. Once the strapping was off her wrist and ankles she took to going out for long evenings to a new bar on the other side of town. Soon she and Randolph were getting gigs again; a couple of agents he hadn't bitten turned out to have been in the Ragazzo that night, purely, of course, on business.

Annabelle worked on her eyebrows and just wasn't all that hungry. No-one was going to be able to say she was losing control; she just wanted to retreat for a while. It was chilly out, and she knew perfectly well that in this sort of mood she had just to look out of the window at the raindrops to start catching a cold. Feeling ill on top of her depression would never do. She didn't want to be out on this city's streets when they were full of lunatics, and the city was not as attractive when its sky turned grey.

Each evening she went to bed early, which meant that she took off her dressing-gown and slipped under the covers instead of lying on top of them. She didn't get to sleep, though, for hours; just lay there going over things in her mind while getting the sheet rucked up under her and losing her temper with the shape of the pillow. She thought, if I am going to go back to thinking badly about myself then it should happen about now, and counted, and looked down at her body and in a mirror at her face, and, though she was no more cheerful, what she was dreading just did not ever quite kick in.

41.

An insistent rapping woke her from a doze. She put her less sordid dressing-gown on, rumpled her hair into some sort of order, and went to the door.

'Natasha,' she said. 'Oh God, I suppose it had to be you. Alex is off taking off all her clothes somewhere. I was asleep, sort of. What time is it? What is it, anyway? Where have you been? Sure, you're welcome, of course. Come in.'

When Annabelle had put her lenses in and could see Natasha properly she didn't feel at any sort of disadvantage, even while picking sleep and dead mascara from the corners of her eyes. Why, the girl was positively unkempt. Her eyes could never have been meant to look like that, and there were smudges on her blouse that looked suspiciously as if she hadn't done a good job of cleaning off splashes of spaghetti alla vongole.

Annabelle couldn't feel bitchy for more than the second it took to form the thought, because Natasha was clearly very upset. So upset that she was just being quiet and subdued, rather than playing it for bravura and fioritura, the way she did over parking-tickets and minor debts. Annabelle had to feel sorry for her; it was to Annabelle that she had come, which sort of meant something to the ego, said something about Natasha still being her friend, though it was not to her that Annabelle had felt able to turn over the events of the previous week.

It was hardly a surprise to Annabelle that something awful had happened with Carlos, and no breath of having told Natasha so was going to pass her lips. She just couldn't be a hard-nosed, hind-sighted smart-ass with Natasha lying there on the bed looking sort of disarranged and sobbing and sniffling. All Annabelle could do was go to a drawer and get her a large white linen handkerchief. Sherry was all there was to drink; once she had polished off the current bottle of gin Annabelle had decided that she had not better keep any more in the place until she cheered up a bit. She poured Natasha a glass of sherry, and herself a larger one, and put the bottle in easy reach; this had the potential to be a marathon session. Start subtly, then, with the obvious informed guess.

'So he ripped you off?'

'Yes. The bank manager rang about the account being emptied so suddenly and so fast. He'd noticed that it was always Carlos' signature, and hoped I didn't think he was being impertinent but he'd seen partnerships go sour before, and he thought he should make sure I knew what was going on. Really, though, he was only covering his own ass, you know. Being sensible. Because if head office in New York ever heard how many times I fucked him to get the original loan...'

'They'd probably,' said Annabelle, 'come over all nostalgic for the good old days of their own early careers in banking. But what did he say?'

'Carlos said he had "come to the decision"' – there was a vein of malicious imitation in her recital that boded well for her rapid recovery – 'that he had invested sufficient time in the business and emotion in the relationship to justify pulling himself out of both and taking an adequate recompense, they both having proved to be essentially non-viable. He doesn't regard taking my money as any sort of breach of faith, he says. He says I owe him a lot for his hard effort on business and sexual fronts; I'd pay a therapist, he said, and he'd been spending a lot of time being therapeutic. He had his lawyer with him, and the lawyer said that if it came to court his defence would be the stress contingent on Carlos' being involved with a person of my type. With the right judge he reckons that would be admissible. Of course, he's gambling on my not being able to take that kind of public humiliation.'

'He's right, though, isn't he?'

Natasha nodded. 'Carlos had some snappy one-liners rehearsed about the way I look first thing in the morning; he told me some of them. He has character witnesses from the store to say how haggard he's been getting.'

'Mr. Salvatore, I suppose.'

'Probably. How did you know? Never mind; Carola, I guess. Then he got abusive. He was really nasty and there was some girl with them listening in on the extension and she was giggling as if she thought it was real funny. I hope he gives her a real hard time when it comes to be her turn for his shit.'

'So he's got your flat, as well?'

Natasha had the grace to blush a little at past disingenuousness. 'No, well,' she said, 'it never got really much past the stage of discussion. It was an idea that came up and he was insistent, whatever I decided about it, that I not have you round.'

'And right then you actually didn't want me around a whole lot yourself, and you thought I'd accept it more readily if I thought it was coming from him. Nice to get that clear. Have another drink, Natasha.'

'Hey, listen, Annabelle, sweetheart, you needn't think I came over just so you can ooze compassion over me and feel good about yourself for being nice to someone who's let you down. From what I hear you've not been doing so hot yourself. You needn't sit around playing Pollyanna with that "Miss Social Competence of the Year" look on your face.'

'Nice to see you back to normal, Natasha,' Annabelle said. 'I was worried about you there for approximately three nano-seconds.'

'What I was going to ask, unless you are totally in love with this scuzzy little room, was if you would be interested in paying me a little rent, because I don't think I can entirely handle being by myself right now, and you don't seem to be in all that hot a mood either, and you could do with some help. I mean, I did let you down, actually, sort of, and it was all his fault really and....'

The tough line of talk got progressively more staccato and eventually Natasha started crying again and smearing what was left of her eye-makeup all over the handkerchief.

Annabelle said of course she'd love to come and stay. Natasha smiled and bounced up and down with pleasure and then cried some more and fell asleep in the middle of Annabelle's bed. Annabelle poured herself another drink, finishing the bottle of sherry. She was already beginning to think that moving in with Natasha, while not something she especially felt like getting out of, was not, perhaps, the smartest move she had ever made.

42.

No-one else seemed to think it was an especially good idea either.

Alexandra started off by talking about nursing vipers and then apologised to Randolph, who had put on as much of a hurt expression as a reticulated python is capable of, which is not all that much.

'I always thought they were deaf, anyway,' said Annabelle.

'He may be deaf,' said Alexandra in a tone of stern rebuke, 'but he's not utterly insensitive.'

'She is my oldest friend in this country, after all,' Annabelle shrugged. 'It was her idea that I came here. The time I spent being let down by her was very educational, and I'll never be so foolish as to trust her entirely. I owe her, sort of, not least for these' – she gestured in the general direction of her breasts – 'and she surely owes me, and my moving in seems like the best way we can both pay. And I've been thinking: after what happened that night maybe I shouldn't have stayed on in the same hotel, never mind the same room. Not a smart idea. You and Randolph are supposed to be off to Florida soon, or so you've been saying, and even if you were thinking of asking me along, which I'm sure you were, a pale thing like me couldn't possibly stand all that sun. Blisters all over. But, oh, Alexandra darling, I'm not forgetting you and how kind you've been to me. I couldn't have survived without you, you know that. I don't think I'm making any sort of choice between you.'

Annabelle was hugging her friend by this stage, and getting her hair tangled in Alexandra's sunglasses.

'Don't get all sugary on me, hon,' Alexandra said, disentangling herself and pulling back. 'I can't stand it when you get all kissy. People have been making very caustic and hurtful remarks, did you know that, about how close I'm getting to the English girl, and haven't I been warned about private girls' schools and what they get up to in the dorms?'

They pecked each other restrainedly on the cheek, and Alexandra helped Annabelle pack and take her bags down to the lobby. In the elevator she started to tell a long story about the time Mexica was sharing a flat with some Filipina bitch, and they got into a fight about using each other's tweezers. It was all starting to look very broken-bottle for La Divina when Alexandra put Annabelle's bags down in the middle of the carpet and said, 'Look, hon, I'm sure it won't be a bit like that between you two. I'm just being an old misery, spreading alarm and despondency. Tell me to stop it; I'm sure you'll get along fine. Just visit your mother occasionally; I get alone and inadequate sometimes too, you know.'

She sniffed sonorously and Annabelle had to dig in her handbag for yet another of the large white linen handkerchieves.

43.

It was on the second morning that tension first arose. Natasha insisted on drinking herb tea first thing, and sitting around striking vaguely yogic poses while drinking it very slowly, and seemed to expect to be appreciated for the elegance with which she was doing so. Annabelle flung on one of her new black outfits, pulled a black beret over her hair, which she had brushed only a hundred times, and jammed a pair of dark glasses over her eyes, which she had not made up.

'Where are you going,' said Natasha, 'looking like that?' She hadn't finished breakfast yet but was already in serious competition with the cover of the copy of *Vogue* the postman had just delivered. If Carlos was genuinely critical of how she looked first thing in the morning, not even Eve on the seventh morning of creation, adorned in pristine dew, would have passed his test.

'Well,' said Annabelle, who was wearing dark glasses partly to avoid being blinded by so much beauty first thing, 'I was just popping over to Carola's for coffee.'

'Are you getting into bad habits?' asked Natasha, touching her ears with her feet.

'Gosh, no,' said Annabelle. 'I don't do drugs at all, hardly.'

'By bad habits,' said Natasha, 'I don't necessarily mean spending money you haven't got on cocaine you shouldn't be taking. I don't even mean drinking coffee, which is especially bad for someone of your size and nervous disposition, or the cookies she will undoubtedly force on you out of sheer perverse opposition to my will. I mean gossiping. About me.'

'Well,' said Annabelle, stretching out on the sofa for a few moments before facing the outdoors, 'it is of course true that it is impossible for me, your flatmate, to talk to Carola, your oldest friend, about topics of mutual interest without your name coming up from time to time, just as, say, Mark's does. If you don't trust us to be thinking of you primarily in the context of our deep sisterly feeling for you, and only secondarily in terms of tearing you apart with our tongues, then I guess you

had better stick some clothes on and come round with me.
Then the three of us can bitch someone else up. You don't have
to touch the coffee or cookies.'

'You know,' said Natasha, 'you know perfectly well that
there is a deep gulf fixed between me and that person.' The
perfect calm was gone, such a relief.

'But now you're agreed on what a toad that man is...'

'That,' said Natasha, setting her jaw with unbecoming
hardness, 'does not alter the fact of her betrayal.'

'But she'd really like to see you. And you know that whatever your feelings are about it as a habit at this moment, sooner
or later you're going to tire of clean living and want to get a
good deal from her. So why not peck and make up now?'

Natasha went on being what she thought was principled
and Annabelle thought was petulant until suddenly she got an
evil glint in her eye. 'What's all this about Mark?' she asked. 'I
hope you haven't any presumptions of cutting in on my dear
friend Hennie, not that you can compete with her.'

Rather than pursue this line of conversation, or throw
something at her hostess, Annabelle went down to Carola's by
herself, which was what she had wanted to do in the first place
anyway. Predictably, the role of a peacemaker was not a more
popular one in this quarter either.

'I am of course deeply biased about the whole thing,' said
Carola, who, thank God, slutted around mornings in the tee-
shirt she had slept in. 'I think you're being a lot nicer about
That Girl than That Girl deserves after what has happened to
you, poor wounded chile, all alone in this sinful city, through
her wicked neglect and betrayal. You're not going to get
canonized for all this saintliness, you know. We don't get
canonized, I'm told.'

'Oh, you're exaggerating,' said Annabelle. 'True, she let me
down, and she has acknowledged that she let me down. I can
take an apology, and I can forgive; it doesn't seem very much
for me to do, especially when it means that I get to live in a
luxury apartment. Even if it is a long way from the ground and
I can't bear to look out of the window with the drapes open.'

'I've lived with her, darling. You know it'll be apricot face-
masks without the option every time she thinks you're looking
dry, and you'll always suddenly need a good drastic facial scrub

whenever you argue about whose turn it is to wash the kitchen floor. She likes things tidy, That Girl, but she's a princess too, always glad to have a pair of perfectly-manicured hands around that she can yell at until they do things for her. Don't let me put you off; you can always come round and gulp Vs when the pressure gets too much for you.'

After this, Annabelle felt it would be disloyal to have more than one cookie.

44.

Annabelle had been avoiding Mark. Carola attempted to set up supper a couple of times, but Annabelle always found an excuse to stay at the apartment and do her nails, or have a migraine or something. She couldn't face the idea of romance; she particularly couldn't face the idea of getting into some situation where the object of said romance was more interested in this Hennie, whoever she was. None of what had happened had been her fault, or his either: he wasn't going to think the worse of her; he knew the score and, if he was in partnership with Carola, he was hardly going to be shockable. She really just didn't want to see him yet.

He wanted to see her, though. He tracked her down in the bookstore where they had met before; she was still going there a lot, even though it was some way from the apartment. This time when he came up behind her suddenly he had the sense to stand far enough back that she couldn't automatically kick him in the shins for surprising her.

'Hi, Annabelle,' he said when she turned. He was looking cute and adorable, and wearing the sort of white sweater she associated with cricket heroes in the Sixth Form.

'Hi, Mark,' she said. 'How have you been keeping?'

'Well enough, how about you? Carola told me about what happened. I didn't know why you were upset last time. I'm sorry, I was probably insensitive.'

'You couldn't have known. I suppose we might as well go and have a drink.'

He sat on the opposite side of the table. Either Carola had told him to treat her like spun glass or it was only as a friend he

wanted her anyway. Given the existence of Hennie, probably
the latter.

He wasn't very keen on her living with Natasha, which at
least meant he was interested enough to feel he had the right to
comment, not that that means very much. 'Annabelle,' he said,
'I think you're wonderful. Go with it, just as you are, and don't
worry about what she says about your looks and style. One day
you'll be even more fabulous because you'll have realised you're
okay. You don't have to hang around that tight-assed plastic
bitch to pick up her crumbs. Do you really want to end up
another Barbie doll?'

'Oh no, Mark, that's not it, not any more, not really. I like
her, and she is my friend in spite of everything. I'm not blind to
her faults, but then I have plenty of my own.'

'Don't put yourself down. Carola and I have noticed you're
always putting yourself down.'

Annabelle ignored him; she knew her faults perfectly well.
There was just not much point in detailing them right now.
'Anyway,' she continued, 'she's had a rough time too, and her
pride has taken a beating. I could do with a change of scene; I
move flats quite often in London. I'm just looking after myself
really, because when you've been hurt the very best thing you
can do is try and look after someone else, isn't it? And I'm
giving her that chance too, you see.'

Mark shook his head, downed his bourbon, patted her on
the hand, and told her that she was crazy, but if that was what
she wanted to do then she should just get on with it, he
guessed. He'd be around.

After he'd gone she had another three drinks. She hadn't
really wanted him to go away at all; she could have listened to
him giving her good advice about thinking well of herself all
night, even on opposite sides of a table.

45.

A few days later Annabelle decided she needed her hair
trimmed; it was getting too long to be cute and perky. She went
along to the hairdresser with Natasha, who was having her
purple streak changed to an orange one because she felt like

giving herself a slight change of image to celebrate being rid of Carlos. She owed it to herself, she said. Usually when she was depressed she went to a man and had more silicone put into her cheekbones, but he was out of town, skiing at Aspen. Looking at the cheekbones, which were already a trifle too spectacular, Annabelle considered a smartass crack about ski-jumps, but thought better of it.

When they got back the flat was a lot less full. Carlos had never returned his key, and clearly felt he had a right to the presents Natasha had given him when they were living together. After that they changed the locks, just in case his sense of his rights got broader.

Natasha was firm with the doorman.

'Look,' he said, unrepentant, 'I mind doors, I don't read minds. If you don't want people here, tell me. But if I don't know, I'm not about to stop people who used to live here taking their furniture away. Just who is supposed to be living with you, anyway?'

Annabelle thought it would be tactful to smile during this, and slip him a gratuity next time she passed his desk.

Without the lithographs and the mobile and several of the sillier tubular steel chairs the flat was more pleasing anyway. Annabelle could walk around it without ducking prisms and without being tempted to snigger at pink and purple trees. She still had the problem of needing to stay in the half of the room where one was not compelled to look down thirty storeys, but this was a matter of practice. She persuaded Natasha that that was the half of the room best for her yoga, and occupied the unregenerate chaise-longue that Carlos had never managed to purge. She spent many idle and enjoyable hours ensconced on it; she gave up thrillers for Proust and allowed Natasha to believe it was purely because she was trying to keep the tone of the place suitably aesthetic.

Natasha had given up the sort of Zen twig-and-half-a-thistle flower-arrangements that Carlos had told her were the correct form for young professionals. She had gone back to masses of expensive alleged wildflowers that she kept paying for in spite of the season and her debts. The flat was full of light even when cloud was low, and it smelt of summer.

Annabelle was aware that she wasn't one of the world's

stars when it came to doing the washing-up or hoovering into corners, and for a while it was quite refreshing in a moral sort of way to live with someone who didn't let her let these things slip. By the time Natasha had creamed her hands and put on a pair of rubber gloves and wrapped a silk scarf round her face because she had an allergy to dust you realised it was actually less tiring to let her bully you into doing it than to watch it being done. It also got tiring being told each time about how Mexica once shared a flat with a slut like you, and one day simply got fed up and turned the fire-hose on her.

Natasha's complete inability to take pleasure from food was a problem. Earlier flatmates had considered Annabelle's cooking a redeeming feature, but this only ever worked for Natasha when guests were round and complimented them both on the food.

One evening when Annabelle had just put together a scratch chili, Natasha turned up with a tanned, elegant woman in an artistic-looking long blue sweater and a belt and nets and men's evening dress shoes. This turned out to be Hennie, just back from Amarillo. Natasha was clearly intending shock treatment of some kind, and the evening was likely to be sticky.

Either Hennie didn't know that Annabelle had a crush on Mark or she was just tired of Natasha's games. She asked after the meal how Annabelle made chili that was so hot yet didn't leave your stomach feeling like a mangle after a hard day's wash. Annabelle explained about putting in milk, and they had a long and friendly chat about Indian food and the effect on world cooking of lactose-intolerant variations. Natasha yawned ostentatiously.

There were other problems around food. Natasha had the attitude of the white American suburbs that eating offal was either an admission of social and economic failure – unless done in very expensive French or Italian restaurants – or indicated something a bit dodgy about your ethnicity. The streak of racism that people had always told Annabelle existed in white Americans just below the surface was observable in Natasha on the occasion that she found Annabelle boiling pigs' trotters for her special cassoulet recipe. Remarks about polka-dot bandannas were tossed in among complaints about the number of bones there were going to be in the garbage, and queries about whether some of them would be appropriate for the throwing of the Book of Changes.

Natasha had never got a taste for English cooking either: she collapsed in serious giggles when Annabelle told her dessert was to be Spotted Dick, and looked unwell when told about Toad in the Hole. Still, even in the Gloucester Road it had been clear that living with her was going to be a foreign country.

46.

When the flower-shop sent round her account for the second time, with the total underlined in red and no complimentary cloth-and-wire orchid, Natasha came cleaner to Annabelle about the economic situation. Annabelle knew something was up when Natasha poured them both a drink with no-one else in the room; the garter-belt and black stockings under her white towelling dressing-gown were some sort of hint as well. At least it meant that yoga exercises would only be in the offing at the cost of snapped elastic.

'Look, sweets,' Natasha started, 'I know you're still getting over things and this is probably not really your sort of thing – not that it's precisely mine, of course, except that being naturally talented at everything I'm really rather good at it. But I asked at Sachs today and they're not hiring on any of the makeup concessions for at least a month. And that bastard really cleaned me out. I know you haven't been spending that much, but you must be going through that collection money just helping me with the rent. I'm going to put on my black plastic trench-coat and go down to Whitey's. Come with. One of these nights you might need entrée, and if you come there with me they'll know you're alright. In spite of everything.'

Natasha was strict about the look for Whitey's, so strict that Annabelle picked up a reasonable idea of the sort of place it was. The whole look was Inge's sort of thing, only done in a more officer-class sort of way – brows plucked to death then painted back in in deepest black, the palest foundation you could find that wasn't actually clown-white, and nothing, but nothing, worn that wasn't black and shiny, or at least black, with possibly the smallest bit of bright red trimming.

'You're very tall, of course,' Natasha said, appraising Anna-belle as if she were a used car, 'which helps. And your legs aren't too bad, and it might not matter too much about what's left of the flab if we pull you in a bit here. You'll do, you know; you really will. With help: it's amazing how good I am at makeup. Don't worry about the other thing; they can't afford to be fussy, and it's mainly sisters that do it in this town anyway. Where do you think I got the money to get things together in the first place? Not down at the Chatterbox or the Ace, I can tell you, sweets.'

She was taking all of this very fast.

'Hang on, a second, Natasha love,' Annabelle interjected. 'This is all very interesting, of course. But is this the sort of thing I want to get involved in?'

'Don't be silly, of course it is; it makes money, sweets. First of all Whitey's is safer than the Chatterbox, not full of lowlife scum and peg-leg pool-players. Second, I'm not asking you to get involved in anything; just asking you to come along and keep me company. And to have the right sort of look so you don't feel out of it, or people wonder why I've brought you along. I mean, if someone offers you a drink on the strength of the look you're not going to turn it down. We both know you that well.'

'Thanks a lot. Where do I sign on for detox?'

'Now I think of it, better tip Frank to make it mixer only after the first couple, because Whitey likes people who stay sharp and don't get bombed: he makes more profit on the bar that way. And third, well, sweets, let's be candid: one reason why I'm going back there is because right now I kind of like the idea of beating up on a few men. I'm owed for what that shit did, is how I see it. I'm sure you could come to dig that after what happened; you wouldn't even have to try very hard.'

'I'm not into violence.'

'Not the story they tell on the street, sweets. And I'm not asking you to get involved, but doing it for money and quite enjoying it at the same time doesn't mean you have to end up a total whacko like Inge. We all know that she goes too far and gets completely out of control. Her brothers have to cover for her and get the guy into this hospital they own, and make him say it was an accident shaving, or in the shower. Whitey won't even let her in the place anymore, except for the Christmas party, and even then he has Frank frisk her at the door. That razor of hers could damage a lot more than tinsel, if you take my meaning. Of course, though, I forget: you're the poor little non-violent flower that just happens not to be afraid of her, right?'

There are times when it is better just to bow to the inevitable, and Annabelle was wearing black a lot these days anyway.

47.

Whitey's was a glum enough place for anyone to be trying to have any fun in, but Annabelle supposed she just didn't understand how it felt to be perverse. It was a pretty standard executive cocktail lounge tucked away somewhere round the back of uptown. The upholstery was black leatherette rather than the usual beige, and the lighting was all blue neon and red bulbs, so that your teeth shone and your lipstick looked a nightmare.

The men drinking there all had an air of deep intensity and adolescent eagerness; when they drifted up tentatively to speak to Natasha, who had clearly been missed, they fawned harder the more she sneered. Annabelle felt left out of all this. She stopped smiling and started practicing curling her lip and looking down her nose, until Natasha told her not to pull faces and to take this seriously because there was money in it.

The floor show was tiring and tired; the usual two blondes in black leather scanties dragged on the usual slightly run-down muscle-boy in a red leather jockstrap by his pierced nipples. They slapped him a few times; he rode well in advance of the blows, but the audience didn't care to notice. The blondes tied him up with a few not very convincing half-hitches, and one of them stood on his chest in her high heels as a better vantage point for staring into the other's eyes and stroked her buttocks with a riding crop. A not especially well-paced performance of the slow movement of the Rodrigo Concierto De Aranjues crackled over the loudspeakers the whiles.

Annabelle reflected between sips of her gin-ration that the hardest thing about the evil world of sexual exploitation and degeneracy into which she seemed to have fallen was how bored you always seemed to get while it was going on. If Ariadne had made it all sound a bit less glamorous while warning her off... Annabelle supposed you had to have been there to know about the tedium.

During the long minutes of the interval a tall and elegant man in a grey business suit and a blue shirt scurried up to Natasha and knelt at her feet. She gave him permission to speak, but not to raise his head from her shoes while he did so. She then had to teeter dangerously on her bar-stool as she leant forwards, on the pretext of tightening her ankle-strap but actually to catch what he was saying.

Annabelle kept a tactful distance.

'I may be gone some time,' Natasha said. 'I'm sure you'll find something to do. Don't drink too much.'

There followed some more flustered whispering from her feet.

'Oh,' Natasha continued, 'he says he'd really like you to come and observe me deal with his naughtiness, so that you can tell me if I'm not being strict enough.'

Annabelle reflected that at least back at the apartment she could make herself a cup of decent coffee rather than having to drink all the non-fattening soft drinks she'd be stuck with if she stayed. Adopting a sinuously military posture, she stalked behind Natasha and the john to a waiting taxi.

Natasha made the john wait in the hall of the apartment so she could go into the lounge and pull the drapes to and turn the lighting down.

'Now,' she said, gesturing for him to enter

The man hastened to remove his clothes. She gave him another glacial sneer as he folded them neatly and put them out of the way on one of the smaller chairs. His tailor could be recommended because without his suit his body was rather disappointing. He had big pores, and his body hair was matted and slightly unsavoury-looking even before Natasha got busy with the hot candle-wax. Annabelle had wondered why candles had made their appearance on the dining-room table just before they went out; her naïveté worried her sometimes. The john kept his socks on, which had the effect of making him look even more naked and silly, just like books always tell you it does.

Annabelle had gathered that her role in all of this was to sit still well out of the way and look sinisterly uninvolved. Once the man had a blindfold on she used the opportunity to get on with reading Proust.

She didn't think hog-tying was ever a skill she would need to acquire, but after a while Natasha gave her an imploring look and Annabelle wandered over, dropping on the way the dressing-gown into which she had changed, and put her thumb on the knot where the cords came together in the small of his back. At Natasha's raised eyebrow she thought better of it, stood up and put a stiletto heel on the knot instead.

'Thanks, sweets,' said Natasha as the man groaned with the vague beginnings of pleasure, then, louder, added, 'Come here, bitch.'

Annabelle realised that the blindfold had slipped during the man's writhings, and that she was now committed. She felt a little sulky about this, and so just stood there passive and impassive while Natasha stroked her breasts and thighs. Gradually the groans of the hog-tied wreck on the floor increased in tempo and in intensity, and quite suddenly it was all over and Natasha was mopping up with tissues. Annabelle could put her dressing-gown back on, finish her coffee, and sit reading *A l'Ombre des Jeunes Filles En Fleur* while Natasha made out his American Express slip.

'You were wonderfully quiet and sullen,' said Natasha when he had gone. 'That's just what they like from the other one. He was very pleased and paid us twice as much. Are you quite sure you've never done this before?'

'I must just be naturally talented,' said Annabelle, and marked her place in Proust with a piece of discarded thong.

48.

'It would be real convenient if you could help out like that more often,' Natasha said as they sipped their hot chocolate before going to bed later that evening.

'I don't think,' said Annabelle, 'that I do that sort of thing. Not as a general sort of thing anyway.'

'But you have a natural talent. You said so yourself.'

'I swim quite well too. I always have. But I don't go swimming very often, all the same.'

'Anyone who looked at your waistline, sweets, could tell that,' said Natasha. 'But think about it. Beats working for a living.'

When it came down to it, as it ended up doing once Natasha moved on to lectures about the proper spirit of deference a guest should have to a hostess's wishes, and since her role was so largely confined to splendid inaction, Annabelle capitulated. She found it involved no especial emotional strain, and rather less histrionic skill than her sixth-form Portia. Natasha was pleased for a while, and then got ratty again. Since Annabelle had given in on this she felt less need to make concessions over her share of the washing-up: there was a particularly charred saucepan over which they looked daggers at each other for several days. Then Annabelle wised up to the possibilities implicit in the situation. While Natasha went to repair the ravages that a battery of feigned emotion had wrought on her mascara, Annabelle partially un-hog-tied a tired executive, told him she had bought him from Natasha, allowed him to lick her instep, and told him to get busy with the steel wool.

After a couple of weeks Natasha got a job on the Clairol concession and started going out to work again, but her former regulars had got used to the idea that she was around and had put her back in their little black books. Annabelle had met enough of them in the line of duty that they knew who she was when she answered the phone to them if they rang after one too many lunchtime martinis. She had to learn to put a corset on quickly by herself, and sometimes rather more elaborate makeup than she especially cared to in order to pass an inspection in daylight, but that was better than having to do the housework herself. She lacked the edge of sheer ill-temper that made Natasha so handy with a riding-crop; there were, she thought, occasional disadvantages to having such a sunny disposition. It was clear that the johns thought of her as second best, as being for rainy afternoons only. On the whole she didn't find that hurtful: it fitted her picture of the world and her place in it.

Natasha was finding readjusting to the retail trade a bit stressful, and her frazzled nerves made the evening sessions progressively more frenetic; she got keener but also crazier, the more she got irritated about fat suburban housewives. She started actually beating Annabelle where the client could see, instead of taking her where he couldn't contort himself into a clear view and saying 'Take that, bitch' while whipping the arm of the sofa.

Looking at her back in the bathroom mirror one morning Annabelle followed this lateral process of thought from the parallel tracks of weals: she had successfully made peace between Natasha and Carola. The reconciliation meant that Natasha had the option of stopping in for refreshments at Carola's on the way home from the store. The glint in Natasha's eye, her constant need for tissues – which she had explained in terms of an attack of hay-fever – these could be taken as solid evidence of the resurgence of a certain habit. Annabelle decided that enough was enough, turnabout was fair play and other bits of the proverbial wisdom that occur to one when one's back is hurting. One more time, she thought, just one, and she'll pay.

That evening a john came over and it all started again; blows were raining down on Annabelle's back, fast, snappy and stinging. Annabelle reached round and dug a fingernail into the sensitive hollow of Natasha's wrist-joint until she dropped the riding crop. Then she twisted her friend's arms up behind her back, forced her to the floor, knelt on her and lashed her thumbs together with the usual spare thongs they kept laid out and ready on the coffee-table. In the process she noticed the pleasure she was deriving from the glossy texture of her friend's back, and decided that this was perhaps not something of which she should make a habit. Annabelle slapped Natasha repeatedly across the buttocks with an enthusiasm limited only by her feeling that she should be feeling inhibitions. The john almost expired, blue with the joy of it all.

After complaining about the carpet burns on her elbows Natasha did agree that she had been getting a little out of control, that Annabelle had been right to take vigorous steps to call it to her attention, that she had been a selfish little girl, and that next time Annabelle could have some coke too.

'That's better,' said Annabelle, and removed the small screw-clamps she had found in a drawer with which she had been experimenting on Natasha's nipples. It's partly a matter of talent, she thought, and partly having access to the technology.

'Don't get too smart, missy,' said Natasha, once untied.

49.

Annabelle never found cocaine becoming more than an occasional interest; she was working hard on reading Proust, and the drug metabolized for her at irregular rates which caused odd glitches in her understanding of, and tolerance for, his longer sentences. By contrast, there was much to be said for the feeling of a champagne-bottle going off inside your head, and for letting the cork and bubbles ricochet gently round and through your brain, even though, since Annabelle and Natasha were her friends, Carola was letting them have very good deals – though they still had to take what she could get. I wonder what the vintners buy, thought Annabelle, one half so precious as the stuff they sell – more and better wine, stupid Mr. Fitzgerald. Because the little contretemps at the airport had quietly involved the middle-men, Carola had sometimes to take stuff that was a bit cut; and on occasion Annabelle found herself stuck, at the end of evenings that had been wearing enough for her to have indulged, with a leftover insomnia and manic determination which meant that for the first time the tiles in the bathroom shone so bright even Natasha could hardly complain.

After a couple of complaints that were no less definite for being diffident and servile in their expression, Annabelle and Natasha avoided both of them using cocaine on evenings when they were working as a pair. Johns seemed to feel that their tendency to giggle was a little too girly to be entirely consistent with rituals of male debasement and female vengeance. Mostly they did it round at Carola's; they would go over and smoke or do a couple of lines while listening to music, note by note, on her expensive stereo.

Mark was often there as well. He would pat Annabelle's knee or peck her cheek in a friendly but distant way. Often he brought Hennie along too, when she wasn't working herself; she was supposed to be sorting out furniture for his new apartment, or so he said. Annabelle could hardly blame him for his disengagement; apart from the obvious problem, she had given him the chill when he did seem to be interested. He still had that charming half-smile; perhaps she should have swallowed her doubts back then and just pounced.

Evenings at Carola's were always pleasant. The music was mostly slightly laid-back jazz. The cooking almost always consisted of pork chops in differently unpleasant sauces, and thankfully a lot of salads: vegetarianism had more appeal after dinner with Carola. Annabelle decided that she would give up all drugs entirely the moment that Carola's cooking started to taste okay; she could only support so much derangement of her senses.

She was finally enjoying herself, in spite of minor tensions about cleaning the cooker. Part of the point of coming here had been, had it not, to sit around feeling mildly and snugly wicked after years of being safe and plain and quiet and that other thing in the Civil Service. Some of all of this was a bit tacky, but compared to a month or so ago it had the whiff of sin without the dangers. The people with whom she was spending her time were criminals, if not in ways that did all that much immediate damage to people: but they all knew from their childhoods that what they were doing was very naughty indeed. They stayed up late as well.

50.

There were a lot of really nice things about living with Natasha, and one of them was constant access to the quintessentially American experience of being driven along long straight roads in sports cars with the tape-deck blaring. In London Natasha's constant prattle about the respective advantages of the different sorts of gearshifts in TR-7s and Porsches had been one of those bits of her conversation that had made Annabelle go politely glazed or start quietly tearing up matchbooks; it had made her reflect on the possible truth of Magda's analysis of the whole issue in terms of education for materialism. But oh, for a life of sensation rather than thought, was what came to mind as they hit the speed limit on the freeway with a tape of old Stones numbers belting out in competition with the motor's roar and the rush of the wind.

When Natasha was driving she was more relaxed and less concentratingly cool. 'Cars made all the difference back when,' she confided in the sort of yell necessary for her to be heard. 'The fact that I could drive around instead of just hanging out meant I could sort of let ideas creep up on me rather than having to sit and brood about them. That's where I scored over you, Annabelle darling. I mean, it's practical to be able to drive but it's also a way of making a getaway.'

'Well, yes,' Annabelle yelled back, 'but in my case, if I'd tried to think about serious stuff when negotiating even the simplest of clover-leaves I'd have ended up as a statistic. Some of us, Natasha, are just not born to be drivers. It's not in our natures.'

'My dear, you are, once again, underestimating your versatility and adaptability. Various of us have, in the past, rebuked you for putting yourself down,' Natasha said as she steered them into a drive-in.

Annabelle was slightly surprised when Natasha proceeded to order a quarter-pounder with cheese, large fries, a doughnut and a Coke, even more so when Natasha did not look askance at her for doing the same – minus the fries and the doughnut because Annabelle did not believe in pushing her luck. But Natasha called the waitress back and ordered them for her.

'No-one diets in a road movie, kid,' she said, slumping expansively in her seat.

51.

In general, though, Natasha had little tolerance of, or understanding for, the attacks of sheer greed that used to come over Annabelle the morning after a particularly active night. Natasha could, herself, make do with a cup of black coffee and half a stale bagel on mornings when she had to work, and she would normally not even think about lunch. On mornings when she didn't have to go in to work she would much rather stay in bed, thank you very much, than do anything so gross as eating.

On this particular Saturday off Annabelle had brought her coffee three times and she was still not getting out of bed.

'Why can't we go for brunch?' whined Annabelle. 'I'm really hungry.'

'You're always hungry, dammit. And you're getting fat again, sweets, you're getting fat as a pig. Pretty little porker you'll be.'

'So sit and watch me eat. You don't have to, after all. You can sit and practice disapproval. Your sneer is never so good that it can't be improved.'

'And bacon gives you cancer.'

'Says, no doubt, "A Doctor" in the *Depressive's Home Journal of Gardens and Hypochondria*.'

'No,' said Natasha, 'it was in the *Sun-Tribune*.'

'Whatever. You do not, darling, have to eat breakfast yourself. You can brood over a cup of decaffeinated at the ingratitude with which I am chewing my way into a self-hating, but, let me assure you, extremely satisfied early grave.'

'You can't go out without makeup. At least put on the "I'm not wearing makeup because it's too early in the morning" look I taught you.'

'If that means you're coming,' said Annabelle, 'it's a deal. But what about you, oh fairest of the fair?'

'I'm just naturally wonderfully beautiful, Annabelle. Besides last night I only took my eye-makeup off; my chart says it's the time in my cycle to let my skin get really caked and then clean it out thoroughly.'

Annabelle compromised by doing her cheekbones, lips and eyeliner, and Natasha slung on a sweater and some designer jeans and, after testing the waistband, decided she could afford to have a cheese Danish after all.

The Submarine Surprise and Delight was a ways down Clark, near Hyde Park; its name was a joke about a joke, and the original joke was the decor. At some point someone had decided that a diner which sold subs should celebrate Our Brave Boys Under The Sea, and had stuck up a lot of photos of torpedoes and periscopes. A later owner had added sea-shell mosaics and, in a moment of fantasy, a mural of King Neptune, Davey Jones or some such personage, which dominated the back half of the diner, and which caused competitions for seats which did not oblige one to look at it.

These competitions were an added complication to the already-complicated rules of precedence and territory that had been established over the years by the predominant clientele; the diner was habituated by the better class of trucker and a sort of middling class of hooker, and, after incidents, it had been more or less mutually decided that non-communication was the best policy. No-one was here to work; no-one got asked to drive either.

For some years Natasha, Carola and the others had snaffled the bit of the whores' territory nearest the juke-box; Mexica had originally made them sit there in order that they might gently dissuade other working girls from putting on Tammy Wynette, to whose music she had a pronounced aversion. You might not like the table-manners – though their lack was less glaring than it could be in the Oak Tree – but people were less out to be competitive here. You might find certain shades of nail polish and eyeshadow, and certain kinds of high-pitched squealing, a little much first thing in the morning, just before noon, but at least you always knew where you were going to have to sit, and that there would be a seat for you.

That particular morning the table was almost empty except for a skinny vision in mauve hair and sunglasses that drooped like cheek-guards.

'Hi there,' it cooed. 'You're English. I'm Tiffany.'

'I'm always glad to meet people from different nationalities,' drawled Natasha.

'No, it's my name. In hommage to Audrey.'

You could hear the second 'm'; obviously this person had at some time walked too near a film school and could probably pronounce 'auteur' on a good day.

'I'm sure she's honoured,' said Annabelle.

'You're Annabelle,' said Tiffany. 'You used to be in the Chatterbox.'

'Yes, indeed, and now I'm not.'

'I and my friend Sharon – she's from California too – used to hear your accent and think it would be real nice to listen to it close up.'

'But you did not.'

'You were sort of unpopular, you know, and you and that other one, the one with the hands, you just sat there working. You didn't even try to be friends. We didn't want to get on the wrong side of the others.'

'Obviously not.'

'But here we are now, and I have met you after all. So it was all karma, destiny and stuff. And your beautiful friend,' she added.

'Annabelle, do we have to sit here,' said Natasha, in spite of the compliment.

'But, Tasha darling, this is really most interesting, and shows us how we misjudge people. Tiffany here is telling me about how friendship works. All the time I was being bitched up by Nazi Sicilian psychos in that piss-smelling hellhole, Tiff – you don't mind me calling you Tiff, do you? – and her friend Sharon were feeling really warm feelings towards me, and thought it might be nice to talk to me, but didn't. And now I'm supposed to be delighted that they like my accent.'

'Well, excuse me, Miss Thing,' said Tiffany. 'But the way you talk is real neat. Are you a writer or something?'

'Not right now,' said Annabelle.

'Because you talk like you're a writer; I used to think it was just your accent or that you talked slow because you were on downers, but you sort of plan what you're going to say, don't you?'

'Oh, pancake special with double pork links,' Annabelle said to the waitress, who had come over to take their orders. 'And scrambled half-dry, heavy on the syrup, no biscuits, coffee. Sanka and a cheese Danish for my friend. And?'

'Oh, that's real nice,' said Tiffany. 'I'll have another Coke.'

'And a Coke for the lilac wonder,' said Annabelle, who had decided that, in a lot of ways, Tiffany was a pleasant child with a heart of something like gold. Just don't trust her, is all.

'That Inge,' said Tiffany, looking over her shoulder first, 'she thinks she's so tough. In LA I knew girls who used to be with the Angels, big girls with tattoos and all. I mean to do all this after you've been with the Angels, it takes some kind of nerve. A couple of chapters actually issued decrees about it, said it was bad for morale. Rosalie-Ellen – and you always have to call her that, in full, because she doesn't like to be confused with this tough black called Rosalie-June – '

'I'm sure we'll try and remember,' said Natasha.

'If you're ever on the Coast,' said Tiffany, 'you really had better. Rosalie-June used to carve people when she was doing angel dust, and Rosalie-Ellen thinks that drugs prove you aren't clean-living enough, and that knives are sort of soft, and mean you've let yourself get out of shape and out of tune with the wishes of the Goddess. She reckons the Goddess take special interest, you see.'

'How nice,' said Annabelle.

'Anyway, my loves, what I was going to say is that Miss Inge out there with all the airs and that silly little straight-edge she keeps in her boot, Rosalie-Ellen wouldn't even have to look at her. Rosalie-Ellen doesn't lever the tops of bottles with her teeth, she sort of squeezes them in the joint of her thumb until they shoot off because they wouldn't dare do otherwise. She brought me some flowers when I was in the hospital and said she'd got all the other girls to subscribe and that she'd see to business for me if I wanted.'

'Oh, so you've been in hospital?' said Annabelle, unable to keep a tinge of envy out of her voice.

'Oh wow, not for that, not yet, my loves,' said Tiffany. 'I mean this is California where I was living, right? There's no socialised medicine like I gather you English girls get eventually. It must do terrible things to your spirit of independence, I always think. No, haven't you noticed how I walk?' She got up and limped a few steps as sexily as she could manage. 'I mean, that's why I sit so much. The pin in my spine.'

'What happened?' asked Natasha. 'Car-crash?'

'Uuuh, no, though you could sort of say I hit a car. No, it was that one I was telling you about, Rosalie-June. Now, I don't do drugs, not anymore anyway, because of my medication, and I wasn't using then, because Rosalie-Ellen had told me very firmly that I couldn't afford not to be clean-living. No offence if you do drugs; a lot of people I know on the Coast do drugs and it seems to suit them, but I promised Rosalie-Ellen that I wouldn't, except she said I could do the odd downer occasionally, because I get so excited, and that bores her. Let me tell you, when you make that girl a promise you don't break it, even if you're a thousand miles away, because she has ways, doesn't she? And she can be a real bad enemy. She says she does it for the Goddess.'

'So she's pious about it all?' said Annabelle.

'Oh, surely,' said Tiffany. 'Rosalie-June, she got it into her head that I was doing something, because I stay so thin all the time – and ain't I skinny though, and the next time that'll be a Diet Coke, thanks not to mention, don't worry, lover. She thought I was on some kind of dynamite new speed or something, and when I got to my apartment she had bribed the super to let her in, and she was standing on the armchair in some sort of superhero costume –I'd say super-heroine but I always thought she was kind of butch, considering. She said that my hour had come, that the weed of crime bears bitter fruit, and who was my supplier, and she was going to clean up this town, and if there was some dynamite new speed around it was hers to have first. I said she didn't, just didn't, have the right to be in my place if I didn't go busting into hers. What did she think she had done with her eyebrows, I said, and that she was the sort who got us all a bad name. I didn't make any cracks about her being black at all, not hardly.'

'How restrained of you,' said Annabelle.

'She got very upset and this friend of hers came out of the closet with a sleeping-bag, and they said last chance, and I said that I didn't – 'scuse my language, I know it's not ladylike, but that's what I said at the time – fucking know anything about any fucking speed, and I wouldn't be doing it and I wouldn't tell her anyway. So they did it.'

'What did they do?' asked Natasha, because Tiffany had paused and was obviously waiting for a demonstration that everyone was jolly interested really.

'Well, my apartment was on the seventh floor, and they shoved me in the bag, and they dropped me out the window. I was lucky because I hit a couple of awnings on the way down, and it had rained the night before, and the soft-top was up on this sports car I landed on. Someone heard me scream as I went out the window, and so I got an ambulance at once, and they were pretty surprised, I can tell you, that I wasn't completely quad. I guess that's what happens if you live right and stay slim, neat and light on your feet, because if I'd been any heavier I'd be in a chair and doing poopoo in a bag, wouldn't I?

Those two just thought it was so funny that they were sat going hee-hee-hee in my apartment when the police came to check on the crime-scene, and now they are doing some hard time, because the weed of crime does bear bitter fruit, doesn't it? I was very good about it and I told Rosalie-Ellen that enough was enough and I really didn't have any business I wanted taking care of, and that the time was going to be quite hard enough for them without any help from me. They were sisters, after all, and the Goddess wouldn't want us to be mean. When I said that Rosalie-Ellen said she guessed I was right, and she was so moved by what I'd said that she wrote Rosalie-June in the pen and said she'd take care of the Dobermans for her.'

'She had Dobermans?' asked Natasha.

'A lot of us do, on the Coast. They're attractive as an accessory as well as making you feel secure, and you can let them out in the yard and they won't get eaten by coyotes. Poodles are nicer, but coyotes eat them. Dobermans eat coyotes. Rosalie-Ellen got them back from the City before they could gas them, and now she goes everywhere with them straining on these leads with spiked collars and slaver and all. She's got them trained a whole lot better than Rosalie-June ever could, and they're another reason why you don't make promises to Rosalie-Ellen and then break them. She calls them the Hounds of Heaven; I think that's a joke. She has this honour thing going, you know; she helps you even once and then she owns your ass ever after. She tells you do something, and you do it. She says the only way we girls are ever going to amount to anything is like that, because we need discipline or we just fall apart, she says. Lots don't like Rosalie-Ellen because they think she's just a big bully who gets her kicks out of shoving pretty little ones around, but I think she's real neat, honest. She doesn't think I should be punk because she doesn't think that's the right image for me. She doesn't feel real strongly about it, though, or I'd have had to do something. She made remarks a few times, and I didn't feel like taking the hint, so I thought I'd be away for a while till she gets hip. You know how we girls are, always so sure we know what's right for each other.'

Annabelle had another coffee and Natasha another Sanka. During Tiffany's story Alexandra had come in from the rain; she ordered herself a lemon tea and a saucer of milk for

Randolph, whom she had taken to carrying around snug in the extra inside pocket she had had put into a mink she had got from somewhere. She and Annabelle hadn't seen much of each other lately; someone had told Annabelle the details of the rather complicated set of events through which Alexandra had got the mink, but Annabelle had forgotten all of them, save that they were the sort of events about which it might be best not to make tactless enquiries. So all she did, when Tiffany paused for breath and sipped her coke, was say 'Hi' and smile..

'Hi yourself, hon' said Alexandra. 'You've been a stranger.'

'Oh,' said Annabelle, 'I've been sort of busy.'

'So I hear,' said Alexandra. 'I've been busy too.'

'Yes,' said Annabelle. 'I do like the coat.'

'So you heard about all that?'

'Well, sort of.'

It was raining hard outside and no-one was going anywhere. The truckers were talking about whatever it is that truckers talk about, and were not showing very much interest in what was being said around Annabelle's table, except for one who was evidently listening because one of his buddies whispered something harsh and punched him in the arm to get his attention.

'When Mexica was out on the Coast,' Tiffany started up again, since no-one had been saying anything of interest to her, 'to do that second album cover...'

'The one with the guitarist dressed up as a dinosaur, and the piles of burning tyres?' asked Alexandra.

'Yeah, and her being Fay Wray, which is pretty silly if you ask me, when what you've got is some scrawny Chicana bitch with legs they had to unbow because of all the food they don't give them when they're little. When Mexica was out there Rosalie-Ellen came calling. She went real respectable: businesswoman's suit, chauffeur car and only one of the dogs. She went to ask her a favour because she thought it would be real nice if Mexica came round her house to meet some of the young ones who hang out there, to give them some idea of what they should be working towards. Mexica reckoned that that wasn't at all the thing to do because she had better things to do with her time than prove to social inadequates how inimitable she is. Well, that was sort of what she said. Rosalie-Ellen took this tyre-iron out of her clutch-bag and said that if Mexica was going to be like that she could reduce her skull a whole lot more. Mexica narrowed her eyes – she does that real well since she had the slants put in – and she laughed this real spooky little laugh and said that she didn't recognize that as any sort of reason to do anything she didn't want to. Rosalie-Ellen said the way she said it was so like Callas doing "Carmen sera toujours libre" that she was really greatly moved and came away quietly, even though Mexica did this whole evil "Look at me, and then look at you; on the floor, doggie" sort of number and was really unnecessarily unpleasant. Normally Rosalie-Ellen doesn't let people get away with doing that sort of thing, but the next day there were these two pimps she had to have words with, and she broke their arms and legs, so she cheered up after that, and said she reckoned Mexica was in the hands of the Goddess. It was all kind of a shame really, because Mexica and Rosalie-Ellen are both sort of magnificent in their way, and you'd have thought they'd get on. Anyway, here we are sitting around and the day is waiting. Any of you kids like to smoke?'

It was agreed that, actually, they did all like to smoke, and so Tiffany asked them back to the hotel room she shared with her friend Sharon. They took a cab: lucky to catch one in the rain. The room was in the Chesterfield, and it was quite like the one Annabelle had had except that there were a lot more empty boxes from the takeout pizza place on the floor, and a lot more empty cans of Diet Coke than Annabelle had ever let accumulate even at her most depressed, but then hers hadn't been Diet Coke.

Tiffany really did have some dynamite grass. She introduced everyone to Sharon, who was tall and blonde and wearing a black baby doll. She was even thinner than Tiffany, except for her boobs. These were water-filled, apparently, which is why they had not gone hard now her chest was tight from dieting. Tiffany made a point of explaining all this in the course of the introduction because, she said, she thought it was important that sisters know all about, and acknowledge, each other's good points. This was one of Rosalie-Ellen's main principles.

It turned out that, even after they had got through the end-less subject of Mexica, there were all sorts of people Sharon and

Tiffany had known on the Coast who had been to New York and were known to either Alexandra or to Natasha. There was this pair of identical twins who both became sisters even though they weren't in touch at the time, which had, everyone agreed, to prove something or other.

Annabelle wondered what that must be like, growing up with someone and thinking you knew them better than anyone else in the world, but going through the torments of the damned alone and not letting it show. Realizing that they no longer knew you as well as you thought you knew them because you never let them see; only later discovering that they had been exactly the same as you all along, even in this. So sad, and so wonderful, when you found out in the end.

Annabelle didn't know any of the people they were talking about. None of them had ever been to England except for Natasha, and she had never wanted to meet Annabelle's friends like Cee and Glo because she reckoned they were real low-rent. No-one was going to be going anywhere because of the rain, and it would have been rude to take Proust out of her shoulder-bag, so she sat stroking the back of Randolph's head where he lay snoozing on the mink, and concentrated on the Nina Simone tracks that Tiffany had playing on her tape recorder. She had never learned to cope with patches of dead time, and grass sometimes made her lethargic enough that dead time just got deader.

52.

Next morning, since they had both had such a terrific time the previous day, Natasha thought they should demonstrate reciprocal hospitality, and so she made some phone-calls and told Annabelle to fix a late lunch.

'Do it real well, sweets,' she said, 'and I won't say a word afterwards about how we ought to fast for a week to make up for it. Under my direction you've really come on a long way, and I suppose I shouldn't expect miracles. You can afford the odd few ounces more as long as you do something to your skin to make up for them.'

Getting a nice big chunk of beef was easy enough, and Annabelle found some fairly solid-looking potatoes. MFK Fisher says that you might as well use frozen peas if you don't pick your own five minutes before they cook, and so she did. Americans seemed not to eat parsnips much; they took a bit of looking for. Horseradish was going to be absolutely impossible except all mashed up with beetroot in Jewish delis, but Annabelle followed a hunch and looked in a little black store that said it sold health food, where they recommended it as a charm for warts and as a hex for roaches.

As she was coming out of the store she saw Inge on the other side of the road.

'Still working at the brujeria, are we, English?' said Inge.

'Heavens no,' said Annabelle. 'I'm getting the fixings for Sunday lunch.'

'What are you going to do with that, then?' asked Inge, looking with horrified fascination at the nub of yellow root that was sticking out of a brown paper packet.

'Oh, I thought I'd grate it and whisk it up with a bit of sour cream. Why don't you come round? There'll be plenty and I'm sure Natasha won't mind.'

'I'll pass.'

That was the trouble with Americans; they had these strange reactions to English food. Annabelle had known they might find Yorkshire pudding a bit of a shock – "Say, Annabelle, what do we do with the popover?" – but she was honestly surprised by how many of the party assembled found foreign the idea of parsnips and potatoes roasted under the joint. However, they ate everything and they all said it was very nice, and so she felt she could let Natasha do the dishes. Annabelle went and lay in the bedroom, partly because she was tired and partly because she was just a shade replete. She dozed until she woke to the tingling sensation of hands caressing her spine.

'You look done in,' said Mark. His moustache crinkled as he smiled and showed all those perfect teeth.

'I haven't meant to be unfriendly,' said Annabelle, 'but I've been busy, and you know how things are.'

He stroked her behind the ear and leant across the bed to kiss her on the lips. She thought about this and whether it was, as seemed likely, what she really wanted. She didn't move away from him. Then Hennie strode into the room, pulled him around by the lapel of his jacket, and slapped him in the face.

'What the hell do you think you're doing, Mark?' she shouted. 'If we're going to be an item I'm not going to have you fooling around.'

'Oh, for Chrissake, I was only giving Annabelle a backrub.'

'Look, buster,' said Hennie, 'you said it was me you were interested in, not this gang. You said they were your friends, but that at the end of the day authenticity counted for something. I mean, Annabelle, you're really nice, and I'm sure you haven't led him on, and thanks for a super lunch, and is that really how you eat it over there? But you do see what I mean, don't you?'

'Not really,' said Annabelle.

Hennie chose to ignore this, and turned her attention back to Mark. 'I mean,' she said, 'how could you be sitting in there giving me attention, and then suddenly go off with her into the bedroom? Particularly when she's someone who's, well, false, just pretending.'

She sobbed, a trifle theatrically, Annabelle thought, for an advocate of the wholly genuine, and then dashed from the room. Mark kissed Annabelle full on the lips, but only briefly.

'Gotta go after her,' he said. 'I'll be back.'

He patted Annabelle's bottom and got up, tidied himself like a cat, and sauntered off after Hennie.

He came back a few hours later. Annabelle had ended up doing the dishes anyway, because Natasha and Sharon and Tiffany and Alexandra had all got caught up on the question of whether the Francesca they had gutted in Detroit was the one who used to shoot out the chandeliers with a BB gun, and whether they gutted her for anything she'd actually done, or just as a warning. Tiffany stated to go green at the clinical details and came over and tried to help at the sink, but the regularity with which she dropped dishes seemed to indicate either that her heart wasn't in it or that she had been stretching her promises to Rosalie-Ellen again.

Annabelle was not in a good, or a receptive, mood when Mark kissed the back of her neck. She took her rubber gloves off, thought about hitting him across the face with them while they were still wet, didn't, and looked him straight in the eye.

'God,' she said, 'you think you're just so cool and chic. You sit around being perfect and batting eyelashes until I'm moist in my jeans, then you go off with the lovely Hennie, and then you reckon you can waltz back in a couple of hours later, for coffee and feels.'

'You've got to understand,' he said, 'you've got to understand, Annabelle, that it's difficult. I like you and her both. You're so different, the two of you – and I don't mean that way either, really, or not mostly. Though in a way it makes it easier to go with her, you know. Like you said, you had that bad time; and there are things I'm not used to. Look, I brought you some Benedictine, and a copy of *Heavy Weather* – you know how you liked that when we played it. And I really don't mind about you and Natasha, what you get up to... Oh, come on, can you really put your hand on your heart and say all that's just business, really? But okay, I won't push that...'

Whatever could he be implying? Gosh, some people have an infinite capacity for misunderstanding completely innocent matters. But she went soggy somewhere in her stomach, and she let him stay the night when he asked. As he said, it was all quite difficult, but the bones in his shoulders were pleasingly hard.

And he really did not mind about, well, that, but didn't pay too much attention to it either, when she moved his hand away.

53.

Carlos kept sending Natasha curt little notes. The payments on his suits were coming due, and he thought she really ought to honour her commitments and go on paying for them, and for the lithographs he had bought as an investment. Whenever she heard from him she sat around in black not doing her eye-makeup properly and making little sobbing noses in her throat. Sometimes, as often as she could without actually waiting on the stairs to intercept the post, Annabelle would find the bill, or the cheque, and tear it up and tell Natasha not to be so stupid.

'Gosh, you're so weak,' Annabelle said on a day one slipped past her. 'He's ripped you off and you just sit there looking like Garbo in one of her more obscure movies – and I wish to God it was a silent one – and you think you're being good as well as gorgeous by helping him do it.'

'You don't understand,' said Natasha. 'Where you're sitting you're just able to play at emotion.'

'How much more are you going to take from that shit before you wise up and tell him to fuck off? All you seem to enjoy these days is telling Tiffany about colourful creatures from your past or beating hell out of some client. What's happened to your ambition? When you came into my life you had so much drive. I know it brings in the money, you being rough with men, but there's not much point if all it means in the end is that you spend the money on the guy who made you mad enough that you can bear to beat them in the first place, or is that the second place?'

'Annabelle, you're sounding just like Carola. She keeps lecturing me too. You're both so ungrateful; your charts say so. This cooker's dirty again. I don't know why I put a roof over your head.'

'I'm sorry, Natasha, but it's because we both care, and if you weren't being so damn self-indulgent you'd know it was your turn to clean the cooker this week.'

'But I'm sad,' said Natasha, 'and you can't expect me to do it when I'm being sad. Ouch, that hurt. I'd never have asked you over here if I'd know you were one of those girls that tickle.'

Fairly clearly, Annabelle had started to realize, she was one of those girls that tickle, and pinch.

She was not quite sure how she felt about that...

Next morning Natasha got up early and went out so quietly and secretively that Annabelle woke hours later to find her gone. She rang later, however, and Annabelle met her for lunch at a diner downtown. Natasha was looking smug, though this was only partly a matter of the expression on her face.

'What do you think?' she said. 'How does it look?'

'How does what look?' said Annabelle.

'My cheekbones; I had more put...'

'Well, I'm sure it looks very nice,' said Annabelle. 'But he's done so subtle a job that an amateur like me could never tell.'

'Yes,' said Natasha. 'Not wanting to bring you down, but an amateur is all you'll ever be.'

*

54.

Hennie was quite different when she was running her antique store; sharp suits with serious shoulders, and patterned stockings to die for.

'I'm not at all sure that I want to talk to you, Annabelle,' she said. 'Mark and I were alright, off and on, before you turned up. I suspect he and Carola used to occasionally, but that's almost okay by comparison – I know that's not your fault, and something time will remedy – and they are in business together. He and I used to have our spats; he'd probably understand if I worked for him all the time, but somehow he resents it more that I just help out occasionally or work when I need extra funding for some piece. I worry about him and what he does, and – you don't. You don't care about the things that matter about him, not really. Can you put your hand on your heart and say you're not just using him to boost your confidence about things? That's awfully selfish, you know. He's got a good name to lose and people can be very cruel about that sort of thing in this town. And I love him.'

Annabelle had gone round to Hennie's store to try and sort out what she should do about it all. If you really liked the higher bric-à-brac it was all quite tasteful, and Hennie had done the main showroom in some rather nice hand-painted grey-on-grey wallpaper. Calling round to see her was one of those decisions which you continue to question even after you've walked through the door and are committed; it all feels a little too much as if you're looking for extra complications.

'Well, I know that, Hennie,' she said, 'and I am feeling bad about it all. Which is why I called round. Since you're prepared to raise that aspect of the situation in so tactful a way, you may as well try and see it from my side. It's not as if I chased him, after all. It all sort of crept up on me. But, yes, it does help the way I feel about myself, you're right. And there's no way I could possibly get through to you how good it feels not to feel bad all the time about who you are.'

'Shouldn't that be "whom", since we are being so correct and everything?'

'Well, no, actually, Hennie, it shouldn't,' Annabelle said. 'There really wasn't much point in my coming round, was there? All you're going to do is tell me to stop seeing him, and I don't know that I'm prepared to do that.'

She had a tear in her eye by this stage. It wasn't a piece of deliberate theatre, though it happened to be rather convenient.

'Oh, shit, Annabelle, you think you can just come round here and be polite and look wistful and I'm going to say it's alright and you can have him out on loan?'

'I guess that's what I'm asking,' said Annabelle, 'though I suppose I needed to know who you are too. You can't make decisions if the people you're making them for are not quite real. Rivals almost never are real, because you're not let to know them.'

'I really should get angry and throw things, you know,' said Hennie.

'Surely not from your high-quality and expensive stock?'

'Well, no,' said Hennie. She smiled, and Annabelle knew she'd won. 'Okay, yes, I do sort of know how it is; he is kind of cute when he smiles, and most bitches wouldn't try and face me about it, even your sort of bitch.'

'We could have a drink,' said Annabelle, looking at her watch.

'Okay, kid,' said Hennie. 'Let's be nice. You know I'll get him in the end, though.'

'Darling Hennie, it's nice you are so civilised, but don't be smug, all the same.'

55.

Annabelle decided that it would be the act of a friend to go and see Alexandra perform. Alexandra was quite right to be annoyed with her: she had been neglectful lately, and her extreme busyness had only been a partial excuse. She didn't think she had tired of her friend, but it was nice living with Natasha, to whom you didn't have to explain on every occasion who, say, Ingmar Bergman was – not that either Annabelle or Natasha ever mentioned him save in more or less ritual tones of commination.

Alexandra had areas of enthusiasm rather than anything you could call culture, and her areas of enthusiasm tended to be marginal. If you wanted a solid and well-argued case for the importance of Isadora Duncan's dance or the Crowley Tarot you might well get that from her; the difficulty would be in shutting her up once you had got her started. Outside those areas of autodidacticism, however, she was blank; charming, but blank. Carlos had been unutterably bad for Natasha's self-esteem and bank-balance but he, and the sort of predecessor who had made her vulnerable to him, had compelled her to acquire a late education which, even if she tackily saw it as some sort of social gloss, Alexandra still lacked. It is a serious flaw in me, Annabelle reflected in the taxi out to the night-club, that there are limits to how far sterling character and kindness will take people with me.

She sat around at a table waiting for the cabaret. A rather boring PR man from Minneapolis sat next to her, bought her several drinks, and explained how Minneapolis was a company town in most respects, and how you couldn't afford to jeopardise a respectable position there by tomcatting around. So he came to Chicago once a month, and wasn't it a shame how the whole place was getting so sober and how there were all those fags everywhere? Annabelle pointed out that even if she was a working girl – and he seemed to know her from someplace – she was not working tonight, thank you very much, and money and gin might buy much, but not her silent complicity in antiquated sexual prejudices. So he fucked off.

Backstage, which is where she decided to go rather than risk being imposed on by another bore, she found Alexandra wandering round in a fetchingly nude tizzy because Randolph had gone under the floorboards, and though he had re-emerged looking frustrated, she wasn't entirely happy working in a club where they had rats, was she? Annabelle convinced her that she didn't know that; maybe the manager, who lived on the premises, bred gerbils, or maybe Randolph just thought he smelled something – or did snakes go by hearing? She remembered they'd discussed this before.

Alexandra's performance wasn't radically different from the ones she had done at the Ace, except that she started with more clothes and ended with none, except for an elasticated thong you wouldn't have believed could hide everything. She seemed to be feeling more on top of things than she had back then, and somehow all her movements were just that little bit crisper and more organised. She really didn't need a snake anymore, though presumably he gave her confidence; she had a capacity for mime that would have given the impression of his being there even if he hadn't been.

Afterwards a man called Jerry, who was very tall and thin and had a dark scarlet Dralon leisure-suit on, and who seemed to be taking care of Alexandra in the matter of minks, took her, and Annabelle too, out to dinner at a restaurant that did enchiladas and close harmony vocals. He seemed nice enough; the food was hot, the jazz cool.

'Isn't she a good one, though?' he said to Annabelle when Alexandra was off washing her hands. 'What do you think, Annabelle?'

'I've always known she was a terribly good dancer, ever since I met her.'

'And what are you doing in Chicago?' Jerry asked. 'What talent are you going to surprise us with?'

'Nothing much,' said Annabelle.

56.

When she got back, she found Natasha about to go to bed, and Carola and Hennie camped out on the cushions sipping hot chocolate dressed in the sort of faded tee-shirts so many people relegate to sleeping wear.

'Could you make sure we get up at five in the morning?' Natasha said. 'Only there's this guy who's hiring us for a yacht party, and that's when we have to leave to make the rendez-vous.'

'Can't you just get the operator to ring you?'

'Well, I already did that, but you know how useless we all are at getting up, so I figured if you made yourself responsible for it there'd be more chance of us actually getting it together in time.'

'Pretty please,' said Hennie.

'And what's this yacht party anyway?' asked Annabelle.

'Oh,' said Natasha, 'it's this guy I've done business with a few times in the past who wants three girls for him and the guys he's going fishing with. They're all pretty conventional, which is why I can't use you.'

'For once,' said Carola, 'she's not just putting you down: she's right. I only agreed to go because she couldn't get anyone else, because the guy knows my background too, and got awfully sniffy last time. I hit my head on a bulkhead and had a migraine for days. Anyway, you're sensitive; you wouldn't want to cope with the smell of that lake, I can tell you.'

Hennie said nothing further but sat up on her knees, looking sphinx-like.

It was all the most awful imposition, so Annabelle made it much more of one by sitting up and brooding for the relevant few hours. After a bit she got bored with watching people sleep, innocent as the slumber-party made them all look, and went and stared at the city from the window. Somehow the darkness negated her habitual vertigo. There was a lot of glittering going on, even at this hour, and over in the slums there seemed to be another fire. You couldn't usually hear sirens on this floor. She went and made herself another cup of mint tea.

A few hours later she packed them off, grumbling and bundled up in the best possible compromise between sensible warm sweaters and what their client presumably expected by way of business entertainment. She went to bed and slept until Mark came round – how nice of Hennie to tell him she was going away, or maybe it was Carola. They did a couple of lines and went out for afternoon tea and a stroll around the rather nice Art Deco buildings in the financial district, which, he said, needed cleaning, but seemed okay really. Then they went to bed.

Two days later the trio returned, looking bedraggled. Carola had managed to ring quickly during one of their restroom stops, and, though Mark had just been leaving anyway, Annabelle was grateful for her tact. They had the amount of money promised and there had been no unpleasantness, but they had all caught stinking colds. Annabelle believed firmly in the inadvisability of ever getting on a boat for fun, and had laid in a quantity of whisky and honey and lemon juice just in case, and they all blessed her and sat around, still snuffly, but happier.

*

57.

Over the second round of toddies Carola asked a question that had occurred to Annabelle from time to time.

'Hennie,' she said, 'how did a nice, clean creature like you get into doing all this? I mean, we three have the excuse that it's often difficult for people in our position to do much else. You were always busy with your antiques gig; I was too, but not at quite such a grand level. There are advantages to doing the odd bit of work from time to time, or even a lot if you can keep it together. But where, my dear, where in all your time at Vassar and Smith and those places, did you ever get the chance to find that out?'

Hennie took a long sip and a deep breath. 'When I'm asked that question,' she said, 'I usually just tell people it's really not any of their business; or that whoring is a useful way of not having to take out a bank loan every time I think I've spotted a piece worth having. It's a good story though, with a moral. There are times when it becomes clear that Someone is trying to tell you something, and it always seems to me that when that happens you'd better start listening good, or She might send a more forceful messenger than those you've already had.'

All of them were used to the telling of stories; they slumped back comfortably to listen.

'It was when I was first with a gallery in New York, and I had an opening to go to. There was the most cunning little black woollen number that I was dying to buy. I wanted to look my best because I was thinking of trying for another job, and the guys who ran the new place were going to be there. I was only kind of a gofer where I was, and that didn't leave me room to pay out two hundred on a dress, not the same month I'd had this real bargain on Chinese red lacquer, anyway. I had just accepted I wasn't going to get the dress, and people were going to have to take me in my brown wool suit or not at all, when there I was, dropping off an Early American bullet-pouch one of our clients wanted to have on a stand in his office, and explaining to him – again – that we couldn't authenticate the part of the provenance that interested him, which was the claim that it was made from the skin of a Huron who fought with the British. Just the idea that it might be seemed enough for him, though, and he said how nice I was looking, and how refreshing it was that there were all these career-girls around who didn't feel they had to dress like starlets, and who wore sensible shoes. He said he'd ride down with me in the elevator. He seemed kind of shy and stood with his face averted, looking down at the floor and not at my face or my tits. Halfway down, the elevator stopped moving. He said it had been acting up but he'd thought it had been fixed or would have used the other one. Then he started to get anxious. He was wearing a three-piece suit and he fumbled in his vest pocket a bit, looked relieved, then dropped onto his hands and knees. I asked if everything was alright and stepped back out of his way; at which he said "Oh dear" and explained that he was in the first stages of an attack of angina, and that he'd dropped his medication, which he had loose in his vest pocket because you can't go around with bottles in your pockets because it spoils the lines and might make business rivals think you were getting weak, and that they could put one over you, like wolves. All this and he's still on the floor, right? He asks me to raise my left foot, and I do, and he says that, sure enough, I've trodden on the pill and it's crushed into the sole of my shoe. Well, you can imagine how embarrassed I felt, because it wasn't going to do my career even as a gofer any good to have clients expiring on the floors of elevators because I'd trodden on their medication. While I was standing there in consternation and on one leg, he sort of lunged forward and clutched at my foot and, while I struggled to keep my balance, he licked at my sole and my instep. The lift started again, and, by the time we got to the bottom he was back on his feet and looked like a new man. I wasn't really sure what had actually happened even after he'd stuck a hundred dollars in my hand and I'd noticed a small moist spot on his hitherto immaculate trousers.'

'So that was it,' said Carola.

'Hang on,' said Hennie. 'I told you that the dress cost two hundred dollars, didn't I? Later that afternoon I was going out to dinner in the suburbs. I wasn't planning to change because it was going to be sort of informal, and I had no intention of putting out, so I had the same outfit on. I was wandering around Grand Central, because I'd missed my first train and there was twenty minutes before the next, when a man came hurrying out from one of those little archways, carrying a clipboard and a small piece of machinery. He said "excuse me ma'am" and could I come over there a second? He flashed some sort of badge – you know how it is when people flash badges at you. He asked me to restrain my alarm, but he was one of a group of inspectors who had been called in, and they were trying to do their job without causing a panic, because probably a panic was what was wanted. Anyway, these terrorists – I think it was the Croatians he said – had phoned in and said they had scattered a bag of plutonium waste hither and yon throughout the station at the start of rush-hour. By the time the inspectors got there it would have been tracked all over everywhere – if it was there at all, which they didn't think. He had a Geiger counter, and could he check the soles of my shoes, because if I'd picked any up then I and half New York was going to be in mortal danger. Well, he sounded very convincing, didn't he? And I'd seen a movie just like that. I lifted my shoe onto the little stool he provided, and he brought up the machine, and suddenly he lowered his head, and you know the rest. I took his hundred dollars and the hundred dollars from the first guy and I got the dress and I got the job, because these guys said they liked people who took the trouble to look good at openings. I paid attention to Her hint. It really couldn't have been more obvious, could it? The nice thing about having my own place is that it means I can wear sneakers and jeans whenever I want to.'

58.

One night in Whitey's Annabelle and Natasha picked up a guy from Cincinnati who said he wanted them to do a show for him. Whitey said he came recommended by Peter in Minneapolis; in fact, he came so highly recommended that they could take his cheque, and they knew how rarely Whitey was prepared to suggest that about anyone.

He was over in Chicago on business and was living in one of those entirely anonymous company-let apartments – all stripped pine on the walls, and onyx ashtrays on glass coffee-tables. This was the sort of very tall, very fat man who probably doesn't ever look at his surroundings very much because he is too busy being conscious of the bulk of his body, and being rather pleased with it as a demonstration that he can afford to let it be comfortable, and dress it so that it doesn't sag too much, and from time to time let it get horny and, even when not laid, at least aroused and entertained. He looked kind of strong in spite of the weight; they were both rather glad that he had no plans that they involve him in the proceedings.

He told them to sit down on one of the sofas and they did so, feeling slightly uncomfortable; it was the sort of pseudo-velvety upholstery that your nets rub up the wrong way. He laid out eight lines on a mirror lying on one of the desks; he couldn't easily have reached down to the coffee-table. He did one and a bit lines himself, rather hurriedly and snufflily, and was really insistent that they do all of the rest, straight away. They looked at each other, a bit reluctant because both had been trying the last few days to restrict their intakes. Natasha felt that any moral debts to Carola had long since vanished up her nose, and Annabelle wanted neither to take advantage of Mark, nor to be dependent on him.

'Hey, look,' the man said – his name was Gunderson – 'I'm paying and so what goes, goes, because I say so and that's how it is. Oughtta be enough. I mean, lotta girls on the street're glad to stick candy up their noses or anything anywhere else I ask 'em to. Don't see why Whitey said you two were so special.'

So they snorted the lines he'd laid out.

'And I want to see some real action,' he added, and they got the impression that he was into being the referee or something. 'I'll sit here, and you play to that mirror over there and ignore the lights. Even if they get in your eyes.'

They started off with the usual routine of wrestling for dominance while calling each other 'Bitch' and 'Slut', but somehow it just wasn't quite right. The coke was very obsessive-making stuff, and it wasn't really a night for wrestling and slapping and Chinese burns so much as for stroking and tickling and showing a lot of interest in the nicer and more glossy parts of each other's skins. Natasha used the whip a bit, but she never got past the flirtatious stroking stage onto the causing of at least a sunburn tingle; her heart was just not in it.

Annabelle was slightly more in control of herself and said,

making some effort to get on with the script, 'Come on, mis-
tress, hurt me, hurt me.'

Natasha had great difficulty turning the fit of giggles which
followed this declaration into a snarl of animal defiance.

'Okay, hey. Cut,' said Gunderson. 'Cut this, alright; take
time out. I wanted something serious, not some penny-ante
soft silk dyke show. Which, if what Whitey told me is true, is a
pretty sick idea with you two anyway. I'm not paying for you
two to fun each other around; I want some sweat and some
pain and some tears and maybe a bit of blood. Come on now.'

'Gosh, I'm sorry,' said Annabelle, because Natasha was lying on her back on the sofa blowing little giggly bubbles. 'But if
you would insist on our getting completely deranged you have
to take responsibility for what comes out. It's all theatre, you
know, but if you will get us ripped what you're going to get is
going to be closer to a piece of the truth. I don't know what
Whitey has been telling you about us, and indeed I wouldn't
like to think, but Natasha and I don't bleed for anyone. You're
not paying enough, frankly, for us to take the time off work to
heal up, and there is a limit to what I think is worth doing,
except in the spontaneous heat of the moment, even for so
charming and generous a gentleman as yourself.'

It's always a good idea to remind them that you have manners, because it might suggest to them that they should have
some as well.

'You really are English, aren't you? I thought it was an act
like that silly little Sicilian bitch with her Martin Bormann
schtick. Aye wood nort laike to thenk...' – why do Americans
think they can even begin to imitate English accents? 'You
know, I'm really disappointed in you two. You owe me money,
way I look at it, because you've not delivered, and I've wasted
the evening, and you've used my drugs. I don't know what
people are into in this city, but it certainly isn't anything we'd
pay money for in Cincinnati. But just to show I'm a big soft
teddybear at heart I'll let you go now, and I'll be real generous
and give you fifty each, which you are not worth.'

Annabelle watched carefully as he went over to another
desk, pulled out his wallet, and wrote out a cheque. He didn't
seem the sort of person with whom it is appropriate to argue
the toss, so they put their clothes back on, tucked the whip back

into Natasha's bag, and were sufficiently crestfallen that they did not repair their lip-lines and gloss until they were in the lift.

Natasha had stopped giggling. 'Annabelle,' she said, 'I think we got off lightly. That guy's a psycho; I think sometimes he gets girls up there and doesn't let them go until they really hurt each other. I think it was probably a good job that you can come on like a glacier even when you're ripped. I think that Whitey knows what he's like. I don't trust Whitey, not any more. Maybe it's his way of saying we don't show him enough respect when we give him his third.'

'Um, you know best, I suppose,' Annabelle answered. 'But mightn't that just be the drugs talking there, darling, and not anything to do with reality?'

'I don't know. He gave me a feeling of doom is all, though I suppose that was what he was going for, psyching us out.'

59.

Two mornings later Natasha's bank manager rang to tell her in his usual tone of vague regret that the cheque from Gunderson had bounced. Of course bank managers don't usually ring you to tell you things like that but, as Natasha had pointed out to Annabelle before, she and her bank manager had a special relationship, and Annabelle suspected that by now Natasha had got him conditioned so that he got off just on the sound of her voice.

They finished their morning coffee and got themselves together and went back round to Gunderson's apartment-building. They knew there was unlikely to be much point, but it was the principle of the thing. He'd told the doorman not to let them in, or indeed anyone else much, it seemed. The doorman stuck by that, even after the offer of a quickie from Natasha, who was looking devastating in her fox jacket and leather trousers, her face ivory in the cold against the collar and the dark and purple hair – she had decided that purple suited her better than orange, even if it had been Carlos' idea.

Annabelle was feeling quite pudgy and lank-haired by the side of her. She reckoned, though, that dark glasses and the hair clipped to one side and a scarf piled up around the ears, and paring her nails with something that looked long and sharp, and leaning against the wall with one knee up was probably about the right style. The doorman had seen all this sort of thing before, however, and was not about to be even slightly impressed.

'I told him,' he said wearily. 'I told him thirty times in the couple weeks he's been here. Treat your bitches right, I said, or take 'em someone else's place. The other good people that pay me to keep 'em safe and clean, they don't appreciate even elegant bitches cruising the lobby. Dropping curses like litter. Trying to get me to let 'em get to Mr. Gunderson. And they really don't like crazies like the broad with the eye-patch. He never listens, and that's how it is. Real, real sorry, ladies, but that's how it is. Now you got thirty seconds to get out of my lobby and then I call the police.'

They went across the street to a little patisserie Annabelle had spotted; Natasha didn't make any remarks even when she ordered a cream cake with her coffee. When Gunderson came out of the building Natasha charged out after him, but he showed a surprising turn of speed in getting to a taxi, and it was pulling out by the time Natasha had dodged traffic to reach his side of the street.

Annabelle hadn't even bothered moving.

That evening they went and complained. Whitey poured them both a drink. It was evident that Natasha's suspicions as to his complicity had been groundless from the fact that he refused to let them pay.

'Well, I'm real sorry, of course,' Whitey said. 'You can't please everyone, and you two are kind of weird together, you know that. Johns ain't complaining, but they do mention it.'

He folded his hand on his stomach and looked like a rather annoyed priest.

'What Gunderson did was way out of line. You don't have to pay me the thirty-three bucks. He did come highly recommended, and I shall speak most severely to Peter from Minneapolis. I'm not having anyone say I don't look after the girls. Gunderson has been spreading bad paper with girls all over town. I talked to Jimmy, but he did pay us, and we're neither of us put out enough to cross Peter over it. Maybe you girls should club together for a contract.'

He obviously found this idea hugely amusing.

They checked up. Gunderson had managed somehow to get around everyone they knew in an astonishingly short period of time. No-one liked to admit being taken, but once Annabelle and Natasha had, others were quite prepared to share the misery.

'I don't have to take that stinking shit from anyone,' said Inge. 'Sure, I'm Sicilian – everyone knows that – but the whole Nazi image the sort of johns I work with go for, and the Brotherhood protected me inside, in spite of everything. He laughed at me and he snapped the elastic on my eye-patch right back into my face.'

Tiffany had turned up with a box of home-made cookies and had obviously cleaned out the bowl with the batter in. 'Honest, lover, no-one thinks any the worse... So what if you are Sicilian? You wanted to be a Nazi bitch sadist and with a lot of hard work and peroxide you were one. It's the American way.'

No-one talked to Inge like that, even at a council of war, and Annabelle and Alexandra independently but simultaneously kicked Tiffany on her good leg. She squealed, and Inge smiled like a jaguar.

Hennie had been out for funds she needed for church brocade, and was particularly indignant. 'He got me to undress, and then said he thought I was one of you but that they'd done a really good job. He laughed when I said I wasn't, and said that's what you all say. Not that I mind, in a sense, but I'm not, am I?'

Everyone agreed that she wasn't and tried to look sympathetic.

'I know some guys,' said Inge. 'I've checked, and we're not allowed to do anything very much, but we could probably push it as far as a knee, and with him being that size that'd be real cruel.'

Annabelle had what she thought was a better idea.

'Natasha has this terribly good visual memory. He paid for his drinks in Whitey's with Visa, and she can tell you his American Express and Mastercharge numbers as well. We looked at his wallet and we've got a lot of copies of his signature; there must be some way of putting all of that together.

Why break a leg when we can bust his credit?'

'That's typical,' said Inge, looking pityingly through the monocle she had taken to wearing instead of the eye-patch now that ice had taken the swelling down. 'Shopkeeper mentality. I thought you were supposed to be this real hotshot bruja, what with the roots and all.'

'Ah,' said Annabelle, 'but he's a toad already.'

Inge lost the ensuing vote, though she insisted on Randolph's not being counted. Alexandra said that that wasn't fair, because Gunderson had threatened to sit on him if she didn't do things she wouldn't dream of doing with a snake she respected. They gave way to Inge on that one, and she was very gracious, and insisted on paying for coffee.

It all went like a dream. Jimmy and Whitey cooperated, and only took their regular third. It was all very illegal but Annabelle felt rather smug, like the naughtiest prefect in school. The money was really very handy for everyone, though they were tactful enough to have their celebratory drink in Whitey's. When Peter from Minneapolis rang up about it Whitey just said that Gunderson should be more careful in future, and Peter from Minneapolis let it alone. No-one loves a welsher.

60.

Annabelle was starting to lose her temper; the lace had torn off a garter and she had never been very good at sewing, even on the rare occasions when, as now, she had not exhausted herself and her patience getting the needle threaded in the first place. She knew stitches were supposed to be small and delicate, and she tried, she really did, but somehow they ended up being rather large and crooked. She just wasn't able to concentrate with Natasha sitting on the other side of the room looking sickeningly self-indulgent and tragic with an evening skyline behind her.

'You know, sweets – and I do know he's a rat and all that, but I still have an aching to see Carlos again.'

'Oh God,' said Annabelle. 'Why?'

'Because he made me so happy for a while in there. It was

almost worth the money to feel warm inside like that.'

'Natasha, darling, how could it ever be that way again?' Annabelle said, being restrainedly nice in the face of idiocy. 'Even if you lifted the phone and grovelled at him, it was he who left you; he betrayed you; what you want has nothing to do with the case.'

'I could do something about it, surely.'

'No, not really. Look at how it is now with you and Carola: you're never going to be able entirely to forgive her, and the betrayal there wasn't even that important. It's not as if you were ever going to bed with her, not as far as I know anyway. You and Carlos – it's over, love. It really is. Or is that not what you want to hear?'

'What I want to hear,' said Natasha, 'is that it's months ago and I'm just waking from a bad dream and none of it ever happened and I never let him think he could get away with pulling that sort of thing without getting the coffee-table laid upside his head and I never let him touch a cent of my money. But you're right, of course you're right.'

'About Carlos I seem always to be more or less right,' said Annabelle. 'What brought all this on? Did you see him?'

Natasha looked even more tragic. 'Yeah,' she said, 'the other day, in the Art Institute. He was standing looking at some Monet water-lilies with this tiny little oriental thing tucked up against his shoulder, and she was giggling. He was doing his riff about why Monet wasn't any good really, because even then you could do all that with photography, more or less, and why bother to do it with paint when it wasn't how the eye saw it, and how that was the trouble with the nineteenth century, and how Europe always did things the hard way. Well, I didn't actually hear him say all of that. But I caught the odd line, and I had that talk from him myself one time so I guess that was what he was saying, because I don't see him thinking up any new lines just for her.'

'Did he see you watching him?'

'I pulled my collar up and then I sort of slunk over and peeked at them through the glass on one of those big wood doors they have just around the corner from that painting, so I guess not. I can't really be sure because my eye started hurting.'

'Oh, really?'

'I got some stuff in it or something, and I had to go to the restroom to get it out and then wipe up and do my eyes again. When I came back, they had gone. I didn't feel like hiking through more than the odd couple of rooms to look for them: when we used to go there he'd take me through to the Goncharova to tell me what was wrong with that, and they weren't there, so I guessed they'd gone.'

'What are you going to do about it?'

'Nothing, I guess. Like you say, it isn't up to me, and there'd be no point.'

'We going out tonight?'

'I'd rather not.'

'What are we going to do, then?'

'Ring out for pizza and beer, or teriyaki, or spring roll, and stuff our faces and watch the late movie?'

'Sounds fine to me. Do be careful though, love. We don't want him hurting you any more, okay?'

61.

One lunchtime when Natasha was out working at one of her occasional straight jobs the phone rang and Annabelle answered.

'Hi there,' she whispered throatily, and in as Mid-Atlantic a voice as she could manage.

'Where's Miss Natasha?' some man asked in a very thick accent that sounded sort of Balkans.

'She isn't here,' Annabelle answered, and then, in a more conciliatory tone, 'Can I help?'

'Who are you?' the man went on. 'Do you do bidness? Are you' – it sounded like – 'kwin?'

'Well...' Annabelle was not sure quite what to say. She had assumed Natasha didn't usually mention her past, because either they knew or they didn't, and she would never have thought Natasha would call it that, as nor, usually, would she. '...yes.' She put extra dignity into her voice. 'If you want to call it that.'

A queen, how undignified to have to call herself that for a john, but, well, always money, not pride.

'I find myself in Chicago with a free lunchtime,' he went on. 'Could I call?'

'By all means,' Annabelle replied, reaching for her makeup case.

When he arrived the john was a trim man with a goatee and sideburns and wire spectacles. Hard to say which side of fifty he was.

'Zo,' he asked again as if it were some sort of big deal, 'you're kwin.' Only this time there was more of an 'i' in it, as if he were not saying queen at all, but...

She looked at him apologetically and clutched her kimono tightly about herself. 'I'm awfully sorry,' she said. 'Yes, I am clean.' He looked far less apprehensive. 'But that's not what I thought I heard you say.' She let her kimono fall open, showing first her breasts, at which his eyes looked sparkly, and then her black lace knickers, out of which she stepped.

If she had to fight him off, well, he was quite short – this might turn nasty after all.

He goggled slightly.

'I thought you said queen,' she explained with a shrug. 'I am sorry to have wasted your time.'

He was very courteous about it. 'Zese things happen,' he shrugged.

Then he stared hard at her breasts and her face, and then looked over the rest of her again, and then looked at his watch.

'I really wanted to haff sex this lunchtime.' He shrugged again. 'I'm sure it vill be okay'.

It was.

The john rolled over onto his elbow and looked at her.

'Hey, girl,' he said. 'I think you're wery nice, you know that?'

'Well, thank you,' she said. 'My name is Annabelle and I told you that already. And yes, I do know that I'm rather neat, in my own way. It's sweet of you to tell me so, though. Actually.'

'Ekshually. Oh, sorry I'm sure: no offence meant. I just really love the way you say that.'

'Why, thank you. Anything else, before you go?'

'Vell,' he said, 'I vas wondering...'

'Yes?'

'Could ve do it another way? I'll probably never do it again, not with a girl like you, and it seems like a waste not to. Would you mind if I asked you to go on top second time?'

She didn't normally do that; wouldn't usually do it even for money. In the circumstances, though, it seemed churlish to refuse.

'Well, that's a perverse thing to ask a girl in my position, really... You are a naughty little boy, aren't you? The sort of naughty boy who gets his bottom smacked if he's very careful.'

'Please.'

'Well, I hope you're as flush as you are naughty, because if I'm going to do that for you it's going to cost you a little more. What doesn't come naturally doesn't come cheap.'

'Okay.'

Why was she doing all this, Annabelle asked herself. Though the money would be kind of useful; there was that rather nice fox down at the thrift store she had her eye on, and most of Gunderson's money had already gone into a black-and-silver dress to wear to concerts. The streetlights outside the window made shadows across the smooth skin of the guy's back; odd when his chest was so hairy.

Afterwards he volunteered to take her over to the coffee-shop for a sandwich, and this was sufficiently unusual in its thoughtfulness that Annabelle accepted. They were both nibbling on fresh croissants when Hennie walked in.

'Hi Annabelle,' she said, and then, tightening her lips a little, 'And how are you, Max?'

He blenched slightly.

'Annabelle,' she said, 'some girls might resent having their toes trodden on, you know.'

'Well, gosh, Hennie; but he doesn't come stamped or branded, you know? Max, why don't you buy Hennie a coffee and a croissant too?'

Hennie shrugged, and then smiled and sat down.

'Now, Max,' Annabelle said, 'I think we've both seen quite enough of you for one afternoon. So just gulp your coffee and pay the tab. One or other of us will see you soon.'

He scurried off, and they spent a pleasant hour tearing him apart.

Hennie was full of questions.

'You didn't...?'

Annabelle looked smug.

'I wouldn't have thought he'd – '

'Apparently, he would. He was very keen to have sex instead of lunch. Twice, and the second time we – '

'I didn't know you ever did that.'

'I don't,' Annabelle shrugged – it seemed appropriate to pick up the MittelEuropa thing – 'But I like Max.'

Hennie's eyes grew slightly beady.

'And Mark? Do you like Mark like that?'

Annabelle was shocked at the idea, and aware of how silly it was that she was shocked. 'No, of course not.'

Hennie relaxed, some dreams intact.

'Not much to be gained from confrontation, is there?' Annabelle went on.

'Now who's being smug?' said Hennie.

62.

Sometimes Natasha just wanted to drive, late at night, round and round the city; or out to O'Hare and back, to watch jets take off to somewhere else. She couldn't drive as fast as she would have liked, but it was simply being on the road, and having to watch the road, and not having to just sit at home and brood. Annabelle sometimes got carsick, but on the whole she thought it best that she come along. Natasha wasn't going to do anything silly, she was sure of that, but someone had to be there to make sure she went home when she was tired, and didn't fall asleep at the wheel. Driving, just driving, was part of America. And Natasha didn't expect her to look at her best.

Sometimes they'd stop for a Coke or a Big Mac, and then Natasha would start up all over again. Probably she never stopped thinking about it, inside. 'I get so jealous about him, sweets. Sometimes I just want to sleep with him one last time, so I can do something dreadful to him.'

'He really isn't worth fretting yourself over,' said Annabelle, 'let alone getting into trouble over. Which is what you'd be doing.'

She poured ketchup over her fries and sucked it off one,

meditating on the sheer trashy sensuous pleasure of junk food.

'Christ, Annabelle,' Natasha said, pointing a plastic fork at her. 'Stop being so darn sensible for a second, won't you? This isn't some kind of game like the one you're playing with Mark and Hennie, you cold bitch. Okay, so I'm being self-indulgent, but sometimes I don't think you feel at all. You're cold, heartless and immoral.'

'Natasha, I feel. I've made a decision to bear what I have to. There are areas in which I face facts and you seem not to be able to. You should find what you really need and go after that, not after him.'

'What I need is to hate him and to be close to him and to think of something really rotten to do, like what Mexica did.'

'Is there no end to... Okay, what did Mexica do to her man who done her wrong? Rooty-toot-toot, I suppose.'

'No, sweets, much better. There was this guy, a pimp, and this was when she was young and scrawny and hadn't had anything done. He reckoned she was on his bitch's turf, so he slapped her around and dumped her in a can with the garbage. Said it was appropriate because she was garbage too. Years later, when she was beautiful and all, so that he didn't recognize her, she went back. He'd done quite well, had a real stable by then. She threw herself at him, and when that girl throws herself at guys they don't let her bounce off the wall, do they? When he was asleep afterwards she rolled him onto his front, and reached into her bag, and she took out this tube of Superglue and...'

'Natasha, I don't want to hear any more of this story.'

'And she said he was an asshole, so it was appropriate.'

63.

Solti had been very good in concert that evening. His Mahler 9 was a bit flashy for Annabelle's refined and austere taste, all crashes and languor and not nearly enough structure, but it was a lot better than nothing, and she'd probably never have gone in London. Afterwards, she and Mark went promenading in the crisp air, she in her new multiple fox with all the tails hanging and the black-and-silver dress that was just so snug, and Mark in his tuxedo looking sharp. And she knew the score, really she did; she wasn't living on dreams, just on what she could get. She knew perfectly well that the reason she had got in on the free tickets he'd been given by a client who played the double-bass was that Hennie only listened to electronic, free-form, aleatory and pre-classical, and wouldn't have been seen dead...

'Well my, what a handsome couple,' a well-known voice said smoothly close behind them.

'Oh, Mark,' Annabelle said, barely turning to acknowledge its source, 'I can't remember if you are acquainted with...'

'Carlos? We've had our business dealings, but I guess I don't – '

'This,' said Carlos, 'is my Mariella, and this is my good friend and patron, Mr. Salvatore.'

Annabelle turned to study Mariella, who was small and finely-chiselled, almost to the point of disappearing altogether. Mr. Salvatore was, down to the tie-clasp and the last leaf on his boutonniere, exactly what she had expected. Soigné; the only word, and it caught both the precision and the affectation. He was trying so very hard to be Rossano Brazzo and he was more or less succeeding. If Carlos grew up to have more heft and money, she guessed this would be the sort of look he'd end up going for.

'This is Annabelle,' Carlos said to the others. 'She's the English girl I told you about, the one who's looking after poor Natasha.'

'I'd put that the other way round, I think. And do have the taste, Carlos, to find another adjective to describe my room-mate. One referring less to financial dealings.'

'Oh,' he said, ignoring this second comment, 'I'm sure she would say she was looking after you too, and I guess she has managed some kind of improvement. Wouldn't you say so, Mark?'

Mark looked him in the eye. 'I can't say,' he said, 'that I have ever known Annabelle to have less than her present style and poise and class.'

She felt like kissing him for the lie. Very delicately, and just at the hinge of his jaw, she did so.

'I think that perhaps the three of us should be going,' Mr.

Salvatore said in a tone of velvet and ice. 'I would ask you both to dine with us, but I fear we had some difficulty in getting ourselves reservations as it was. And Marcel is most exigent when you have ordered langouste.'

'That's quite alright, thank you,' Annabelle said graciously, flashing her new bridge-work. 'Mark has an allergy anyway, and I ordered us a murgh masala two days ago because he'd never tried it, and I owe him. For the concert.'

'You English girls like it hot then,' said Mariella, attempting to buy into the vague atmosphere of tension people seemed to be trying to generate.

'Just so,' said Annabelle, and turned, foxtail trophies swinging, on her stiletto heel.

64.

Annabelle sat on Alexandra's unmade bed while Alexandra got ready to do a show, shaving parts of herself that were never allowed to get hair on them. Randolph slithered over into Annabelle's lap and she stroked his perfect head, enjoying the feel of his scales against her fingertips. It was strange how quickly she had got used to experiences which would once have had her screaming with terror.

'Honestly,' Annabelle said, 'I really just don't know what to do. I like him a lot and all that, and the sex is just about alright. I couldn't say that I'm in love, though, and I know that to a very real extent the whole business is just him playing around because it happens to seem to him to be vaguely smart right now. Also I think a lot of the time it's just him playing mind games with Hennie.'

'So what's that to you,' said Alexandra. She had moved on to doing her makeup, and drew a sudden sharp line under her left eye.

'I know you think I make too much of such things, but I really do have qualms of conscience about being used by him to give her a hard time. I'd call it unsisterly, but people wouldn't understand my meaning, or they'd doubt my bona fides. I'll just say I have a vague feeling I'm being shitty, particularly since I do quite enjoy the sensation that I'm doing well in what is at least notionally a sort of competition.'

Alexandra put her liner-brush down and paid a little more attention.

'You don't suffer from the delusion of being in love, right?' she said. 'And you are at least sort of getting laid once in a while by someone you quite like? And he isn't, so far as I can see, other than easy on the eye. Well, okay, kid, what's to worry? Lucky kiddy is all I can say. Look, here's your old mother getting all painted up so I can twitch my snake and my person at a whole bunch of boring Shriners with watch-chains. I'm more or less alone right now, and I have to work my butt off, and not get laid save in the course of... If you weren't so Miss Prim about making money from what you stick up your nose with what seems to be a fair measure of enjoyment, I'm sure you could get him to – '

'He doesn't like me that much.'

'What have you asked him for lately?'

'Well, nothing, but I couldn't. Apart from anything else – '

'So he sits pretty and you fluster around having moralistic snits. You're real good at handing out advice, judging from the highlights you give me of what you say to Natasha. So take some. You don't know when you're well off, kid. I mean, you paid a very few dues in a very short period of time, and they weren't nice, but they weren't too heavy either, and really it all came together for you pretty well. We all know you have that ticket tucked down your boobs somewhere, so if it ever did start to come down heavy on you again, chances are you would flutter off before that flawless skin got itself marked.'

'Well, thanks a lot.'

'Oh, Annabelle, it's not that you've got spoiled or anything, but you do seem to be more or less lucky these days. There are people out here, my dear, who have been waiting in line for years for that kind of luck. Just don't you and this Hennie go leaving that boy on the sidewalk while you swan off to be refined and cultured together, okay? There are people who would eat him up in a second if you get careless.'

'Oh, God,' said Annabelle, and put her arms round Alexandra. Randolph slithered to a less emotional part of the bed. 'I don't want you to feel like that. You were good to me. I couldn't have survived without you, and I think it was important that I did stay and didn't run away. I'm sorry I've been neglectful, but you know how it is.'

'Sure,' said Alexandra, and hugged her back. 'You've been busy; you have commitments to him and to Miss Wonderful. Don't worry. I'm just a bitch. You make your mother so proud is all, you and your new eyebrows, and sometimes she could scratch you for it.'

65.

Natasha was out of town for two days. Her bank manager had introduced her to a senior executive from the branch in Detroit who liked to do it on a swing on the front porch on days when it was misty enough that the neighbours probably couldn't see.

'I'll detour down to Peoria on the way back, because there's this guy in Peoria who likes to be given enemas. Don't wait up.'

It was slow down at Whitey's, but if you were patient, and pretended to be really interested in whatever they had to say, and waited through enough repetitions of the floorshow and a lot of diet sodas, you could always walk out with a john.

Annabelle got back to the apartment with a john at about two a.m. Lying across the foot of the door was Tiffany, in shorts and a skimpy top, and looking so much like a broken blossom that Annabelle's concern as she rushed forward was mingled with annoyance at both herself and Tiffany for being obliged to think in such clichés, and then guilt for being so callously judgemental. Tiffany was breathing, but only shallowly; Annabelle kept an eye on the movement of her chest as she fumbled for her key.

The john was being tediously laid back.

'Who's this piece of trash, anyway? Friend of yours?'

'Sort of, I suppose. I really don't know what she can be doing here in this state.'

'I guess I'll just have to excuse her manners, then,' he said.

'Here, help me lift her.'

'She's real skinny,' he said. 'It would be like making love on eggshells.'

'Over there on the chaise longue, with her head up. Wait around if you like, but I'm going to have to call the parameds.

Hello, is that Emergency; could I have...'

'Hey.'

Annabelle looked across at him while continuing to talk to the emergency operator; he really wasn't very prepossessing, with that floppy brown Michael York cowlick, and in his eyes that terrible swinger's glaze.

'Could we make it while we wait for them to get here? I haven't much time and it would be kinda interesting to do it with someone dying in the room. In fact, why don't we, well, make it a threesome? I know I could trust you to give her her cut later if she makes it – she'll need it for the hospital bills; or tidy her clothing if she doesn't. No-one wants to be ripped off, right? Why don't I – '

'No,' said Annabelle. 'I won't say anything else. Just no. Please leave.'

'Hey, you've no call to get like that about it. She's only a junkie, right. I thought it would be kind of neat. Where do you get off on being moral anyway, you – '

'Hold it right there, honey.' She used a tone of voice she had found could stop armed juvenile delinquents in their tracks back when she was a supply teacher in Lambeth. 'The parameds will be here in just a moment, and they'll probably want names because there might be the police with them. A smart young professional like you shouldn't be here when they do – you shouldn't be hanging around with trash like us. But I suppose you're right about one thing: I am absolutely sure you would only have needed the time it takes them to get here, and they're here now. Your loss. They've come, and you're going.'

Tiffany was very pale under her Harvest Rust blusher but she was still breathing when they took her downstairs on the stretcher. All Annabelle could tell them was that no, she didn't know why she was there, or how she had got in, and they were welcome to check her own arms for tracks if they wanted, but really that was not what she was into herself, and she only knew the kid slightly. She lived at the Chesterfield, she thought; perhaps she came over ill in the street and just pushed the doorbells outside until someone let her in; she really didn't know. Annabelle's air of innocence seemed to convince in spite of the fact that the left shoulder-strap of her black dress kept slipping and she had rouged her nipples that evening, dammit.

They went away. She poured herself a quick and large gin and tonic and rang Tiffany's flatmate Sharon. The man at the Chesterfield said she had gone back to California two days ago. She got a number for the forwarding address, and it turned out to be Rosalie-Ellen's. Rosalie-Ellen said gruffly that if that child Tiffany had been OD'ing then she was beyond help, and Rosalie-Ellen was just not interested. If it was anything else, well surely call again, and love the accent, honey.

When Annabelle rang the hospital next morning they asked if she was a relative; she said that she wasn't, just the person who had called in the emergency. They weren't supposed to tell her anything very much, but the rather gentle, camp voice at the other end prevaricated until a superior was out of the room, then said that it had turned out not to be drugs at all, at least not directly; had there been a head injury in the past, did she know, at the time when the spine was cracked? Annabelle rang Rosalie-Ellen and got her to talk to the doctor about it.

Rosalie-Ellen rang back later and said that Tiffany had been taken away by her parents, and no, there wasn't any forwarding address, but she would sort it out, and not to worry. She sounded nice; Annabelle reflected that it must be fine to be strong enough that you could really take on board caring and doing something about things at the same time.

66.

Carola had gone blonde again, and she was spending the odd evening down at Whitey's these days. It really didn't suit her, but the johns didn't seem to notice.

'Sorry,' she said, 'pork chops is really all I can offer you. Oh, and a V if you take them. Mark says we've got to take it easy for a month or two so I'm keeping the place really clean. We may close down altogether for a while. But he'll have told you all that, of course.'

'Well, no, actually, Carola,' Annabelle said. 'We don't have that kind of conversation. I was brought up to believe that it was vulgar to talk about trade.'

'Oh, pardon me, Miss Thing.'

'Besides, if I don't know things I shouldn't, I can't be indiscreet. I suppose they could still make me a material witness or whatever they call it, but if all you two ever talk to me about is jazz and films they're not going to get very much joy out of using me. His views on which sidemen Miles Davis went wrong with, or yours on which is the proper point in *Enfants du Paradis* for a girl to start crying might be indicative to some sort of super-subtle shrink, but they're hardly anything you could call prima facie, are they? Yes, of course I know where the money comes from, but like I say, in the circles in which I move habitually it's considered vulgar to discuss such matters.'

'That's sweet. Hey, terrible about that Tiffany thing. How bad was she?'

'Pretty bad. She had a seizure with a john in our building, and he threw her out onto the stairwell. You know her parents took her.'

'Oh Christ, poor bitch. She's been running for years; they're Mormons, and they don't like at all what became of her on the road – shaved her legs along the way and all that. If they've got hold of her again, well, that's it for Tiffany, for the person we know. That sort of Christian'll do anything to their kids to keep them on the straight and straitened. Holy Mother Church has her limits since you stopped getting zoning permission for walling people up, but they don't. Exorcism and lobotomy both if they have to; they'd feel they were doing their child a kindness. We wouldn't know her if we saw her again. Sure, the kid could be a pain, but they'll turn her into a robotic superstraight. If she dies, and maybe she'd be better off if she did, it won't even be her clothes they bury her in.'

'Rosalie-Ellen said she'd take care of it.'

'I don't see the Queen of the Dobermans making it past the Utah State Police, let alone the Avenging Angels. But you never know.'

'Anyway, what else could I have done?'

'Nothing, kid, that's the shame; nor could the hospital when they needed consent. Silly bitch should have known better than have real next of kin on her ID, given what they thought of her. In the end she must've had a death wish. We all have, I guess; that's why I deal and why you hustle. I mean, we don't have to, not really, do we? Some of the others, maybe, but not two smart cookies like us. We could be in grad school or something.'

'I was in grad school,' said Annabelle. 'And it didn't suit.'

'That was then and it wasn't really you, was it? Different now, surely?'

'That could be a problem too, you know. Names on degrees and all of that, and problems with references.'

'You worry too much, Annabelle; there are a lot of people who aren't cool, but there's always a way round things if you look for it.'

The phone rang. Carola answered. 'Hi. Carola here. God, you sound really weird, Natasha. Yes, she's here. I'll put her on.'

'Hi, Natasha, what's up?'

'Annabelle, sweets. I've been silly, and I just wanted to say thank you and goodbye.'

'Why, where are you going?'

'I'm going to kill myself, you insensitive bitch. "Where are you going", indeed. I don't know, but I don't want to stay.'

She was very drunk. Carlos had called round and said it was time they were civilised about things, and would she like to see his new apartment. He had decided that high-rises lacked the right sort of historic elegance, and elegance was it now, surely. They sat on the sofa she had given him; he thought it just about went with the new place, and they drank a lot of not very good Californian fizz. He suggested a quick one for old time's sake. He'd always thought bondage was good for her, he said. After all, she needed a submissive side, and anyway it made a change, given the lifestyle. She was drunk enough to go along with it, reckoning that if this was what he wanted now, then maybe Mariella wasn't giving it to him, and that would be a way back in, would it not?

Once he had her tied to the brass bedstead he started to be really insulting, telling her she didn't fool a soul and that everyone thought she was absurd. He laughed at her, and Mariella came out from where she had been hiding in the bathroom and laughed at her too. They made love on the bedroom floor, and though she shut her eyes she could still hear them. They spat on her, and they said horrid things, and they poured bad champagne over her, down her and up her.

'They left me there and went to dinner and said they'd do

more to me later. I don't know what they'd been taking. I only
just got myself untied; that boy never could tie very good knots
but they were quite tight, and he doesn't understand about not
letting the circulation get cut off at the joints. Or maybe he
does. My clothes are ruined, and I really don't see much point
in living if it's going to be like this all the time.'

'Natasha, don't be silly. What's the address, Natasha?'

'Oh, leave me be.'

'Natasha, if you'd wanted to be left to die alone, you
wouldn't have rung up in the first place, would you?'

'I just wanted you to know. Don't get smart with a doomed
girl, missy.'

'What's the address, Natasha? Or I shall get annoyed with
you.'

Carola had Carlos's new address for business purposes, and
she scrawled it on a piece of paper, which she waved in front of
Annabelle's eyes.

'I'm coming straight over. Just get your clothes on, clean
up, and don't do anything.'

The cab driver giggled incredulously when they told him to
step on it; he didn't bother with remarks about not being in the
movies, but he clearly thought them very loudly. Carola hadn't
wanted to take the car because, well, it had been used for
deliveries on occasion in the past, and if they were taking notice
back then, she couldn't afford to have it further associated with
trouble. Annabelle found herself shivering with the feeling that
serious things were going on, and the knowledge that there was
nothing she could do except wait for the cab to get there.
Which, eventually, it did, though stopping at half the red lights
in Chicago on the way. The cab-driver seemed about to say
something mordant as they paid and tipped him, but they
looked at him in a serious way that changed his mind.

Annabelle gave him another fifty, to wait.

They ran up the path to the entrance to the apartment-
block, which was set back from the street and had built-in
wings. When they got to the front door they had a problem
because the doorman had gone off duty, Carola couldn't
remember the number of the apartment, and Carlos hadn't
bothered to put his name up on a little card among the other
doorbells.

'Probably still agonizing over the most socially prestigious typeface,' said Carola. 'Caslon minor can be death in this town.'

She could remember the phone-number though, and ran across the street to dial from a call-box; Natasha didn't answer. On the way back Carola had to turn down two two-hundred-dollar tricks, as a Porsche and then a Mercedes screeched to competitive halts. Annabelle reflected that Carola's ego was now going to be unbearable for the rest of the night.

They were standing in the cold, freezing with frustrated worry and trying to think what to do next, when the door of the apartment building crashed open and Natasha fell through it with one arm out of her fur coat, and looking like a dictionary definition of dishevelled. The door slammed shut behind her.

'I fixed him good,' she yelled.

So much for any hope of making ourselves unobtrusive.

'What have you done, Natasha?' Annabelle asked patiently. 'We thought you were going to hurt yourself. We were worried.'

'Well, I was going to, when I talked to you. Then I thought, well, that's what he wants, isn't it? So I went and poured cold water on my head, which ruined my coiffure but got me a bit together, and most of the crap off me. And I took those stinking lithographs – they really are bad, aren't they? You were right about them, Annabelle, though you were a real lamb and never said anything. I don't know what I could have been thinking of, buying crap because some guy with almost no taste tells me to – and I smashed them against that dreadful sofa and tore its upholstery. He took away what he gave me, right? So it's only right, really.'

She was carrying two handbags.

'Whose is that one, Natasha?' asked Annabelle.

'His bitch's. It's only fair.'

'It's also theft, Natasha. You have to give it back to her and hope they'll let it ride. It's a shame you let the door swing shut, or we could have – '

'S'easy. If you insist. I left the window open and turned the heating off so they'd have a nice cold wreck to come home to. S'only the second floor. Look.' Natasha concentrated herself back into array, took two steps backwards, and a hop forwards and a loop of the arm. 'Shoot a basket like that any time, easy.'

Then she was sick into the nearest frost-covered flower-bed.

They took her by the arms and got her properly into her fur coat, then staggered with her half-dead weight back to the cab, which was still waiting, because this was a town in which fifty dollars buys most things.

She smelled a little, so they drove to the nearest Burger King and took out a lot of black coffee which they poured into her.

'Carola,' said Annabelle, 'I don't want to be alarmist, but could you think of some place to leave her that no-one will think of immediately, and possibly stay there with her? I think we can expect callers, and I don't want to have to cope with that and be holding her head over the toilet at the same time. I don't want to talk to policemen with her hiding under the sofa, or teetering down the service stairs. Okay? I would also suggest that the act of a friend would be not to let her have any valium.'

67.

Annabelle got another cab and went back to Natasha's apartment and tidied away any incriminating implements of a flagellatory kind. Three quarters of an hour later there was a very official-sounding banging on the door. Annabelle placed a peacock feather between the pages of *Albertine Disparue*, checked the wave at the front of her hair, and opened the door.

It was Bunckley, fatter than ever, and with a shark smirk on his face which seemed to indicate that he was here for fun.

'Why, good evening, Detective Bunckley. What can I do for you on this cold night? A glass of hot toddy perhaps? Or what?'

'Nothing you'd like, kid, but this time I'm not looking for lemons. Where's that other bitch?'

'Natasha, you mean? Why, she went out several hours ago, to visit with her ex-boyfriend at his new flat – sorry, that's apartment, of course, isn't it? She was going for dinner, but, to judge from the time, she may have stopped over. Is something wrong?'

'You just bet there is. See this? It's a warrant for her arrest. He's sworn out charges of malicious damage against her.'

'What has the girl been doing? Oh, and she really isn't here

by the way. You can check if you like. Now sit down like a good
policeman and tell me what she's supposed to have done.'

The balance of dominance had shifted over the months.
Nervously, Bunckley did what he was told. I should have done
the schoolteacher voice at him in New York, she thought, and
things would have been very different.

'Sofa, couplea pictures. She did a good job on them.
Matchwood.'

'Gosh, officer. I don't want to seem to be trying to teach you
your job or anything, but it wouldn't be these pictures and this
sofa, by any chance?'

Ananbelle had checked through Natasha's files and then
popped over to the all-night copy shop; except for the books the
girl had always kept her paperwork in good order. She had
never really needed Annabelle at all.

'According to these, you see, officer' – and she showed him
cheque-stubs and receipts and certificates of provenance for
the lithographs – God, how pretentious! – 'she paid for them.
Now, when it comes to their being in his apartment, well, he
may say they were a gift, but then again, suppose she just left
them there in storage for a bit, or say he borrowed them
without permission and then she went round there and on an
impulse just decided that she really didn't like them? You or I
might not smash them on the spot, and it was very emotional
and deeply antisocial of her. But it's hardly criminal damage to
smash what you own. In the case of these particular lithographs
you might even call it a public service. Now, why don't you get
on the phone to that boy Carlos and check whether he wants to
go on wasting your time? And isn't that an offence over here?
And do you have such a thing as wrongful arrest?'

Bunckley didn't look especially delighted, but Annabelle
knew from his failure to answer immediately, or to interrupt,
that he had been listening to her case. So she went for the
clincher; she had had, rather belatedly, the idea of ringing Mr.
Carpets, who hadn't even regarded it as clearing the favour he
owed her because it made him laugh. It had been a long shot
against a rainy day, and now it paid off, but that's how the
breaks go if you're a wise virgin.

'Oh, and I got round to the phone-calls. Your helmet will
arrive at the precinct house any day.'

Once you've got the shits smiling, you've got them.

68.

The Gunderson business had been invaluable to Annabelle in the way it had put people in her debt. Inge would probably have helped out anyway; she seemed to have no especial liking for men except to arm-wrestle with, and there was some kind of complicated dispute over dynastic precedence between her lot of cousins and Mr. Salvatore's. But with obligations established, and mutual respect shown, there was no question. It was always best there be no question with Inge, because otherwise she might suddenly find some of her odd principles and dig six-inch heels into them. Annabelle met her – Inge insisted on their sharing tortellini with a nameless stuffing and some sort of chili sauce – and asked her advice on how to proceed.

Inge sucked red fire off her fork. 'I'm sure I'll think of something. But it's for you, English, not for that other prissy bitch.'

She had a crime reporter on tap, though taps were rather less than the hold she had on him, and he looked punch-drunk all the time even though he was the soberest journalist in town. Inge turned up at the apartment with what he had written at her behest; Annabelle looked over the typescript and smiled.

The colloquies with Carlos' lawyers were oiled in their passage by a demonstration – Annabelle was a terrible ham when she read aloud, but it was time she indulged herself just a little – of how, were the whole sorry business to go any further, Carlos' glittering career in talc, cologne and tasteful gents' toiletries might be hindered by the imputation that what he and Mariella had done to Natasha had been not a mere harmless jape played on a tediously-persistent former inamorata, but the prelude to some Lovecraftian act of ritual murder. Inge's journalist was fearfully disappointed when Carlos backed down; he had put a lot of work into the story and now he'd never get the Pulitzer. Inge said she thought she could think of something to console him, something lingering and involving boiling oil.

Carlos' behaviour during the whole episode lacked its usual suavity. When Annabelle and Natasha, wearing matching dark suits and dark glasses, encountered him in the corridors, he ranted. They needed no legal advice to act with sweet restraint; they knew it would annoy him more.

'What can the deranged child be taking these days?' said Natasha, quite possibly out of his hearing.

She, Carola and Hennie got the chance to go fishing again. It was Annabelle who took the brunt of Carlos' phone calls in the middle of the night.

'Hello, Carlos, no, you didn't get me out of bed. I knew you were going to ring so I didn't go to bed. Takes the point out of it really, doesn't it?'

'Where's that other bitch?'

'Not here, dear. Not just not in to you, but actually not here. Will that be all?'

'You think you're so fucking smart.'

'This is true,' said Annabelle.

'I'll get you both for this,' said Carlos.

'Perhaps,' said Annabelle, and blew a whistle down the phone. Carlos didn't ring again, and he didn't turn up at any symphony concerts for a week or two either.

69.

Mark had stayed away during all of this. Annabelle could see how he might need to keep a low profile, and she could see the advantage of not involving him in her little chats with the police. Once all the excitement was over, however, she saw little harm in popping down for breakfast to the croissant shop where he often ate, and in taking a little extra care over her eye-liner just in case.

He wasn't there, even after the second brioche, but Hennie turned up. It was clear from the knowing smile that crossed her lips as she silkily pulled up a chair that she hadn't seen him either, and was relieved to find Annabelle sitting around being gluttonous and disconsolate as well.

'I gather,' she said, 'that you've been involved in all sorts of alarms and excursions.'

''Appen,' said Annabelle, then realised that a stonewalling return to her blunt Northern roots would be merely incomprehensible. 'I mean yes, that is the case. Would you like a pain au chocolat, Hennie? I gather they're just out of the oven.'

'Thanks,' said Hennie, and munched for a while. 'Well, he's not going to turn up, is he?'

'It looks that way,' said Annabelle. 'Shall we do a gallery together?'

'Let's go for a drive,' said Hennie, and fastened her large, flat hat more securely to her head with hat-pins. 'I promised Mother I'd look in for lunch one day this week. And you know which fork to use, more or less.'

It was a long drive, through progressively flatter countryside that Vivaldi concerti failed to make more interesting the way they do in the adverts, and it was more like high tea by the time they got there. Annabelle realised she had never fully appreciated just how utterly Hennie was slumming most of the time. It wasn't the creamed lobster sandwiches or the Spode they were served on, nor even the housekeeper or the way Hennie's mother's accent was so New England that a mere Oxford accent felt vulgar; it was the placing of the garden chairs so that the light fell on the meal just so, and the grace with which Hennie's mother asked her to bring her friend back again some time.

'Don't let her put you down,' said Hennie as they drove home. 'You managed really well. I let you meet her because I trust you. Just don't say anything about her to Mark. He'd take advantage, or he'd try to. We can't really trust him, either of us; we can't afford to. Though he is ornamental, isn't he?'

On the way home they took a detour so that Hennie could call in on a dealer she knew in Elgin, and it was quite late by the time they pulled up at Hennie's store.

'Come in for a drink,' Hennie said, and smiled as if she had several moves planned ahead.

'I think I'd better get a cab home; Natasha may have cooked dinner, and be worried,' said Annabelle.

'Just a drink,' said Hennie. 'I'm not going to eat you. Quite the reverse, possibly. We don't need him, after all, do we?'

'Perhaps not, but I'm sorry, Hennie. I do know, and I find it confusing. You know how things are with me.'

'I'm not asking you to compromise on any of that, am I, Annabelle dear? Take it as a compliment.'

'I can't,' said Annabelle. 'But thanks anyway. For everything.'

'You'll be sorry you didn't,' said Hennie, with that damned confident smile.

'Perhaps.'

'Not anything I'll do, I don't mean. You know that. But you'll regret it.' She kissed Annabelle on the lips, and went into the shop.

Annabelle walked down the block and hailed a cab. The shiver down her spine made her wonder whether Hennie might, in the end, be right.

70.

'Seen Mark lately?' asked Carola on the phone. She was using the particularly tedious throaty voice which usually meant that she believed whatever she was about to say was going to be highly significant.

'Well, no,' said Annabelle. 'But then, often I don't. One is a chic sideline to him, not a grand passion. It's a good job one is also a realist.' It was early in her morning, and she always felt rather third person until the second glass of orange juice. 'You should ring Hennie, though when I last saw her she hadn't seen him for a while either.'

'I did, and she still hasn't. She spoke oddly fondly of you. Seen Alexandra?'

'Not for, oh, a week, or even two. She's been boring me with how cushy things are for me now, and how tired she is of her terpsichorean ventures. No quiz-games, darling; cut, as I believe you say, the crap. Where have they gone together, and why? This is a very tedious way to tell me.'

Oddly, she wasn't at all upset. Two focuses of vaguely guilty feelings had been improbably and simultaneously removed.

'Well, I thought I should find out first whether you knew and were playing little games with me.'

'How could you think such a thing of an innocent like Annabelle?' said Natasha over the extension. She had picked up some of the accent, but the irony still needed work.

'Well, anyway,' said Carola, 'they've gone off. With my half of the money. His note said he was trying to double my investment. Nothing to be done about it except wait and see, I guess. I'm not vindictive, heaven knows.'

'Why with Alexandra?' said Natasha. 'I mean clearly his taste is a little off, but... Sorry, sweets, only teasing.'

'Because neither Annabelle nor Hennie works with a snake,' said Carola.

'Are you giving us information,' said Annabelle, looking hard at her roommate, 'or feeding me straight lines?'

'Someone offered Hennie some gemstones. She's careful about never touching anything even slightly warm, but she mentioned it to Mark the next morning over croissants. He was thinking of changing his line of work anyway. Alexandra got him an artiste's work-card as a partner in her dance-act. They've taken off for parts unknown, and that unfortunate reptile has rubies and emeralds bruising its gut.'

'Alexandra would never hurt Randolph,' said Annabelle.

'Annabelle, you have a sweet and forgiving nature, and we all love you for it, but really? Anyway, I'm sure the worst he would get would be constipation or the odd chipped tooth from a crunchy mouse. They've gone, alright, taking my life of crime with them.'

'So what now, Carola, back to antiques?'

'Maybe sometime. Hennie offered. Right now? Doctoral programme at Northwestern.'

'You fixed that up rather fast.'

'Real groovy criminology department they have there. Services rendered. And they reckon they can give me credit for the last five years as a participant observer.'

71.

In the Submarine Surprise and Delight Annabelle was eating her second chocolate nut sundae. Natasha was glowering, but was respecting what she assumed to be deep grief. Annabelle didn't undeceive her; all she had to do was to wear more black even than usual, and she didn't know when so opportune a moment for sheer gluttony would come again.

She was just grinding her spoon into the bottom of the glass for the last traces of chocolate sauce when Carola, who was sitting facing the door, gasped. Natasha turned and joined her in a chorus of aghast surprise. Annabelle took note, without surprise, that the theatricality was there even when the emotion was genuine. Annabelle swallowed her last mouthful and turned in her chair.

Clumping towards them on an aluminium walking-frame, a crocodile bag slung from its front, was a woman with the most beautiful face that she had ever seen. The face was beautiful even though it was also a geometrical model of how a beautiful face might most advantageously be laid out. She had extremely large but firm-looking breasts, a tiny waist and almost no hips. Her ankles were many inches around; from the knees down her legs were puffed into cones. Even so she had a presence that was in itself a command.

Carola and Natasha bustled about the diner – asking the owner for an especially comfortable chair, getting coffee brought over, showing sharpened nail-files to a trucker who seemed to think something was amusing – the courtiers of a monarch in exile. Annabelle just sat and waited for what she sort of knew came next. Her role in all this was minimal.

'Annabelle,' said Natasha, pushing her forward. 'This is Mexica.'

'I'm very pleased to meet you at last,' said Annabelle.

'Oh,' said Mexica. 'English sisters now?'

'You won't remember,' said Natasha, 'but we met, Mexica, oh, I guess five years ago. When I was very plain in New York.'

'Sure I remember, kid,' growled those perfectly bee-stung lips. 'You didn't change that Goddamn much, you know. You borrowed my favourite lip-gloss, and you remembered to give it back.'

'Oh,' said Natasha.

'S'when I knew I was a legend,' said Mexica. 'Normally some bitch takes every bit of your paint first chance she gets. Whatever. Someone said the sisters hung round here in the daytime. Thought I'd look in, because I'm making my calls right now.'

She used both hands to lift her coffee-cup; there was a slight tremor even so.

'I just wanted to keep the story straight this time,' she went on. 'There was all that crap when I had bits of bone carved from my forehead; you'd think they carved my head off or something, versions that go around. This time I wanted to keep things straight. And I've got nothing better to do with the next couple of months than visit.'

'What happened?' asked Natasha.

'The legs? Butt and hips drifted. The cheap quack cheated and gave me industrial in those shots; the tissues can't take the weight of that forever. I can't even break his hands for it; he died years ago. There was some guy who wanted to be an amputee, so the sawbones chopped his arms off, only the guy bled out, and he ran off to Panama. Or that's what I heard. Like I said, you know how it is keeping the story clear. Details, anyway. The legs are a bore, but they don't matter. Other things went wrong, nothing to do with that. The legs aren't killing me. Better than being some skinny wimp wetback trying to come on macho. I was the most beautiful in there for a while, wasn't I?'

'Yes,' Natasha and Carola said.

'Yes,' Annabelle added, because she knew she should, but missing the beat.

'You don't have to agree, kids, though it's nice. No-one'll ever be that again; too many now to judge clearly. Sorry 'bout that, Natasha dear, but that's how it is. Crock of shit anyway. Hey, but what isn't? It was worth it, even for a little while. I wasn't about to do anything else, was I? I got what I wanted, and, like they say, you've got to pay sooner or later, right? One way or another. Well, it was nice talking with you.'

She finished her coffee and they trailed behind her as she moved slowly to the door; a large black driver lifted her into the back seat of the Mercedes that was waiting outside.

'Thanks, kiddies. I'd love to stay and bitch, but you know how it is. I've got calls to make and I want to get to California; then he can have the car.'

The driver closed her door and she waved at them through the glass. He got into the front seat and started the motor. The windows darkened automatically as the car drove away.

Natasha wept; it was the end of something.

*

Back at the apartment that afternoon there was another man in a dark uniform. He was from special delivery with a letter for Annabelle. In it was a cheque to her for a thousand dollars from a bank in Utah. From Tiffany's parents. It was for saving the life of their wayward child; it would have been more but she didn't need more, being damned.

'Fucking blood money,' said Annabelle.

'So tear it up,' said Natasha.

'Things go in threes,' said Annabelle, 'and I'm not a foolish virgin anymore.'

72.

'I thought we'd go for tacos,' said Hennie, standing dominant in the doorframe in a Dietrich-in-tuxedo sort of way.

'What a neat idea,' said Natasha, emerging from the bathroom in Annabelle's best silk kimono.

'Yes, do come too, Natasha,' said Annabelle.

'I suppose a trio is more discreet,' said Hennie.

'And more choice of entrées,' said Annabelle.

'Quite so,' said Hennie, lingering just slightly over the friendly peck.

Hennie was being very bright over the enchiladas and sangria, but then so was Annabelle. There's nothing like trying to bring your partner in depression down even further for raising your own spirits. Though at least Hennie had something to be authentically cheerful about: the chest she had bought up in Elgin that night had proved to have under its lining-paper galleys of a suppressed pornographic *Oz* book. She was off to New York to split the proceeds with another dealer, which meant that all the paper on her store was paid off.

'It just proves that She, you see, is back on my side again,' she said. 'It just shows that you have to pay attention to Her little hints when they occur.'

Annabelle thought about Mark, and bit a hot pepper to explain the sudden tear in her eye and the choking in her throat. How could Hennie be content with such cheap consolations?

Halfway through the second jug of sangria a waiter came

and asked for Miss Jones and said that she was wanted on the phone. Annabelle took a mouthful of beans and shredded pork and sauntered over.

'English? That you, liebchen?'

'Oh, hi, Inge,' she swallowed in surprise.

'Sorry to disturb the delicate social manoeuvres.'

'How did you know I was here?'

'You were out so I checked the slummer's answering-machine. I called you because it's you I owe favours to, alright, not the elegant one. I thought you were terrible at first, but it worked out having you around; you're not so dumb, really. You sort of grew on us.'

'Why the elegiac tone, darling?'

'Well, I dropped in for parish tea. It keeps the uncles happy and it's the way things get passed on, mainly. That Carlos is still hopping mad, and he seems to have found a way of persuading Salvatore. You can never trust a stud not to, is what I say. Anyway, there was a price on – oh, let's be polite and say his kisses: she gets hurt; you too, maybe. Nice trick with the whistle, but you don't make friends that way.'

'He's taken out contracts?' said Annabelle, incredulous but shaking.

'Shit, liebchen, no. Course not. Salvatore couldn't organise anything serious without approval, and it's all too trivial for that. You know how they are about domestic stuff, and in the circumstances – well, it wasn't even Salvatore's sofa. But he has permission to hire some street punk to break her face as long as he doesn't come running if it turns heavy. Say if they got unprofessional and did more than just cut her. They said I could tell you. No-one wants trouble, not really; that's why they let me know at all. And you complicate things whenever something comes up. Everyone knows you have a ticket, right, and they tell me you had a windfall this afternoon. Be smart, English, and someday you can show me the instruments in the Tower of London.'

Annabelle went back to their table, gulped another glass of sangria and turned to Natasha. 'Sweetheart,' she said, 'I've been thinking. Maybe it would be nice to go to London. We could live at my place.'

'Some scummy project in where is it, the Lower East Side?

Why on earth would we want to do that?'

'That phone call was Inge. She suggested we leave town. She was being a messenger girl. Carlos and Salvatore aren't pleased with us, and no-one wants trouble.'

'In that case,' said Natasha, 'we'd better go.'

'When She drops little hints,' said Hennie.

'Perhaps,' said Annabelle,' but I don't think She uses the Mob to do it. Even in mysterious ways.'

'I'll drive you to the station this evening,' said Hennie.

Annabelle and Natasha both had their own ideas about what to pack in a hurry and what was essential. That vulgar crystal pendant – oh, it's designer, you surprise me – and *Temps Retrouvé* – no, I'll want that to read on the plane – and a photo of Mom, and of course you don't ditch the Meissony, don't be stupid, because I know this cleaner in London who could shift that, and the heels have gone on those, really, and carry the fur of course; we need the room and we mustn't go overweight. Carola is taking those out to your Mom's, and Hennie can sell those for you, and that can be shipped, and it takes much less space if you roll it, and you can't just leave that in the fridge for the next tenant, and no, don't you go eating it either. We'll eat breakfast on the train.

'Why aren't we just flying direct from O'Hare?' said Annabelle.

'They might watch O'Hare.'

'It's an awfully big airport, and they're supposed to be only cheap punks.'

'Even so,' said Natasha, 'I don't know why you assume we can trust Inge.'

After locking the door and handing in the keys to the super they got into Hennie's car and drove through the neon-lit dangerous streets to the station, and they boarded the train, and they went away from cold Chicago silently and without arguing about it. You have to leave places sometimes; accepting loss goes with the territory.

For a week or two people would ask after them, and why they'd gone. Johns would want to know. The story would get garbled; it always does. Sometimes it would have been Carlos and Mariella and Salvatore; sometimes Tiffany's parents, or

Rosalie-Ellen; sometimes Bunckley or Gunderson or something to do with Mark and Randolph; one way or another the messenger had come for them. The apartment was shut up and the fridge turned off.

As they got on the train Hennie kissed Annabelle one last time, and said they would see each other again: there are always little hints.

73.

The sea was below them, and Natasha had already started bitching.

'You rushed me off my feet,' she said. 'I'm sure I could have worked it out with them. I can't go back now. People would say I was afraid.'

'You were afraid,' said Annabelle, 'and you were quite right to be, really you were. I don't expect you'd have got the chance to try and use charm. Carlos really is cracked; you know that.'

'It's going to be awful.'

'You always quite liked London before. I kept my flat on, and we can just live quietly for a bit. I think I'd like to live quietly, and it would do you good too. I'm sure you can find a job in a store, or there'll be someone interesting.'

She was just prattling and it would do little good. She and Natasha had complicated each other's lives forever, and there would be no forgiving. Sooner or later Natasha would think of blaming her, which wouldn't be fair, not even after the whistle, but neither of them was capable of letting well enough alone. That's how it works.

They had had to leave, and Annabelle needed to anyway. In London at least you could cross the road without walking through an opera or a blood feud. Stories in London were gentler ones; the closest you got to threat was saying good morning to the wolves on the boundaries of the Zoo as you walked in the park on a summer day. They were behind walls. They weren't your friends and your lovers.

She and Natasha didn't quarrel at once, but there was just more cleaning to do in Hackney, and less feeling on Annabelle's part that she had duties as a host. Natasha was as ornamental as ever, but Annabelle was back writing reviews and didn't feel quite the need to turn out in her best every single day. The exotic Annabelle of Chicago gradually became something she kept in the wardrobe and only took out of its bin-liner for special occasions. There were words, and Natasha moved to Chelsea, and to Kew, and to Harrow. She seemed happy enough, but she never let Annabelle meet any of her new lovers, which suited Annabelle just fine.

They did meet sometimes. They rendezvoused one afternoon in Patisserie Valerie. Natasha was looking smug in green leather; she'd had something else done to her face and Annabelle was supposed to guess what it was. In deference to their former friendship Annabelle avoided the patisserie, though Natasha stared at her long and hard until the cakes had all gone by.

'Carola wrote,' Annabelle said.

'What's new,' said Natasha, unconcerned.

'Mariella got really fed up with Salvatore hanging around for another shot with Carlos, and she went for assertiveness training. One day in the store she took out his appendix with a paper-knife, and Salvatore retired to Florida for his health. She got probation and ran off to Aspen to ski and lead a healthy life. Carlos got to be deputy manager for a bit, but then there was this widow, and he went off to Mexico with her. Carola thinks he's painting.'

'So does he, probably,' said Natasha.

'Criminology isn't quite as much fun as she hoped, but there's this peachy professor. Mark turned up with the money. Randolph had to have an emergency enema, but it all sorted itself out and he's alright now. Carola isn't going to go back into business with him; she doesn't feel he's behaved entirely as a partner should, and he's working with Alexandra now. They took her out to California for Mexica's funeral. Tiffany was there; Rosalie-Ellen busted her out of theological college with a bunch of bikers and the Dobermans and re-deprogrammed her. There were a lot of flowers and a mariachi band. She died in the car, and the driver just left it in a lot near the Hollywood sign and rang the lawyer. Carola says people think he showed respect; they say she didn't feel anything much.'

Annabelle and Natasha held each other's wrists a second,

and Natasha started to trace Annabelle's scar. There were things between them more important than cleaning, but they were different people too, and they quickly remembered appointments in different parts of town. They were part of each other's pasts, in another city, another country, another tale.

74.

Some months later Magda and her lover Ariadne met Annabelle for coffee in the Photographer's Gallery. Normally they would have met in the classy feminist bookstore down the road, but there was a signing on by an author whom Ariadne had, many years before, called middle-class in a context and tone of voice roughly appropriate to a summons to the field of honour. Subsequent shifts of The Line had placed them on more or less the same side, but Ariadne felt bad about it, not least because, in an unsisterly way, she still felt that, at the time, at that stage of the evolution of her consciousness, she had actually been quite right. Besides, the café had shut down now. Also, there was always that vague social problem of people's views about Annabelle...

'It might be just about tolerable if you weren't so right-off in so many other respects,' said Magda.

Conversation turned, as it tended to that year, to pornography, and Annabelle as usual irritated Ariadne by her uncertainties.

'Of course, there is stuff that is just incitement to sexual violence, or which is produced in circumstances that are sexual violence or class oppression in themselves, and anything that people choose to do about that is okay by me. Always though, kid, bloody always, there's the problem of knowing how to define what's the aggressive policing of the status quo by exploitative thugs, and what's something else, something that explores and challenges and subverts.'

'Maybe women just can't afford to take that risk. Maybe what you're asking for is the privilege of middle-class bohemian artists to pretend that other women don't face violence and death.'

'Maybe you're ignoring that middle-class bohemian artists

take their chances like anyone else. Saying that things can't be afforded for the duration of the emergency is a bit of a slippery slope. It's saying among other things that you shouldn't be having tea with me, even in the Photographer's Gallery.'

'Well,' said Ariadne, 'apart from the typical way you blackmail us by personalising the issue...'

Magda got bored with all this and tugged them more or less by main force into the bookshop, hoping to calm them down by showing them some Weejees. But Ariadne was now in full flow. She pulled the new Helmut Newton collection off the shelves and flung it open with a melodramatic gesture learned years previously by watching Margaret Lockwood play barristers.

'Look,' she said, 'here's something that's supposed to be artistic and subversive and all the rest, and just look at it. Is that erotica or is it just pornography?'

'Well, actually,' said Annabelle, with a card-sharp's smug drawl, 'it's neither. To me, it's just a photograph of my old friend Alexandra. I wonder what she's up to.'

'Typical,' said Magda, 'Avoiding the issue by personalising it yet again.' But her moral sneer turned into a friendly giggle as she said it.

'Besides,' Ariadne asked, 'who is this Alexandra anyway?'

'She was my friend,' said Annabelle. 'She had a snake. She taught me stuff.'

'I see, one of the minor characters in all those rather sordid adventures you keep being so noisily reticent about.'

'Well, Ariadne,' said Annabelle, 'I suppose so. But I had thought that part of the point of feminism is that there are no minor characters.'

The End

NOTE

This is a novel I wrote in 1988 about my time in Chicago in 1978 and 1980. Most of it happened, more or less, though I don't guarantee the truth of all the stories people told me back then. I submitted it to various publishers, and at least two editors were keen enough on it to take it to full editorial meetings, but it didn't sell. One editorial director said it was cold, heartless and amoral and another that his house had been publishing 'too many quasi-experimental novels about sexual deviants'.

It was another era.

This new version is only altered in a few ways – I wanted to make it far clearer that most of the female characters are trans than I did in 1988, when I quite liked the game of forcing readers to work out that the only cis women in the book are Magda, Ariadne and Hennie. I tidied up some repetitions a little and inserted one major episode; another episode is now closer to what actually happened.

I am, after all, now 35 years older than I was when I met the real-life version of Natasha and the rest and it's a different time, one in which I've published some very different novels.

RK February 2014

CPSIA information can be obtained at www.ICGtesting.com
Printed in the USA
LVOW08s2254100716

495776LV00006B/402/P